Only Twelve Days

Only Twelve Days

Eileen Thornton

Published 2014 by Creativia
Book design by Creativia (www.creativia.org)
Cover art by goonwrite.com

As always, I dedicate this novel to my husband Phil. He is so patient when I sit typing away for hours on end.

Contents

Prologue

December 1977

Sally drummed her fingers on the desk and glanced at the clock for the umpteenth time. It was well past six o'clock; where on earth was Joey's father? Couldn't he have telephoned when he realised he was going to be so late? All the other children had gone home an hour ago.

Jane Miller, who ran the small nursery, had warned her Mr Roberts had a demanding job, which sometimes kept him a little late. Fine! She didn't mind hanging around for ten minutes or so, but this was ridiculous. If only she'd had asked exactly how late he might be, before Jane's hasty departure.

But there had been so little time. Responding to Jane's telephone call to take over the nursery due to her suddenly feeling unwell, Sally hadn't been given the chance to say very much at all. Once she had arrived, Jane simply hurried off, saying she would ring later in the morning.

Sally recalled how nervous she felt being thrust among twelve young children. However, before hurrying out the door, Jane briskly reminded her that she was attending the local college to train as a nursery nurse and this would be good practical experience.

On the whole, the day had gone quite well. The only real problem had arisen when she had asked the children to write a letter to Santa, telling him what they would like for Christmas. Knowing Jane, a retired schoolteacher, had taught the children to read and write, it had seemed a good idea, especially with Christmas being only a few days away.

However, after reading Joey's letter, she wasn't so sure. Instead of the usual gifts, such as toys and sweets, he had asked Santa for a mummy, as he didn't have one. Quite upset, Sally set aside her original intention of inviting the children to read out their letters. Instead, she had told them she would post them to Santa that evening.

When Jane rang later in the morning enquiring if everything was all right, Sally took the opportunity to ask about the children. "Is there anything important I should know? I don't want to do the wrong thing."

Jane told her they were all healthy children and played happily together. "Though, perhaps I should mention Joey sometimes needs a little extra attention. His mother died when he was one year old and because he can't remember her, he believes he never had one."

"Miss Hughes."

Joey's voice jolted Sally back to the present. She looked down at the anxious expression on the little boy's face.

"You won't leave me here by myself, will you? Mrs Miller always stays with me when my daddy's late. He can't help it."

"No, of course I won't leave you. We'll wait here together until your daddy comes to collect you."

Another half an hour crept by. Sally was really angry now. Just what was the man playing at keeping his child waiting all this time? She glanced out of the window just in time to see three men hurrying towards the front door of the building that Mrs Miller shared with two small companies.

"What does your father look like, Joey?" she asked.

"He's big," he answered, his arms outstretched.

"Well I think he's here now." She could see that one of the men was quite portly. "Come along I'll help you with your coat, then you'll be all ready for him when he comes in."

She was fastening Joey's coat when she heard footsteps rushing down the hall.

"I'm so sorry I'm late, Mrs Miller. Please forgive…" the man's voice trailed off.

Sally, still attending Joey, didn't look up. "You must be Joey's father. Mrs Miller was unwell and had to leave." Her tone was brisk. "I'm Miss Hughes and I would like to speak to you about…"

The anger in her voice resided when she looked across at the man standing in the doorway. He was tall, rather handsome underneath that worried frown and… slim. This was definitely not the man she had thought to be Joey's father. By big, Joey must have meant tall.

"Yes, and I can only apologise for being so late," he said, feeling more than a little embarrassed. Obviously she had been going to complain about his lateness.

"My name is Bill Roberts and I'm really sorry, Miss Hughes. I... I had no idea Mrs Miller wouldn't be here. I usually telephone if I'm going to be so late, but today I got caught up in a couple of meetings and couldn't get away. I hope you'll forgive me."

"It's quite all right," she replied, hoping he wouldn't hear the tremble in her voice. "I wasn't doing anything else. I err... I didn't really mind at all." She could feel her cheeks burning. She wasn't making a very good job of this.

"Come along then Joey, we mustn't keep Miss Hughes any longer. I'm already in her bad books." He took Joey by the hand and he began to walk towards the door, but a sudden thought made him turn back. "Perhaps I could give you a lift home?"

"There's really no need, I don't... I haven't got far... What I'm trying to say is, I only live a short distance from here." What must she sound like? He will think Jane has left his son in the care of an idiot.

"Please, I insist. It's my fault you're so late. It's the least I can do."

"Well then, thank you. I'll get my coat." She rushed across to the cloakroom, pulling her lipstick and hairbrush from her handbag. Why hadn't she worn something better this morning?

When Jane telephoned she had simply dropped everything in her haste to get to the nursery, totally forgetting she was wearing a sloppy sweater and an old pair of jeans. Her plan had been to do some revision that morning. Why didn't Jane say Mr Roberts was so handsome? But then why would she? All Jane ever thought about were the children. If Mr Roberts had pointed ears, Jane wouldn't have turned a hair, so long as he was a good father to his son. "Better, but not good," she murmured, tugging the brush through her long, auburn hair. "But it'll have to do." She pulled on her coat and hurried outside.

As Joey was skipping up and down the pavement, she took the opportunity to give his father the letter he had written to Santa. She had already handed the others to the parents earlier in the evening.

"The children were writing letters to Santa Claus this morning. This one is Joey's." She hesitated, wondering whether she should tell him of the contents or leave him to find out for himself. In the end she simply said, "He's only asked for one thing."

"I can guess what it is," Bill didn't get the chance to say anything further before Joey bounded across towards them.

"Can we go for a pizza, Daddy?" he asked.

"Yes, of course we can, son." He smiled at Sally. "But we'd better take Miss Hughes home first… unless you would like to come with us."

The words were out before he could stop himself. Why on earth had he said that? An attractive young woman like Miss Hughes must have lots of boyfriends. Why would she want to come out with him, a widower with a four-year-old son?

Sally hesitated. There must be a thousand reasons why she should say no. But at that precise moment, she couldn't think of a single one. Besides she really wanted to go with them. Joey's father was very nice. She rather liked his shy, pleasant manner, so she found herself saying, "Yes, thank you. I would love to, and please call me Sally."

"In that case, my name is Bill and we're delighted you're joining us, aren't we Joey?"

Joey grinned and nodded his head. He liked Miss Hughes.

At the restaurant, Joey chatted excitedly, telling Bill everything that had happened during the day. His words tumbled over each other. It was easy to see how much the child loved his father.

"We all wrote a letter to Santa and Miss Hughes is going to post them for us, aren't you Miss Hughes."

"Yes I am, Joey," she said. She felt sorry for him. Santa Claus couldn't supply a mother to order, no matter how good his intentions. She hoped the little boy wouldn't be too disappointed on Christmas morning.

Sensing her discomfort, Bill changed the subject. "What's wrong with Mrs Miller? I hope it isn't anything serious. She's a nice lady and has been very good to us."

"She has a bad dose of 'flu," said Sally, relieved the conversion had moved from the subject of Joey's letter. "I've promised to stand in for her until she recovers."

"I must send her some flowers," said Bill. "They may cheer her up a little."

"What a lovely thought, I'm sure she'll appreciate it."

Bill glanced at Joey. "I must say, you've made quite an impression on my son. He's not normally so talkative with strangers. He's very shy when meeting anyone new."

4

"Thank you," said Sally. "I must admit Joey and I got along well today." Sally found herself liking Bill more and more. She was usually shy herself, especially in the company of men. But somehow, Bill was different. Perhaps it was because she sensed he was lonely or shy – perhaps even both. She was rather disappointed when it was time to go. But it was getting late and Joey looked tired.

Outside, she gave Bill her address and they set off in the direction of her home. She was sorry when they turned the corner into her road. "My flat is number ten, the one on the end. Tell me, will you be bringing Joey to the nursery tomorrow?"

"Yes, we usually get there about eight-thirty, if that's all right. We tend to be first in and last out," he joked.

"Eight-thirty it is then," she replied.

Standing by her front door, she watched his car disappear down the road. Already she was looking forward to seeing him again the next morning. Nevertheless, she was a little curious at why she should be feeling this way about someone she had met only a couple of hours ago.

"I don't suppose he'll give me a second thought," she murmured, slamming the door shut behind her.

However, Bill *was* thinking about her as he drove home and he thought about very little else all evening.

Day One

The next morning Sally rose early. After a leisurely shower, she applied her make up carefully before checking out her wardrobe. She wanted to look her best when Bill brought Joey to the nursery.

Pulling out a few dresses, she realised they weren't at all suitable for spending the day with twelve youngsters. They would be expecting her to play with crayons, paints and goodness knows what else. In the end she decided on a pretty blue blouse and jeans. Though the outfit was much more suitable for a nursery, it wasn't exactly glamorous.

She took a final look in the mirror and realised she wearing far too much make-up. Removing some of it, she glanced at her reflection again and frowned. Jeans, flat shoes, hair tied up in a pony-tail and virtually no make-up, Bill would think she was a real frump.

Bill hadn't slept very well at all. He had spent most of the night tossing and turning, recalling his meeting with Sally. She was very attractive. He reminded himself of how her long hair had framed her face, as it fell gently to her shoulders and how her large brown eyes sparkled when she smiled. Even when her hair had been tied back as it was when he first arrived at the nursery, she had looked good. He also thought it rather strange that he had felt so comfortable when talking to her. His shyness usually left him feeling embarrassed and lost for words in the presence of young ladies.

Yes, he quite liked Sally… Well, he liked her a great deal if he was honest. But had she really liked him or had she simply agreed to go for a meal with them last night because she felt sorry for them both?

Plumping up the pillow, he hoped that wasn't the case and tried to push the idea from his mind. Nevertheless, he couldn't help wondering whether it was really possible for an attractive young woman like Sally to be interested in someone like him – a widower with a four-year-old son. After all, she only looked about twenty, twenty-one at most.

It wasn't as though he considered himself old – or at least he hadn't until now. He was only twenty-eight for goodness sake. But since his wife Julie had died, he had totally lost touch with young women. He grimaced. It was not as though he had ever *been* in touch with young women. He had always been too shy. Over the years he had come to feel more comfortable with the Mrs Millers of the world.

After spending most of the night wondering what to do, he had come to the conclusion he must put Sally out of his mind. Mrs Miller would be back at the nursery very soon and once that happened, he probably wouldn't see Sally ever again. Come to think of it, he was taking Joey to his parents' home later this afternoon. He had almost forgotten about that since meeting Sally Hughes.

Joey was spending a week with his grandparents, so he wouldn't be back at the nursery until next Friday. Surely he could cope with seeing Sally for that one day. By the time Bill had shaved and dressed, he was convinced Sally was well and truly out of his system.

Joey was carrying his advent calendar when he came downstairs to breakfast. "Look Daddy. There's a little star behind this door. Now there're only eleven days left until Christmas."

Not wanting to be late this morning, Sally was at the nursery by eight-fifteen. She had only just finished getting all the books and games from the cupboard, when she heard Bill and Joey walking down the corridor. Her heart missed a beat when she heard his voice drifting towards the nursery door. He was telling Joey how he must be a good boy and not do anything that might annoy Miss Hughes.

"Good morning Sally. It's nice to see you again." Immediately forgetting his earlier resolutions, Bill couldn't help noticing she looked even more attractive today. That shade of blue really suited her.

"Good morning to you both," replied Sally, trying to keep her voice steady. She felt like a schoolgirl instead of a fully-grown woman about to take charge of twelve youngsters. "I'm sure Joey and I will have lots of fun today." She told Joey to look at the toys in the corner, assuring him she would join him in a few minutes. Turning back to Bill, she asked him if there was anything special Joey liked to do.

"No," replied Bill. "Nothing special, he enjoys playing all sorts of games. But while I have a few minutes to spare I must tell you I'll be collecting Joey at around three o'clock today. I'm taking him to his grandparents and he'll be with them all next week. They want to see him before they visit my sister in the north. They're spending Christmas with Barbara and her husband, Jack. They have just had a baby and my parents are anxious to see their new grandchild. Joey won't be back until Thursday evening, so you won't have any more late nights."

His friendly smile made Sally go weak at the knees. "You needn't have worried Bill, I wouldn't have minded at all." She was saddened that she wouldn't see Bill or Joey for the next week. Jane could even be back in the nursery before Bill brought Joey in next Friday, which could mean she might never see either of them again.

"I must get off now," said Bill. "I can't be late today. I've an important meeting this morning and I want to take time to stop at the florist on the way. 'Bye Joey! Goodbye Sally, see you at three o'clock."

The other parents arrived with their children and though Sally went through the motions of greeting them, her mind was still preoccupied with Joey's father. Even now, she was looking forward to seeing him again when he came to collect his son that afternoon.

Why should she be feeling like this? After all, she had only just met Bill the evening before. However, she had to admit she liked everything about him: his smile, his shyness, his thoughtfulness and his charm. Oh, she could go on and on about Bill Roberts.

Mrs Miller telephoned during the morning. "I don't want to be a nuisance," she said. "I was just wondering if all was well."

"Yes," Sally replied. "Everything's fine here. Are you feeling better? It sounds as though your voice is coming back."

Jane's voice croaked as she laughed. "It's probably because I haven't been using it. I'm usually talking to the children all day. Oh, Sally, I'm finding it very boring here all alone. You know how I like to be doing things."

It was true. Mrs Miller was a no nonsense type of person and had been busy all her life. Sally knew she wouldn't enjoy sitting around all day. "It won't be long before you're back here Jane. The children will be delighted to see you again."

"I received some lovely flowers this morning from Mr Roberts. It was very kind of him," said Jane.

"Yes," replied Sally, "He said he was going to see the florist. Oh! That reminds me, Joey won't be here for the next week. Mr Roberts is taking him to his parent's home, something about them being away for Christmas this year."

"Yes, that's right." Jane recalled. "I'd almost forgotten about it. His sister has recently had a baby girl. The family were hoping she'd be born before Christmas. I believe Mr Roberts isn't taking Joey up there until sometime in the New Year. He thought it best if everyone didn't arrive at the house at once, very sensible. Is there anything else I should know about?"

"No, I don't think so. Just you keep warm and don't come back too early. I'm managing okay; in fact I'm quite enjoying it," replied Sally.

"I knew you would. Well, 'bye for now Sally, but don't forget you can ring me if you need to – though I may phone you again later today."

Sally guessed Jane would ring several times during the day. But knowing how much the children meant to her, she didn't mind.

The children really enjoyed themselves that morning. They ran, jumped and skipped. Sally was quite worn out by lunchtime. It amazed her how Jane was able to cope with the children every day, especially at her age.

"I think we'll sit quietly now and have our lunch," said Sally, looking at the bright pink faces of the children. "And after lunch we'll all have a nice little nap," she added, hopefully.

By about one o'clock all the children, with the exception of Joey, were fast asleep. They were wrapped in thick warm blankets and lying on a large sheet of foam rubber supplied by Mrs Miller for just this purpose. She always believed that an afternoon nap was very important for young children.

Joey was too excited to sleep. He wanted to tell Sally about his forthcoming visit to his grandparents. "Nanna and Granddad have a dog called Bess and we take her out for walks across the fields all the time. My friend David lives next door to Nanna and he has a rabbit and sometimes I go into his garden to play with it." He chattered on breathlessly about how he would be going to David's birthday party and that his daddy had bought a present for him to give to his friend.

Sally listened in silence. She was thinking how much he resembled his father. Same dark brown hair, same lovely brown eyes that crinkled when he laughed, the only difference was that Joey's hair was curly while Bill's hair was straight. The curls must come from his mother. Her thoughts were interrupted when she realised Joey had asked her a question.

"Have you got a dog, Miss Hughes?" he repeated.

"No, Joey, not now. I used to have one when I was a little girl though," she replied. "I called him Sam."

"Daddy says we can't have a dog, as it would get lonely when he's at work and I'm here with Mrs Miller," said Joey.

"Yes he would." Sally agreed. "But you can always go to see Bess at your nanna's house."

"I'm glad I'm going to see Nanna and Granddad for a little while. We do lots of things when I'm there. Last time we went to see a film about a dog called Lassie," said Joey, starting to yawn.

"Yes I know you're looking forward to it, sweetheart." But Sally wished he wasn't going right now. She would have liked the opportunity of getting to know Bill a little better.

"I like you, Miss Hughes, do you like me?" Joey asked, suddenly.

"Of course I do. I like you very much Joey, I really do," she replied.

Joey thought for a minute then said, "Miss Hughes, do you have a man living at your house like my nanna?"

"No, Joey I'm not married, so I don't have a man living with me," said Sally, a little surprised by the question. She smiled "You see, your nanna and granddad are married, so they live together."

"Do you want to get married like my nanna?"

"Yes of course I do," Sally laughed.

"When will you get married?"

"One day, when I find some nice young man to love me."

"I'll love you," said Joey after a moment's thought.

"Thank you Joey, that's very sweet of you. But you're too young at the moment. You'll have to wait until you grow up, then we'll see."

Joey suddenly went silent and looked rather sad. He was recalling something Sally had said.

"Is there something wrong Joey? Sally asked.

"My daddy doesn't have a lady living with him. Does it mean nobody loves him?" he asked quietly.

Sally was alarmed that something she had said in all innocence had upset the little boy. She put her arms around him. "Oh Joey, you mustn't think that. Of course your daddy has lots of people who love him. You love him don't you and then there's your nanna and granddad and your aunt and uncle, they all love him."

"Yes," said Joey, thoughtfully, "I do love my daddy very much." However, he wasn't sure if that was quite the same thing. Hadn't Miss Hughes just told him he was too young? "Do you love my daddy, Miss Hughes?"

His question rather took her aback. She was certainly very attracted to his father; in fact she could hardly wait to see him again. But love? Could that be love? She felt Joey tugging at her sleeve; he was still waiting for an answer.

"Well," she said. "I like your daddy very much." Wishing to change the subject she added. "You're a very inquisitive little boy," and without giving him time to ask, she added, "And that means you ask a lot of questions. Now, I'm going to telephone my friend, Jo. She'll be wondering where I am. I haven't had time to tell her I'm here at the nursery with you. Would you like to speak to her?"

"Joe is a boy's name." Joey was thinking of one of his friends who lived near his nanna's house.

"Well Jo isn't her real name. It's Josephine, but she likes to be called Jo."

"Why?" Joey asked.

"It's because she likes to play a joke on people."

"How?" he persisted

"Well you see when she calls herself Jo, people think she's a boy and they get a surprise when they find out that she's really a girl," answered Sally.

It wasn't the real reason, but it was near enough. She didn't feel like explaining about the Women's Liberation Movement just at the moment. She picked up the phone and dialled her friend's number; it rang twice before Jo's answering machine kicked into action.

"She isn't at home," said Sally, looking at Joey. "I'll leave a message for her." She turned back to the phone. "Hi, Jo, it's Sally. I'm at Mrs Miller's nursery school. The number is ... " She gave the number and asked Jo to call when she got back.

Putting down the phone, she turned back to Joey. "She may ring later so you can say hello to her then."

"I think I'm sleepy now, Miss Hughes." Joey climbed down from her knee. He was relieved Jo wasn't in. He wasn't really sure he wanted to talk to her. A girl with a boy's name sounded a little frightening to him.

"I'll help you get wrapped up in the blanket and you can have a little nap," said Sally. "Then you'll feel as bright as a button when your daddy comes to collect you. If his meeting goes well, he may even arrive a little earlier than three o'clock."

Bill arrived at the large building, which housed his firm. However, he didn't leap out and rush up to his office as he normally did. Instead, he closed his eyes and took a deep breath. He had thought about Sally during his drive into work. If only he'd had more time to spend with her before having to dash off to the office.

He opened his eyes and stared at the building. But now he had to put Sally out of his mind; his meeting this morning was very important. He needed to focus.

Upstairs in his office he called his friend and colleague, Colin Shaw, to come in and see him. Colin would be attending the meeting with him, so they needed a few minutes together to catch up. However Bill found it difficult to stay on track and kept gazing out of the window.

It didn't take Colin long to notice that Bill was preoccupied with something and was rather concerned. He had known Bill for over ten years now, so he knew immediately when his friend was troubled. He recalled their first term at university together.

He was older than Bill by two years, but he had taken a couple of years off to 'see life', as he liked to call it before taking up his place. As they were complete opposites, the other students were surprised at how well the two young men got on. While Bill was quiet, shy, withdrawn and very easily embarrassed, Colin was an extrovert. He loved meeting people, going to parties and, most especially, dating the female students. He also loved playing practical jokes, or teasing his friends.

From their first meeting, Colin decided it was his role in life to bring Bill out of his shell. He had thought Bill might be finding the work too difficult and need help. However, he couldn't have been more wrong. As it turned out it was Colin who needed extra coaching from Bill, who was a genius when it came to figures. Even the lecturers were astounded at just how quickly Bill could work out the most complicated equations in his head. He was also very sharp at legal issues and could quite easily have studied law, but mathematics was his passion.

Still gazing at Bill, Colin smiled to himself, recalling how he had tried to persuade Bill to attend the university dances; even setting up dates for him with one or two rather attractive students. Yet he had always refused to go, saying he was quite happy to read his books.

Though Colin knew this reluctance was due to Bill's shyness, he teased him about it mercilessly, suggesting he might prefer a date with one of the male students. "I'd be quite happy to organise it for you. Now, let me see, there's that rather attractive fellow reading history; or the one with the beard in the science lab…" Colin loved the way Bill ran a finger around the inside of his collar when embarrassed and not quite sure what to say. However, he had always been wise enough never to tease him in front of anyone else and Bill always took it in good part.

While Bill graduated with a first class honours degree, Colin hadn't managed anything so grand. Nevertheless he knew it was due to Bill's patient coaching that he had achieved far more than he deserved. Left to his own devices, he would possibly have been sent down for playing the fool too often. After leaving university, he and Bill had remained good friends and had even ended up together in the finance department at the Head Office of Websters International.

The company, realising the gem they had in Bill, rapidly promoted him to Head of the Department and, wanting an assistant he could trust and rely on, Bill had appointed Colin. But it hadn't ended there. The firm had grown rapidly over the last few years and Bill was now Financial Executive to all the accounts departments within the whole company.

Bill had been best man at Colin and Rachel's wedding. Rachel looked on him as a brother and concerned he would never meet anyone himself, she arranged a dinner party; inviting both Bill and her friend Julie. With a little coaxing Bill and Julie began dating and eventually married. They had a son, whom they named Joey.

"If you're ready, Colin, I think we'd better go upstairs, they'll be waiting for us."

Bill's voice snapped Colin back to the present, "Yes," he replied, gathering his papers together. "Let's get it over with." Following Bill over to the lift, Colin decided that immediately after the meeting he would try to get to the root of whatever was bothering his friend.

The meeting went well, much better than either Bill or Colin had expected. Often they were long, drawn out affairs with all the heads of departments arguing about how their finances over the next half-year should be spent. Usually by the end of the meeting tempers were hot, however today had been different, everyone parted with a smile on their face.

Bill had been very relieved, having found it difficult to stop his mind from wandering back to Sally. "There has to be a first for everything," he said to Colin, over lunch. "I've never known an interdepartmental finance meeting go so smoothly before."

"I agree," said Colin, remembering how the last one had gone on for two days. "You'll be able to get away early now. Taking Joey to your mother's aren't you?"

"Yes," replied Bill. "He's spending the week there; he's looking forward to it. I'm staying overnight, but I'll be back in the office tomorrow morning."

"Joey *is* well isn't he?" Colin asked, trying to get onto the subject of what was making Bill so distracted. He knew that Joey was Bill's life.

Bill looked up from the finance report sheet he had started to read. He wasn't having much success; his thoughts were still back at the nursery. "Yes, of course he is. Why do you ask?"

"It's just you seem to have your mind on something else today. I wondered if you had a problem at home. If you'd like to talk to someone, you know I'm always here," replied Colin.

Bill hesitated. He didn't know whether to say anything or not. Colin could be such a tease at the best of times, but if he thought a woman was involved, then he there would be no stopping him. "No." he said eventually. "Everything's all right at home. I'm just a little under the weather this morning."

However Colin knew better. Something was definitely bothering his friend and he wasn't going to give up so easily. On the other hand, he was also aware that badgering Bill would get him nowhere at all, so he decided to wait until they were back downstairs in the office before trying again.

Changing the subject, he told Bill how Rachel had been out shopping for a new dress for the firm's Christmas dance being held the following Thursday. "Are you going this year, Bill? You know you could come with us. Rachel would be delighted." He already knew what the answer would be, but he felt he must ask. One of these days Bill might just say yes.

"No, I don't think so," said Bill. "But thanks for asking all the same."

The rest of the lunch break carried on with small talk, but once they were back downstairs Colin tried again.

"Bill, are you sure there's nothing you want to talk about?"

Again Bill hesitated. He would like to talk to someone and Colin was the only one he could trust. "Alright, come into my office Colin. Perhaps you could give me some advice." Once inside, he closed the door and rang through to his secretary telling her he didn't want to be disturbed.

"This sounds very mysterious," said Colin, grinning. "You're not thinking of embezzling any money from the company, are you?"

"Don't be ridiculous Colin. I simply don't want to be the subject of office gossip." He paused, still not knowing whether to say anything. He didn't want Colin pulling his leg about it for the next couple of months.

"Bill," said Colin. "You know I won't say a word to anyone. I promise." He watched Bill run a finger around his collar. What on earth can have happened since yesterday to put him in this state? He feared the worst.

"I know this is going to sound stupid to you," said Bill at last. "But last night I met a girl at the nursery and I can't get her out of my mind. She's standing in for Mrs Miller; she had to go home with 'flu sometime yesterday." He paused; still not sure whether he was doing the right thing by confiding in Colin. He turned away and took a deep breath before continuing. "As usual, I was late collecting Joey, so I offered to take her home. She agreed and we all stopped for a meal on the way." He hesitated and looked at Colin, half expecting him to make some remark. But Colin remained silent. "There's just something about her and it's driving me crazy," he continued. "It's a terrible thing to say, but I was even jealous of my son, as he was spending today with her."

"Well then ask her out. Take her for a meal or something," said Colin. He let out a long breath, relieved and delighted that Bill was at least thinking about women again. After his marriage, Bill had slowly begun to emerge from his shell. However, when Julie was killed in a car accident he had reverted back to his old self, never going out and continuing to take on more and more work at the office. Colin had been at his wits end trying to make his friend see there was more to life than work, so this was good news as far as he was concerned.

"But she's so young, about twenty-one at most. Besides I have Joey. How many young girls want to be involved with a widower with a four-year-old son?" Bill replied. "This morning, while getting ready for work I made up my mind to forget her, but once I saw her again, the resolution was broken. *You* noticed I was behaving oddly so how long will it take the rest of my staff to start thinking I've flipped my lid?"

"Calm down Bill. All you have to do is ask the girl out. If she says no, what harm will have been done? You're not old you know. Some people only marry for the first time at your age. Hasn't it occurred to you that she may have taken a liking to you? She agreed to go for the meal with you last night, didn't she? Besides, some women like '*older*' men." He stressed the word older and made quotation signs in the air. "Look here! I'm older than you, I have a lovely wife and two kids and I'm balding – well slightly," he added, quickly, rubbing his hand across his head. "Yet let me assure you, I do not consider myself past it. So why on earth should you? You have a lot more going for you than I do."

"You're making fun of me now. Perhaps I shouldn't have told you," said Bill, looking down at his desk.

"No I'm not, Bill." Colin said gently. All I'm trying to do is to make you see you're still a young, attractive man. If you like this girl then you should go for it, stop dithering about and ask her out. Sometimes it's very hard to get through to you."

"I'm picking Joey up shortly; I may have a word with her then. I just don't want to make a fool of myself. I'd prefer it if you didn't say anything to Rachel for the moment, if you don't mind."

"Anything you say, Bill. Now get away and pick up that son of yours. Say hello from me."

"I have a few letters to sign and then I'll be off. Oh, and Colin, thanks for listening," said Bill, feeling relieved Colin hadn't come out with any of his usual witty remarks about him and women.

"Anytime, *old* boy," said Colin, grinning and emphasising the word old as he slipped out of the door.

Bill pretended to throw something at him before beginning to sign his mail. He decided he would ask Sally out for a meal when he collected Joey. Looking at his watch, he saw it was only one forty-five. If he got a move on, he could be at the nursery for two-thirty. That would show her he could be early sometimes.

It was almost half past two. Sally decided to waken Joey so he might get himself pulled together in time for his father arriving. Going across to where Joey lay sleeping, she took care not to wake the other children. She wanted him to herself for a while. She rather liked this delightful little boy and was certainly going to miss him over the next few days. She shook him gently.

"Wake up, Joey. Your daddy shouldn't be much longer now," she whispered. "You'll be seeing your grandmother shortly."

Joey looked up at her and stretched out his arms around her neck. "Nanna will have made some cakes for tea. She always makes cakes when we go to see her and Granddad. But I'm going to miss you, Miss Hughes." He gave her a big grin.

"I'm going to miss you too, Joey. It's been so nice meeting you," said Sally, standing up and pulling Joey up with her. "I really hope I'll see you and your daddy again sometime. You know, I like you both very much." She gave him a hug

"Daddy!" Joey had caught sight of his father standing in the doorway.

Sally swung around. "I'm sorry. I didn't see you. Have you been there long?" She felt a little embarrassed that Bill might have heard her last remarks.

Bill walked into the room. He had arrived in time to see Sally awaken Joey and had heard and seen everything that passed between them. He was pleased Joey found himself able to trust Sally. One of his main concerns was that Joey would grow up to be shy like him. It was the last thing he wanted. It was also encouraging to learn that Sally liked him as well as his son. However, to save any further embarrassment he said, "I've only just arrived. My meeting finished early so I was able to get away."

Joey ran over to his father and Bill told him to get his coat from the cloak-room. It would give him the opportunity to speak to Sally about them spending an evening together.

"Sally, I..." he faltered. "I... I was wondering... if you would..." He was interrupted when the telephone began to ring.

"I'd better answer that," said Sally. "It may be Mrs Miller and I'm sure she would like a word with you. She was delighted with the flowers."

Joey arrived back with his coat and Bill helped him put it on while Sally answered the phone. He wished he could be more like Colin. He would have simply breezed into the nursery and swept Sally off her feet. Instead, he was bumbling around trying to ask her out. Straightening up he heard Sally speak into the receiver.

"Hello, Mrs Miller's nursery school," she said. "Oh, it's you Jo. I want to talk to you about this evening, but I'm with a parent at the moment. Can you give me ten minutes?"

There was a short pause before Sally replied, "Fine, speak to you later." She hung up and turned back to Bill and smiled. "I'm sorry about that. It was a friend of mine. What was it you wanted to say to me?"

Believing Sally had been talking to her boyfriend, Bill was lost for words. He felt gutted; almost as though someone had punched him in the stomach. All he wanted to do was to get out of the nursery. However, Sally was waiting for a reply. He swallowed hard and shook his head. "It was nothing... nothing important, Sally. We must leave you to get on ... err... We'll see you next week. Goodbye."

"Goodbye both, I hope you enjoy your visit to your nanna's Joey," said Sally.

Joey ran over to Sally and gave her a big hug. "'Bye 'bye Miss Hughes." He ran back to his father, who quickly ushered him out of the door.

Bill fastened the seat belt around Joey and then climbed into the car. He sat there for a while, staring through the windscreen. He was bitterly disappointed. Of course he had known all along, Sally was likely to have a boyfriend. It was stupid of him to have believed otherwise. Nevertheless, he felt his whole world had crashed before him.

Finally, he started the car engine and set off to his parents' home; about an hour's drive away. Joey chattered to him from his seat in the back, but for the first time Bill wasn't interested in anything his son said. Normally he would listen attentively and answer any questions Joey asked of him. Today was different. Today, his mind was elsewhere.

Twice he was forced to pull into a layby, as he knew he wasn't concentrating on the traffic. On another occasion he bought Joey some sweets simply as an excuse to get out of the car.

What was he going to do next week when he had to take Joey back to the nursery? The way he felt about Sally, it would be better if he didn't see her again. Joey seemed to sense his father was tense and stopped chattering. He sat quietly on the bench by a frozen pond, eating his sweets.

Bill thought hard for a long while before he came up with an idea. If his parents hadn't yet bought their train tickets, perhaps he could persuade them to postpone their trip until the next day.

That way he could pick up Joey next Friday, run his parents to the station and take Joey back to the office for two or three hours. No one else would be there. The rest of the staff would have finished for the holidays. Only the security staff would be around and they were quite used to him being in the office at all hours. Surely Mrs Miller would be back in the nursery after New Year.

The more Bill thought about his idea, the better it sounded. Feeling slightly relieved he may have found a solution to his problem, he told Joey to get back into the car. As soon as I get there, I'll speak to Mum about delaying their journey until Friday, he thought.

Sally watched Bill from one of the windows in the nursery. He was sitting in his car and appeared to be deep in thought. She hoped he would see her and wave before setting off. Joey must be reciting the day's events to his father. If there was one thing she had learned about Joey, it was that he liked to chatter. When Bill drove off without even a backward glance she felt like bursting into tears.

However, not wanting the children to find her so distressed when they awoke, she tried to pull herself together. Hopefully they would sleep for a little while longer. Just then the telephone rang and she rushed to answer it. Lifting the receiver, she glanced around to see if anyone was awake, but although one or two of the children stirred, they slept on.

"Hello, Mrs Miller's nursery."

"Hi there, it's Jo. You seem to be in at the deep end. Are you managing to cope or are you wishing you had stayed in your father's business?"

"Not quite." Having escaped from the family business, nothing would induce her to go back. "It's really good fun, but ask me again at the end of the week." Sally replied.

"I tried calling your flat several times yesterday but couldn't reach you. I tried right up until I had to go out, about eight-ish I think. It was late when I got back so I didn't bother anymore," said Jo.

"Well I was here until six-thirty as one of the parents was very late and I ended up going out with them for a pizza. It was about eight when they dropped me off home," replied Sally.

"That was nice of her, good to know the mother appreciated..."

"No, no, it was a father, he..." Sally broke off. Knowing how Jo felt about men, she regretted the words the moment they left her lips.

Jo was a feminist and then some. She often carried her beliefs to the extreme. The male sex was very far down her list of requirements; she didn't trust them at all. "Most men are only after one thing," she would often say. "When the right man comes along he'll treat you as an equal and see you as a good sport."

Sally wasn't sure she wanted to be seen as a good sport, far preferring to be thought of as feminine. She liked nice clothes, perfume, make-up and everything else that went with being a woman. Jo, on the other hand, always wore trousers, preferably jeans or army style camouflage trousers and was appalled if a man offered his seat to her on the bus. This being the case, it had surprised Sally when Jo decided to take up a career as a nursery nurse. She had always thought her friend would join the army or the fire service or something else that would give her equal status, at least in her eyes. However, even more annoying to Sally, Jo had started telling her whom she should and shouldn't see. Therefore she held her breath waiting for the outburst; she didn't have long to wait.

"What're you thinking about, going out with a married man?" Jo yelled down the line. "He must have thought you were an easy touch."

"He's a widower actually," replied Sally.

"What!" screamed Jo. "I don't believe you sometimes. You really are an idiot. A widower must be the worst kind of man you could imagine. They make you feel sorry for them; single parent and all, and then they pounce. You want to be careful my girl. You were lucky he didn't try it on." She paused. "He didn't, did he? Try anything on, I mean."

Sally sat back in her chair and allowed herself a moment's reflection on the previous evening. Bill hadn't done anything improper, but in a way, rather wished he had.

"Jo, don't be ridiculous, of course he didn't," she said, at last. "He had his four-year-old son with him. Besides, I probably won't see him again. He's taken his son to his mother's for the next week, so there's no reason for him to come back to the nursery."

"Thank goodness for that. And please, don't you go out with any more fathers. You're not safe to be left alone."

"He was rather nice you know, charming, good looking, well mannered. Actually, I rather liked him," said Sally, picturing Bill standing there in the nursery.

"It sounds more than that to me," said Jo suspiciously. "Are you sure you've told me everything?"

"Of course I have." Sally felt annoyed with herself for not having the guts to tell Jo to mind her own business.

"Nevertheless I think I should pop around to see you tonight. He may decide to call on you, especially if his son isn't around. I'll soon tell him what's what."

"No, not tonight," said Sally hastily. "That's what I wanted to say to you. I'm going to have to catch up on some studying. We're going to the lecture tomorrow night and I won't understand any of it unless I do some work. I'll meet you at the Lecture Theatre. Keep a seat for me if you're there first."

"Okay, will do. See you there, but mind what you're doing. If he calls on you, tell him to get lost, or better still ring me and I'll come around and do it for you. 'Bye for now."

Sally sighed with relief when she put down the receiver. Thank goodness she had managed to stop Jo from calling tonight. She wouldn't have let the subject about Bill rest. Already she could hear her friend saying awful things about him. Yet he hadn't struck her as being the type to take advantage her; or any woman.

Looking at the time, she decided to awaken the children. They had slept long enough. She must have tired them out too much this morning. She made a mental note not to do that again. She asked them to sit quietly and draw a picture of their home; she wasn't in the mood to do much else. Her mind was too preoccupied with Bill and how he had rushed off.

If only Jo hadn't chosen that precise minute to return her call. She would have liked more time to talk to him. It had all happened so quickly. He appeared to be going to say something to her, but after her brief chat with Jo, he had changed his mind. In fact, he seemed more than anxious to get away. She kept glancing over to the door, hoping he might walk in again at any moment. But it was wishful thinking. He was probably half way to his mother's by now.

She felt tempted to ring Jane and tell her she couldn't stay at the nursery any longer. It was the only way she would get Bill out of her mind. Perhaps Jane could find a replacement for her. But Sally knew she would not simply choose anyone to look after the children. She would rather come back from her sick bed.

Yet even now the picture of Bill walking into the room last evening was so vivid. She could still see the shy look of embarrassment on his face when she had shown her annoyance at his lateness.

A smile played around her lips when she pictured them at the restaurant. By then they had both been a little more at ease. If only they could have been together for a while longer, they would have got to know each other a little more and... Stop it! Oh my God, she had to stop thinking about him. He had gone; she would never see him again. Let that be an end to it.

Her thoughts were interrupted when the telephone rang. It was Jane's voice that came down the line. "Is everything all right Sally? It's not too much for you is it? I suddenly feel very guilty, having dropped you in at the deep end."

This was her chance to leave gracefully. Jane was giving her a way out. She could say that, yes, it was too much; she hadn't finished her course and she needed to revise for the exams. But when it came to it, she couldn't let her friend down.

"Stop worrying Jane." Sally tried to sound a lot calmer than she felt. "You'll never get better at this rate. Everything is going well here. The children are behaving like little angels. They're drawing pictures this afternoon so they're very quiet. This morning we all had fun and games, I think I tired them all out, they had a long sleep after lunch."

"I'm pleased to hear you're coping well, Sally," she said. "Can I have a word with Joey or has his father already picked him up?"

"I'm afraid. Bi... Mr Roberts picked him up a while ago."

If Jane heard her slip of the tongue she didn't mention it.

"I'm sorry I missed him, I would like to have thanked him for the flowers and wished them both a Merry Christmas. Well Sally, if you're quite sure you're all right, I'll leave it at that, but don't forget if you need any advice, give me a call."

Slowly replacing the receiver, Sally scolded herself for not taking the opportunity to tell Jane she wanted to leave.

"You've got my green crayon." Voices across the room interrupted her thoughts.

"No I haven't, this is *my* green crayon."

"I don't want any fighting please," said Sally. The silence had been too good to last. She looked at her wristwatch. Not much longer now. I think I can hold out another half-an-hour. "Here's another green crayon, there are plenty to choose from. Surely you don't *all* have to use the same colour at the same time."

Walking across to her desk, she sat down. She wasn't really angry with Jane; after all she was a good friend. Not only had she taught her at school for a time, but she had also put in a good word for her at the college.

Jane was always being called upon to give lectures to the students or advice on certain aspects of their courses. Therefore the college administrators hadn't hesitated in offering Sally a place once Jane recommended her.

Sally couldn't let her friend down. Yet there were times when she would like to say what *she* thought, or tell people what *she* wanted. Why was it she always ended up doing what other people said? However on reflection, the answer was simple. She had always led such a sheltered life, thanks mainly to her two older brothers.

Taking it upon themselves to protect their new sister right from the day she was born, they had always being around if anyone posed a threat to her. Growing into a very attractive teenager, she had received the attention of many of the boys at school. However, while she could go to a party with one of them, it was always her brothers who brought her home. No one was going to mess with their sister.

She was fifteen when Josephine and her parents moved into a house a short distance away. Josephine, or Jo as she preferred to be called, joined Sally's school. They soon became firm friends and spent much their free time together. Jo had three brothers. However in her case, she dominated them. They were delighted when she became friendly with Sally, hoping some of her femininity would rub off on their sister. Unfortunately, that never happened. Instead, Jo had taken over where her own two brothers left off.

"When I told Jo about going for a pizza with Bill and Joey, why didn't I tell her it was none of her business?" Speaking aloud, Sally thumped the desk. "Why do I have to explain myself to her? I should be more assertive."

Just then Mrs Johnson appeared in the doorway having come to collect her son. Sally walked across the room towards her, hoping she hadn't overheard her talking to herself.

"Is Michael behaving himself," said Mrs Johnson. "He can be so trying sometimes. Mrs Miller knows how to handle him, but as you are new here, he may try to get away with mischief. If you would rather I didn't bring him tomorrow..."

"Don't worry," Sally interrupted. "All the children are being very good."

"Thank you, Miss Hughes." Mrs Johnson looked relieved. "In that case, we'll see you in the morning."

The rest of the parents came to collect their children and soon Sally was left all alone. She carefully packed the toys and games away in the cupboard. Folding the blankets, she put them into the big chest in the corner. After looking around to make sure everything was in order, she went across the corridor to get her coat.

She was about to leave when the telephone rang. Now what? She looked at her watch. It couldn't be Jane; she would know the children had all left by now. Sally had almost reached the phone when another thought struck her.

What if it was Jo checking up on whether Bill had been in touch. She may even be going to insist on coming over this evening after all. If that was the case, she most certainly didn't want to speak to her.

Sally stood by the desk staring at the ringing telephone, willing it to stop. She covered her ears with her hands. But she could still hear it, as it continued to ring.

When Bill arrived at his parent's home, he found his mother waiting at the front door. She was a slight woman and despite the wisps of grey hair, which had started to appear, he couldn't help thinking that she was still very attractive. During one of their stops, he had telephoned, letting her know they were well on their way. Since then she had looked out for them. Watching the car pull into the drive, she noticed how tense her son looked.

"Hello darling," she said, as Joey ran up the path and into his grandmother's outstretched arms. "How's my little man today? I expect you have lots to tell Granddad and me, you always seem to do so many things between your visits to us."

"Hello son," she said, as Bill bent down to kiss her on the cheek. "I've got the kettle on for some tea, Joey might prefer lemonade."

"I'll get Joey's case, while you go and make that pot of tea. I have something I want to ask you once we're all settled." Bill tried to sound happier than he felt.

However, Anne wasn't fooled. She always knew when something was troubling her son. She hurried indoors to make the tea.

"Is everything all right Bill? You seem rather strained." By now they were sitting in the sitting room and she was pouring the tea. She stopped and looked at him.

"Yes, everything's fine." He smiled thinly. "I'm simply a bit tired, that's all."

"What is it you want to ask me?"

"It's nothing much," Bill shook his head and grinned, trying to reassure his mother. Deep furrows had appeared on her forehead, replacing the normal cheerfulness she displayed whenever Joey arrived. "I was just wondering whether you and Father had booked your train tickets for your trip away next week."

She finished pouring the tea before she spoke. "No, not yet, we thought we would do it tomorrow and take Joey with us. He likes to see the trains." She mother could hear alarm bells ringing and her hand trembled slightly as she placed the teapot onto a large coaster. "Why do you ask?"

Bill hesitated. "I was wondering if you would do me a big favour and go on Friday instead. It would really help me out of a jam."

"Of course we will. You know you only have to ask. We'll do anything we can to help you," she replied, wishing her husband was home. She was growing increasingly concerned about her son. Whether he admitted it or not, something was troubling him.

"I'm okay Mum, really." Realising his mother was extremely worried he tried to sound light-hearted. "It's just that we've been so busy at the office, an extra day would help me out." He smiled and held out his cup. "What about another cup of tea?"

Anne went into the kitchen to refresh the teapot. Bill had said nothing to convince her that everything was all right. He was always busy at the office, far too busy for her liking. So what was so different about this week? There was something else.

She knew he wouldn't tell her; he had always kept his problems to himself. Nevertheless, even when he was a boy she had always known when something was wrong. As she waited for the kettle to boil, she remembered how when other boys of his age were out playing, Bill had preferred to stay indoors reading textbooks. She and his father, John, had put it down to his shyness, believing he would grow out of it, but he never had. And to make matters worse, he had never found himself able to confide in her or his father, much preferring to bottle things up inside. She sighed. If only he could have been more outgoing like his two younger sisters.

Anne recalled how his marriage to Julie had helped to bring him out of his shell a little. But after her death he had become even more withdrawn, taking on extra work at the office, eventually becoming Financial Executive – whatever that was!

She knew Bill's friend, Colin, had tried to encourage him to slow down and certainly the last time she had seen her son, he had seemed a little happier. But now this had cropped up. Whatever 'this' was and he was back to square one.

The kettle clicked to off, drawing Anne back to the present. She decided to phone Colin the next morning after Bill had left for the office. Perhaps he knows what's bothering him, she thought.

When Anne walked back into the lounge with the tea tray, Bill was sitting at the table looking at a pile of papers he had taken from his brief case. Joey was playing with Bess on the floor. She poured some tea and passed it over to Bill.

"Thanks Mum," he said, taking the cup. "I won't be long with the paperwork, but I really need to get a few things sorted before tomorrow morning."

"Would you like some more lemonade, Joey?" she asked.

"Yes," Joey replied.

Bill looked up from his work and frowned at his son.

"Yes please, Nanna," said Joey, realising that he had forgotten to say please again.

"You're a good boy," she replied, refilling his glass. She poured some tea for herself. "You carry on with your work Bill, Joey and I will have a little chat. It's been a while since I last saw him." Turning to Joey she continued, "Tell me what you've been doing over the last few weeks."

"Well, Nanna," said Joey, thinking hard. "I've gone to nursery school and played with my friends." He paused. "Mrs Miller is poorly so Miss Hughes is looking after us all."

Anne failed to notice her son stiffen at the mention of Miss Hughes. "What's Miss Hughes like Joey?"

Joey got to his feet and walked over to where his father was looking at his papers. "She's very pretty, isn't she Daddy?"

"Yes, she is," replied Bill, without looking up. He swallowed hard, wishing they would talk about something else. In his mind he could see Sally standing there in the nursery and again at the Pizza restaurant. It hurt him to think he would never see her again.

Picking up a calculator Joey asked his father what it was for.

"It adds up figures for me. Put it down please," replied Bill, a little more sternly than Anne thought necessary.

Bill had never been seen using a calculator, but for some reason, he always kept one by him.

"Tell me a bit more about Miss Hughes, Joey," said Anne, frowning at her son.

"Yesterday, she asked us to write a letter to Santa to tell him what we wanted for Christmas. Did you know it was nearly Christmas, Nanna?" Joey sounded excited.

"Yes, I know it is. Only eleven days now, it won't be long before Santa comes," said Anne. "What did you...?" She had been about to enquire what he had asked for in his letter, but Bill looked up quickly and shook his head. Instead, she asked what he and the children had done next.

"We played lots of games and drew some pictures and today Miss Hughes let me sit on her knee."

"You seem to be getting on very well with Miss Hughes Joey. Has she been there long?" Anne asked.

Knowing how Joey was usually very shy with strangers, she was rather surprised he had taken to this Miss Hughes so quickly. Her dearest wish was he wouldn't be so withdrawn like his father, so she was keen to learn more about this woman.

"Not long, Nanna."

"Two days," murmured Bill, desperately wishing the conversation about Miss Hughes would end. Every time her name was mentioned, he could picture her lovely smile.

"Why do you have to add up sums Daddy?" Joey asked, picking up the calculator again. "And what's this for?" He pointed at a small tape recorder. "What do you do with it?"

"Joey! Will you stop asking me so many stupid questions?" Bill snatched the calculator from Joey's hand. "For heaven's sake stop being such a naughty boy. Go and talk to your nanna and leave me alone."

Anne was startled to hear Bill speak to Joey like that. For one brief moment, she thought he was going to smack him. She caught her breath as she felt her stomach turn over. Oh my God, something was definitely wrong. She decided there and then to get her husband to speak to him that evening. Perhaps he might open up to his father.

Normally she never interfered in the way Bill raised Joey. Usually there was no reason to; he was always so patient with him. However, today she felt compelled to say something. "Bill, he's only a little boy. For goodness sake, what's the matter with you today? Take your work into the other room if he's bothering you." She looked towards Joey, who had burst into tears. "Come and sit on Nanna's knee and I'll give you a big hug."

Joey ran over to his grandmother and climbed up on to her knee. Tears were streaming down his cheeks. "I'm... s... s... sorry... Daddy," he said in between his sobs.

Bill was stunned. He couldn't believe he had raised his voice to his son, especially over something so trivial. He threw his pen down onto the table, sat back into his chair and closed his eyes. Why was he taking it out on his son? It wasn't his fault that Sally had a boyfriend. He went across to Joey who was still sitting on his nanna's knee and knelt down beside him.

"No, Joey, I'm the one who's sorry," he said quietly, wiping the tears from his son's eyes. "I shouldn't have shouted at you. Of course you aren't a naughty boy. You must ask me whatever you like at any time."

Anne had turned very pale and her eyes, usually sparkling, looked tired and drawn. "What is it, Bill, what's troubling you?"

"Nothing, Mum." He grasped her hand. "Please don't worry, it's like I said, we've been very busy at the office." He knew his mother worried about how much work he had taken on at the office. Her face had grown thinner in recent months and her lovely brown hair was turning grey prematurely. He felt sure it was down to her concerns for him. "I promise you, I'm fine." He picked Joey up from his mother's lap and hugged him.

Joey put his arms around his father's neck and Bill walked around the room, clutching his son tightly. Joey was his whole world; he meant everything to him. How could he have upset him like that?

He really needed to put Sally out of his mind. He wouldn't ever see her again so he should forget about her. How he wished he wasn't staying here for the night. It would have been so much easier to have some tea and go straight back home. At least he wouldn't have to listen to all this chatter about Sally.

Bill couldn't really blame Joey, it wasn't often he met anyone new and when he did, he was usually so shy he clammed up. All the boy wanted to do was tell his grandmother about the new lady at the nursery. He hugged Joey tightly. If only he hadn't been so attracted to her! If only he hadn't liked her quite so much. If only...

"I love you, Daddy," Joey interrupted his thoughts.

"I love you too Joey. Daddy's been working too hard, but it was wrong of me to speak to you like that and I'm sorry." Bill handed him back to Anne and tried to muster up a grin.

"Go on; tell Nanna what else has been happening at the nursery." He walked back to his chair, resigned to the fact he was going to hear about Miss Hughes whether he wanted to or not.

"Miss Hughes told me I asked too many questions – just like Daddy said before," said Joey, sounding more like his old self again.

"Why, whatever were you asking her?" asked Anne. Then, as an afterthought, she added, "She didn't make you cry did she?"

"Oh no, Nanna, she didn't make me cry. I asked her if she liked me and she told me she liked me very much," said Joey.

"I'm sure she does Joey. How could anyone not like such a lovely boy." said Anne, glancing across at Bill. She was still very alarmed at her son's outburst.

"Well, she said she liked my daddy very much as well, and he isn't a boy is he?"

Bill was trying to draft out a letter, but he paused briefly.

"No, he's not, Joey," said Anne. "What else did you say?"

Joey thought for a minute.

"I told her I was coming to see you Nanna... and Granddad as well and I asked her if she lived with a man like my nanna did."

"Joey!" said his father looking up quickly. Catching his mother's quick glance, he softened his voice a little before adding, "You mustn't ask people things like that."

"Why, Daddy?" Joey asked.

"It's not nice. You don't do it," said Bill. He was a little worried about what other questions his son had put to her.

"Don't worry Bill. She'll be used to questions like that if she's working with children, they're always asking awkward questions."

She turned back to Joey. "Well, what did she say?"

"Mother, don't encourage him, it's not right prying into people's private lives."

"Okay," Anne laughed. "I was simply curious as to how she got out of that one."

"She told me she wasn't married like my nanna and granddad so she lived by herself," Joey said. And before his father could stop him he added. "She said she couldn't get married because nobody loved her."

"There now mother, are you satisfied?" Bill looked down at his paperwork. "Now please, let's drop the subject. I really don't think we should talk about Miss Hughes anymore."

He recalled Sally's short telephone conversation with Jo. It may not be a serious relationship, but she still had a boyfriend!

"I told her I loved her, Nanna," continued Joey.

"That was very kind of you, Joey. But like Daddy says, perhaps we shouldn't talk about Miss Hughes anymore. She may not like you telling me all these things about her. Why don't you tell me something else?"

Bill breathed a sigh of relief. Perhaps now he could absorb himself in his work and put Sally out of his mind.

"Daddy's bought me a present to take to David's birthday party. It's a game." Joey had been thinking of what else he could tell his nanna.

"That's nice I'm sure he'll like a game. He's looking forward to seeing you on Saturday," said Anne. "He'll be five years old and is starting the big school next month. He wants to show you his new school uniform. You'll enjoy the party; his mummy has been making all sorts of lovely things to eat at the birthday tea. Joe, your friend from down the road is going to be there as well."

Joey giggled and went across to his grandmother. "Miss Hughes has a friend called Jo," he said.

"How do you know? Did you meet him?" Anne wasn't sure she approved of Miss Hughes taking her boyfriend to the nursery.

"Joey, I thought we weren't going to talk about Miss Hughes anymore," interrupted Bill, without looking up.

Looking across at his father, Joey pressed his lips tightly together, something he always did when Mrs Miller told the children they must be very quiet.

"Joey, your daddy didn't say you couldn't speak, he simply wants you to stop talking about Miss Hughes," said Anne, grinning.

"Well I wasn't going to talk about Miss Hughes, Nanna. I wanted to tell you about her friend, Jo."

"Well tell me quickly. What about him? Did you meet him?"

Keeping his head down, Bill closed his eyes, as his stomach flipped over. Please – not again. He breathed deeply, waiting for the inevitable.

"Well, Miss Hughes said she was going to telephone her friend Jo, and she said I could speak to her." Joey laughed. "Nanna, her friend has a boy's name. Isn't that funny?"

"Yes it is, Joey," said Anne, laughing with her grandson.

Opening his eyes, Bill looked up sharply.

"But she wasn't in, Nanna," continued Joey. "Miss Hughes left a message for her to ring back. I think she phoned while Daddy was there." He looked across at his father. "Daddy, did she ring while you were there?"

Bill leapt to his feet so quickly his chair fell over behind him. His heart was pounding and he suddenly felt cold.

"Bill, what is it, are you all right?" asked his mother.

"Yes… No. I… I think I've made a mistake… I need to make a phone call… quickly," Bill rushed out of the room.

The colour drained from Anne's face and she began to tremble. Her son handled accounts worth millions of pounds every day. Had something gone terribly wrong? Could this be the reason why Bill had been acting so strangely? In her opinion the firm expected too much from him. It was at times like this she wished he wasn't so clever with figures.

Out in the hall, Bill leaned against the wall and thought over what his son had said. His heart was pounding and he took a few deep breaths, He ran his fingers though his hair. It had never occurred to him that Jo was a *girl* friend of Sally's. With a name like Jo, he had simply assumed it was a man on the phone. Should he try ringing Sally now? She could still have a boyfriend. Yet, what if she hadn't? His mind was in turmoil. What would Colin do in this situation? The answer was simple; he would ring her without any hesitation. In fact he would have asked her out this afternoon, whether there had been a boy on the phone or not!

He hurried across to the telephone and stabbed at the numbers on the handset. His hand trembled so much, he hit the wrong numbers and he had to stop and start again. Glancing at his watch he hoped he wasn't too late – Sally could have gone home by now. Bill held his breath, as the phone at the other end started to ring.

Sally continued to stare down at the phone. Still believing it might be Jo she was about to walk away when it occurred to her it could be one of the parents. Perhaps one of the children had forgotten something, or maybe someone was ill. Slowly she lifted the receiver to her ear.

"Hello," she said cautiously, almost praying it wouldn't be Jo.

"Hello Sally. It's Bill. Bill Roberts. I was beginning to think I'd missed you."

"Hello, Bill," Sally's heart almost missed a beat. "Well I was almost out of the door. Has Joey left something behind?" She glanced around the room as she spoke.

"No… It's nothing like that… It's just I was wondering… you can say no… or you can think about it… but… Well I was wondering if you would like to have dinner with me tomorrow night." It all came out in a rush at the end, but at least he had said it. He crossed his fingers.

"Oh Bill, I'd love to." Sally didn't hesitate.

"That's wonderful." He was hardly able to believe his ears. "I thought we could try The Showboat, the new place on the outskirts of town. I've heard it's very good… but perhaps you've been there already?"

"No Bill, I haven't." She knew it to be very expensive and way beyond her budget.

"I'll pick you up at seven-thirty. I promise I won't be late." He vowed he wouldn't be late, even if it meant taking the afternoon off.

"Thank you Bill, I'll be ready. I'm looking forward to it already."

"So am I," he said.

Sally was shaking with excitement as she put down the phone. And to think she had very nearly not taken the call.

Walking home, she thought about what to wear for such an exclusive place, she couldn't afford anything too expensive at the moment. It was then she remembered the rather beautiful black evening dress her father had bought for her recently.

He had taken both her and her mother out to dinner in celebration of a large order having been placed with his company. She decided to buy some of her favourite perfume and hang the expense. By the time she reached her flat, Sally was feeling on top of the world.

After his call to Sally, Bill picked up the receiver again. He dialled directory enquiries and asked for the number of the restaurant. After making the reservation, he sat on the stairs and tried to calm himself. He decided not to say anything about Sally to his mother, although he knew she would be delighted for him. However, if it didn't work out, her happiness would be short-lived.

Anne watched her son closely, as he walked back into the lounge. She noticed he was a little flushed. "Is everything alright?" she asked anxiously.

"Yes." Seeing how anxious she looked, Bill took her hand. "Don't worry, I got something mixed up, that's all. It was a stupid mistake but everything's fine." Bill glanced at Joey, feeling guilty about the way he had spoken to his son earlier. After all, it was only through Joey's chatter he had learned the true identity of Jo. "Joey, why don't you and I take Bess for a walk while Nanna gets our dinner ready?"

Joey gave him a big grin and ran across to his father's outstretched arms. "Yes please, Daddy. Bess and I would like that."

Anne watched from the window, as they walked down the path. The colour had returned to her face and she was less agitated. Bill was certainly more relaxed, but she was still determined that his father should speak to him later that evening.

Day Two

The next morning, Joey was up in time to see Bill before he set off for work. Hugging his father close, he reminded him it was now only ten days until Christmas.

"Have a lovely time at the birthday party son," Bill told him. "And enjoy your trip to see the trains. I promise to telephone you every day." Giving his son a final hug, he set off for the office.

Bill's mother was relieved at how much better he looked. She believed it was something to do with the chat he'd had with his father. Though, truthfully, John had told her nothing about it. "Man's talk," was all he would say. However, this was because he had been unable to get his son to open up to him.

During the drive into town, Bill reflected on the conversation he'd had with his father the night before. John had looked anxious when he followed him into the sitting room and closed the door behind him. Misunderstanding, he had asked his father if there was something wrong.

"You tell me," John had replied, looking up at his son. Though he was taller than his wife, he was still a couple of inches shorter than Bill. "Your mother's worried about you. She asked me to have a talk with you." He paused. "Look, shall we sit down?" He grinned. "Otherwise I'll have a stiff neck later. She told me you how tense you were this afternoon" he continued once they were comfortably seated. "You must tell us if there's something troubling you."

"No, everything's fine," Bill had replied, smiling. "I explained to Mum that I had misunderstood something, but it's settled now."

Changing the subject, John had suggested he should find himself a nice girl. At this point, Bill recalled how he had been tempted to mention Sally, but had decided against it. If their date turned out to be a one off occasion, it would be awkward having to explain to his parents it was all over so quickly. However he had promised his father that he would try to relax and have some fun for a change. Though John had nodded his approval, Bill knew his father was unconvinced, as he had gone on to talk about the amount of work he was taking on.

The company Bill worked for had opened two new branches in the last few months. The directors, not being able to find the right men to manage the Finance Departments for either of them, had called upon Bill to take charge of the accounts until further interviews were arranged. He had told his father he was managing fine. Besides they were paying him a large salary with generous bonuses for his trouble. However, John had simply mumbled that money wasn't everything.

Bill sighed, as he continued his drive to the office. If only he could open up to his parents and share his problems with them, as other people did. But he found it impossible; he always felt so embarrassed when talking about himself. Therefore he kept everything bottled up inside him.

As usual Bill was first to arrive at the office. He was determined to get away early today, so it was important he had this time to himself. It was quite amazing the amount of work he could get through when the office was quiet. By the time the rest of the staff appeared, he had cleared half the work on his desk. He called his secretary into his office and asked her about his appointments for the day.

"You have two meetings this morning and three this afternoon," she confirmed. "They're all to do with accounts for the new branches. I have the files in my office, Colin brought them through yesterday."

"I want you to cancel the three appointments this afternoon, Miss Anderson. I would prefer them to leave it until January. However if they insist, fit them in somewhere next week."

She was quite taken aback; it was most unusual for Mr Roberts to cancel any appointments.

Deciding to delegate the branches' balance sheets to Colin, Bill asked her to send him in.

"Colin is out of the office today Mr Roberts, he has a day's leave."

"Yes, of course, I'd forgotten about that." Colin was entertaining his in-laws this weekend. For a moment, he wondered who else he could depend on.

Though he had a staff of forty-five, most of the people he could really trust with something so important as the branches' finance sheets, already had a heavy workload. "Okay, send Alan Hurst in." It would be interesting to see how he coped with the figures.

Alan was fairly new to the firm. Although he was still very young, Bill had believed him to be both keen and competent when he interviewed him for the post. As with all new finance staff, Colin was keeping a close eye on him and so far his reports had been most favourable.

"He seems to be very willing to learn," Colin had told him. "If there's something he doesn't understand, he asks me to explain it to him. Not like some of the others, who leave it for someone else to do. And that usually ends up being you."

"Come in," Bill called out to the faint knocking on his office door.

Believing he was in trouble, Alan entered the office cautiously, unsure of what to expect. Normally he never entered Mr Robert's room if he was working in there, much preferring to wait until his boss was out of his office. Even then, it was only to leave various documents on his desk.

It wasn't as though he had ever been in trouble. It was just he felt a little in awe of someone who was so highly respected by the Board of Directors. Besides, someone had told him how most departmental heads preferred their junior staff to keep out of their way.

At Websters International, all new staff, regardless of age, was considered a junior until they had been with the company for at least two years. Only an exceptional report from the department head would allow an earlier promotion to Full Member of Staff. However, Alan had heard from a reliable source this was something, which very rarely happened.

"You wanted to see me, sir?" he said quietly.

"Yes, Alan. Come in and sit down."

"Thank you sir," said Alan. Moving across the room, he wondered if it was usual to be offered a seat if you were about to be reprimanded.

Bill waited until Alan was seated before continuing. "Colin is out of the office today and I need to get away early this afternoon. Therefore, I'd like you to check the figures from the branches. How do you feel about it?"

"I'm sure I could do it sir," he said quietly. Though he was relieved he wasn't in any trouble, he still felt nervous. "I would certainly like to give it a try."

"Good. However, I must warn you, they're very seldom straight forward. If you come across any problems, leave the files on my desk until Monday morning. I would prefer you didn't try to tackle anything you're unsure of. Take your time and check everything very carefully."

"Yes sir, I'll do my best."

Sensing something was bothering Alan, Bill asked if anything was troubling him.

"No sir." He paused. "Well only that I must have done something wrong when you called me into your office."

"Not at all! Actually, Colin tells me you're doing very well."

Alan left the office feeling quite elated.

Now all Bill had to deal with were the two new clients and the constant stream of files, which had a tendency to appear on his desk throughout the day. But as long as there wasn't a major catastrophe, he should get away from the office by four o'clock at the latest.

Sally set off to work feeling very happy. She was so looking forward to having dinner with Bill that evening. Jane phoned during the morning. "I thought I would let you know the parents usually pick up their children by about 3 o'clock on Fridays, I'd forgotten to mention it before. You should get away early. Joey is usually the only one left, but as he isn't there, there's no problem."

Sally decided not to mention her forthcoming date with Bill. Jane may not be too keen on the idea of her socialising with the parents. During the children's afternoon nap, she allowed her mind to drift to the evening ahead. She smiled to herself, as she wondered what Jo would say when she told her about it. Perhaps it would be best not to mention it at all until after the event.

However, thinking of Jo reminded her they were due to meet up at the lecture that very evening. Oh no! She was going to have to tell her after all. Deciding to get it over with she picked up the phone. Secretly, she hoped Jo would be out somewhere. It would be so much easier to leave a message on the answering machine. But as luck would have it, Jo answered quite quickly.

"I can't make it to the lecture after all. I'm afraid something's come up." Sally tried to make light of it, hoping to change the subject without having to say what the 'something' was.

"Oh Sally what a shame, I think it'll be really useful. What's happened?" She paused for a moment. "It's the widower isn't it? He's asked you out?"

"Well yes, he has actually." Sally was a little taken aback that Jo had cottoned on so quickly. "He telephoned me late yesterday afternoon and asked me out to dinner."

"Are you mad?" Jo yelled down the phone, "Where's he taking you? Some cheap place I'll be bound. I've told you before, he probably sees you as an easy touch."

"Actually, he's taking me to The Showboat," replied Sally, starting to get a little annoyed.

"Well, I suppose he isn't a cheapskate," said Jo grudgingly.

"Bill isn't cheap about anything." Sally was thinking of his well-cut suits and large expensive car.

Still, you mark my words." Jo almost spat out the words. "He's only after one thing. Be on your guard and get yourself a taxi home straight after the meal. That'll show him."

"How can you say such an awful thing? You haven't even met him. He's really very nice," said Sally. But she knew she was wasting her breath. Jo always thought the worst of all men.

"Well, go if you must. But I'll give you a ring at about eleven-thirty and I'll keep on ringing every ten minutes until you answer. I want to know you're home okay."

"There's really no need to do that. I'm sure I'll be fine. You could do me a favour though. Tape the lecture for me; I may be able to catch up sometime over the weekend." Sally tried to divert the subject away from Bill.

"Yes, all right," replied Jo, sullenly. "But I'll still phone you at eleven-thirty."

"Okay," said Sally weakly, "If you must."

After a few more cutting remarks about her friend's stupidity, Jo hung up.

Sally realised she was going to have to do something about Jo, but what? No matter what she said, Jo always got her own way. On reflection, no matter what anyone said, Jo always had the last word. Looking at her watch, she decided to wake the children. They would have time to play a game or do some painting before their parents arrived.

By ten past three, all the children had gone home and after a final check around the nursery, she locked up. She went straight home to enjoy a long, hot bath, wash her hair and be ready for Bill calling at seven-thirty.

The rest of Bill's day went well. It was more than he had dared hope for. His two morning appointments hadn't been difficult and Miss Anderson had managed to postpone the other three. For once his desk looked reasonably clear. However, he knew when he arrived back in the office on Monday it would be piled high again *and* he had two very important meetings scheduled, but he wasn't going to dwell on those now.

He telephoned his mother.

Ann had decided not to ring Colin after all. As Bill was looking so much better when he had left for the office she had thought it best to leave well alone. She was pleased to hear him sounding happier and more relaxed and told him so.

'If only she knew,' he thought, as he waited for Joey to come to the phone. Joey told him he had seen lots of trains at the station and then they had gone to have a glass of milk and a cake in the teashop. Before hanging up, Bill told his son how he was missing him already and would telephone again over the weekend.

He packed his brief case and went through to see his secretary. Much to her amazement he told her he was leaving the office for the day.

She looked at her watch. It was only three-thirty. He had left early yesterday to take his son to his mother's home. But he had marked it in his diary several weeks ago and had given her specific instructions Thursday afternoon must remain free. This was so spontaneous, it very unlike Mr Roberts. Still it was not her place to question her boss. "Goodbye, sir, have a nice weekend."

"Thank you, Miss Anderson." He smiled. "I think you might as well take the rest of the afternoon off, next week we may be rather busy. Goodbye."

"Thank you," called out Miss Anderson, but she wasn't sure he heard. He was already halfway down the stairs.

It was a little before six forty-five when Bill climbed into his car to drive the short journey to Sally's flat. He was determined not to be late, but he knew the traffic would be building up with partygoers. After all, it *was* only ten days until Christmas; his son had reminded him of it earlier in the day.

He knew he had been lucky to get a reservation at The Showboat. It had only been due to a cancellation a few minutes earlier. He would have hated having to tell Sally it was fully booked.

He arrived at Sally's flat at seven-thirty on the dot and pulled a large box of chocolates from the back seat. He had wanted to buy her something special, but had no idea what to get. He was so out of touch. What *did* men buy young ladies these days? In the end he decided on the chocolates. He paused at her front door and took a deep breath before ringing the doorbell.

Though Sally had been ready for some time, she had spent the last few minutes looking in the long mirror in her bedroom. This was her first evening with Bill and she certainly didn't want it to be her last. Hearing the doorbell, she picked up her evening bag and hurried to the door.

Bill was left breathless when she opened the door. She had changed from the attractive, young girl he had met in the nursery into a beautiful, elegant young woman. Her long auburn hair, swept up at the back of her head, emphasised her swanlike neck, while her make up, delicately applied, high-lighted her large brown eyes. Her long black evening dress hugged her slim figure like a glove and around her neck was a diamond necklace; matching earrings completed the picture.

"Sally, you look absolutely stunning!" Bill gasped. He would be the envy of every man in the restaurant.

"Thank you, Bill." She saw the box of chocolates in his hand. "Are those for me?"

"Err, yes," he said, handing the chocolates. "These are for you." How inappropriate they seemed.

"They're my favourites, thank you." Sally placed them on the hall table behind her. "I'm all ready." Reaching up to the coat stand, she took down a short evening jacket and handed it to Bill. "Would you help me with this please?"

Taking the jacket, he wrapped it around her shoulders. "Your carriage awaits and I promise to get you home by twelve midnight before it turns into a pumpkin," said Bill, helping her into the car.

"Thank you, Prince Charming." Sally laughed. He did look charming tonight in his evening suit and bow tie. He reminded her of James Bond, tall, slim and very attractive.

Bill had trouble keeping his eyes on the road, as he wanted to look at Sally. She looked gorgeous. How lucky he was to be with her.

If she saw him constantly glancing towards her, she didn't mention it. She merely chattered to him, asking questions about his work. She wanted to know what he did. How his day had gone. Had he been very busy in the office? While Bill answered all her questions, he would rather have been talking about her.

Arriving at the restaurant, the headwaiter showed them to their table. Bill could feel the eyes of the other diners following them as they walked across the dining room. He knew they were looking at Sally, but how could he blame them? After all he couldn't keep his eyes off her himself. Though he was proud to be the one escorting her, he was fully aware she could have her pick of any of the young men here tonight. It saddened him when he realised this could be his first and last evening with her. The headwaiter handed them each a menu, saying someone would be with them shortly.

"Would you like a drink while we're looking at the menu?" Bill asked, calling a waiter.

After making their choice from the menu, Bill wanted to know all about Sally, asking her to tell him about herself.

"There's not much to tell," she said. "I grew up with two brothers who took it upon themselves to look after me. The only trouble was, they never allowed me to live my own life." She didn't usually open up with strangers, but she found herself telling Bill all about how her parents and brothers had dominated her for most of her young life. She told him how her parents ran a small business and had insisted that she worked in the family firm, even though she wanted to be a nursery nurse.

"I was almost twenty when I finally told my parents I was moving back to my hometown and going to college. They were horrified and tried to stop me, but I got my own way and with Jane Miller's help, obtained a place on the part-time course." She laughed. "Dad wasn't happy at all about me living in the Halls of Residence that's why he bought me that small flat. I do a few jobs at the college and it helps me to pay my way." Somehow she felt comfortable talking to him and went on to tell him a little about Jo, though she left out what her friend had said regarding Bill's intentions. When at last she paused, she wondered how she could have told Bill so much. "Why didn't you tell me to shut up? I must be boring you to death. Tell me something about yourself."

However, Bill could have listened to her all night. He smiled "Of course you're not boring me Sally. I'd like to hear more." He had been watching her intently while she was speaking and realised he was falling in love with her.

Come to think of it, hadn't he loved her from the first moment he set eyes on her? He longed to take her in his arms, but he knew he couldn't. Not here, not yet. Besides, she had only just met him; she couldn't possibly feel same way about him. Before he could say anything else, the waiter arrived with their meal.

"You don't get off that easily," Sally laughed. "You must tell me your life's history after the meal."

"There's nothing to tell. I'm a bit of a loner, really. I've always been so shy and withdrawn." Bill could have kicked himself. Why on earth he had told her he was shy? It was a stupid thing to say. Grown men weren't shy. What would she think?

They finished their meal and while the waiters cleared the last of the dishes away, Bill ordered more drinks, choosing a mineral water for himself.

"I have to drive," he explained. "And I promised to get you safely home by midnight, remember?"

Sally glanced up at the clock on the wall. Surely it wasn't time to go yet; she didn't want this night to end. She was relieved to find the night was still young.

A pianist had been playing soft music, but now he had finished and a band was beginning to set up their instruments on the small stage. The manager came out to introduce them and their vocalist. The lights dimmed and as the band started to play, Bill moved his chair a little nearer to Sally. He couldn't remember feeling like this about anyone before. Not even Julie. Noticing Sally's hand resting on the table, he wondered whether he dared take it in his own. Reaching out, he gently cupped his hand around hers, hoping she wouldn't move away.

She looked at him and smiled. She would like to have learned a little more about him, but he hadn't said anything else. Once he had mentioned his shyness, he clammed up.

The singer finished her song and then sang another two before asking why no one was dancing. The band started to play a very slow waltz. Bill wanted to ask Sally to dance. He was desperate to hold her in his arms and he looked around the room, hoping someone else would be first on the dance floor. But no one moved. Turning back to Sally, he found himself saying. "Sally, would you like to dance?"

"Yes, I'd love to," she replied.

Walking onto the dance floor, Bill took her in his arms and held her as close as he dared. She looked so fragile, he was afraid she might break. They moved gently with the music. Having eyes only for each other, they were oblivious to everyone else in the room. No one joined them on the floor; the dance seemed to belong to this young couple. They looked so in love, no one would have believed this was their first evening together.

When the music stopped they suddenly realised they were the only two on the dance floor and walked slowly back to their table. Everyone began to applaud, even the waiters and by the time they had reached their seats they were both quite flushed with embarrassment.

Bill couldn't believe he had done that. It wasn't like him at all. Usually he never did anything that brought attention to himself. This lovely young woman was having a strange affect on him. It was so wonderful holding her in his arms and he wished the evening could go on forever. He didn't want to take her home at twelve, if the car turned into a pumpkin, so what? But he reminded himself he had promised she would be home by midnight and he couldn't go back on his word.

However he didn't realise Sally felt the same about him. On the dance floor, she had loved the feel of his arms around her; they were so gentle, yet so strong. She yearned for him to kiss her, but somehow she knew he wouldn't. Not yet. It was too soon.

He asked if she would like to dance again. And once on the floor, he wouldn't let her sit down. By now many other couples were up dancing, but neither Bill nor Sally noticed them. As far as they were concerned, they were the only two people in the room. When they finally returned to their seats they were quite out of breath. He looked at his watch. It was almost midnight.

The time was passing far too quickly. Before long, he would have to take her home. What if she didn't want to see him again? What would he do then? He looked away to hide the pain in his eyes. His thoughts were interrupted when the band began to play a waltz.

"Shall we dance Sally? It's almost twelve, and I promised I would take you home by then." A lump formed in his throat, this would be their last waltz.

Rising from her seat, Sally smiled. "It doesn't have to be the last one does it?" She didn't want the night to end anymore than he did. "We don't really have to go yet do we? I'm having such a wonderful evening."

"No, of course we don't." Bill's heart soared. She was happy to stay on with him. "I simply didn't want you to think I was going back on my word and planning to keep you out all night."

Secretly she wouldn't have minded if he had.

They lost all track of time. It was almost two in the morning when the band played the last waltz.

Outside a hard frost had formed and it crunched beneath their feet. Sally shivered in the cold night air and Bill draped his overcoat around her shoulders.

"You wait here where it's warmer," he said, guiding her back to the doorway. "I don't want you to slip on the frost. I'll bring the car around to the door."

While she was waiting Sally gazed up towards the stars. How large they seemed tonight, much brighter than she had ever seen them before. There were millions of them; all looking like enormous sparkling diamonds hanging by invisible threads in the night sky.

'How beautiful,' she thought, pulling Bill's coat tightly around her. She was amazed she had never noticed before how lovely the heavens were at night. She saw Bill's car coming around from the car park.

"If I could make one wish for every single star," she murmured, tightly closing her eyes. "Each wish would be the same – please make Bill feel the same way about me, as I do about him."

But in her heart, she knew magic and wishes were only for children. Such things were not for the likes of her. She must stop dreaming and face reality. He was a high-powered executive in one of the largest companies in the world, while she was merely a trainee nursery nurse. What could he possibly see in someone like her? It was likely he wouldn't even ask her out again.

They drove a little of the way in silence. Bill was thinking how wonderful the evening had been, so much more than he had ever dreamed possible. He wondered whether she would go out with him again. He winced, probably not. She was a lovely young woman and he was not only several years older than her, but he was also a widower with a young son. Nevertheless, he could...

"Have you spoken to Joey since you left him with his grandmother?" Sally interrupted his thoughts. "I know he was excited at seeing her again. He told me so yesterday."

"Yes, I spoke to him today. He'd been to the station to see the trains. My mother was booking seats for their trip to Scotland. He sounded quite excited. He'd also been to a teashop and had cakes."

"Yes, he told me all about Bess, his nanna's dog and how he might like a dog some day," said Sally. "He also told me he was going to a friend's birthday party and you'd bought a present for him to take."

Bill ran a finger around his collar. It seemed Joey had had a long chat with Sally. He felt embarrassed when he recalled some of the questions his son had asked her. He wondered what else he might have said, but thought it best not to ask.

Pulling up at Sally's flat, he helped her out of the car and walked her to the door. Upstairs the phone was ringing. 'That has got to be Jo,' thought Sally, miserably.

"Is that your phone?" Bill asked.

"Yes," replied Sally. "It's probably a wrong number. I sometimes get calls for an all night Chinese take-away." This was true; the numbers were very similar, but it didn't happen often. "Would you like to come in for a coffee?" she added. She hoped he wouldn't think her too forward, but she really didn't want him to leave.

Bill would have loved to take her up on her offer. However the hour was late and he didn't want her to think he was pushing his way in, or that his intentions were anything but honourable.

"It's very late Sally. I think I should go. Besides, you must be tired."

"Thank you for a wonderful evening, Bill. I've really enjoyed it."

"I've enjoyed it too," replied Bill. "I'm so very pleased you were able to come." He paused, wondering if he dare ask her out again. He decided to risk it. If she said no, at least he would still have the memory of this evening. "Sally, would you like to go for a drive to the coast with me tomorrow?"

"I'd love to." Sally replied, glancing up at the stars, still sparkling brightly above.

Bill could hardly believe it. She had said yes. "Would ten-thirty be too early for you?"

"Ten-thirty will be fine, Bill," replied Sally. "I'll be ready."

He bent down and kissed her on the cheek. Then pulling her closer to him, he kissed her quickly on the lips before walking back to his car.

Opening the door to her flat, Sally watched him drive away. By the time she reached the top of her stairs the phone had started to ring again.

"Hello, Jo," said Sally, knowing it wouldn't be anyone else.

"About time too," she replied. "Where have you been until this time of night?" Then, as an afterthought, added. "Are you alone?"

"Yes, of course I'm alone," said Sally, though she wished she wasn't. "We only left the restaurant about fifteen minutes ago and came straight back here."

"Well I'm glad you didn't ask him in. Goodness knows how it would have ended up. I thought I told you to get a taxi home after you'd eaten."

"There wasn't any need," replied Sally. "I trust Bill. Actually, I did invite him in, but he said it was very late and he should go." She paused for a moment. "I'm seeing him again tomorrow. We're going for a drive down to the coast in the morning."

"You must be mad. Fancy getting involved with a widower, and one with a son as well," Jo retorted. "You know what he's after, don't you?"

"I don't believe it. If that's the case, why didn't he come in tonight?" The tone of Sally's voice rose a little. She was beginning to get angry.

"Perhaps he's biding his time; saving you for another night. He may even have gone to someone else's house tonight. Come to think of it, he's probably got a string of women, all waiting for him to call," said Jo spitefully, ignoring the warning signs in Sally's voice. "If you want my advice I think you should get rid of him, tell him you've changed your mind when he calls in the morning. Tell him you've cottoned on to his little game and you're not going to be his little bit on the side." There was a pause. "On the other hand, perhaps I'd better come over and tell him for you, at least I'll know you're rid of him. I'll soon put him straight!"

Sally was furious! How dare Jo talk about Bill like that! "Stop it! Just stop it right there! As it happens I *don't* want your advice. To tell you the truth, I've never wanted your advice. You barge in and take over and until now, like a fool, I've allowed you to get away with it. But not anymore, I simply won't allow you to talk like that to me. This has been the most wonderful night of my life, and you want to spoil it by being so spiteful. You haven't even met Bill. He's a wonderful person and if you want the truth, I wish he had come in tonight. I really didn't want him to leave."

Sally couldn't believe it was herself speaking. By now she was shaking, but not with fear. She was shaking with anger and she crashed the phone down on its cradle.

At the other end of the line, Jo realised she had gone too far this time. She didn't want to lose Sally's friendship, having already lost too many friends through her sharp tongue. She dialled the number again and it rang for some time before Sally answered. "I'm so sorry, Sally. I promise I won't say another word. You're right. I don't know Bill. But I care about you and I get carried away sometimes." Wishing to change the subject, she mentioned the lecture.

"It was very helpful. I've taped it for you and I picked up a few flyers. I'll drop them into you tomorrow morning, if you like."

"You might recall I'm going out." Sally's tone was icy. "Bill is picking me up at ten-thirty."

"That's okay Sally. I'll come over at nine-thirty, if that's okay?"

"Yes. All right I'll see you then." Sally hung up, not giving Jo the chance to reply. She undressed for bed. However she was far too excited to sleep and lay for some time, recalling the whole evening. But tiredness eventually overcame her and she fell asleep and dreamed about what tomorrow would bring.

After Bill left Sally on her doorstep, he drove home slowly. The scent of her perfume lingered in his car, reminding him of the wonderful evening they had spent together. How he would have loved to have coffee with her, but it *was* late and he didn't want her to get the wrong idea about him. Besides, she had agreed to see him tomorrow. He glanced at the clock on the dashboard. The pointers showed it was nearly three o'clock – it was tomorrow already! In only seven and a half hours, he would see her again. He knew now he was desperately in love with her. Yet, was it possible to be so in love with someone you had only met three times and, come to think of it, had kissed only once? If you could possibly call it a kiss, it had been nothing more than a fleeting brush against her lips. Thankfully the roads weren't busy, as he was reliving every single moment of the evening.

Reaching home he poured himself a drink and took it upstairs, hoping it would help him fall asleep. But he had grave doubts.

Day Three

Despite not falling asleep until around four in the morning, Sally was awake by seven. It was no good; she was too excited to sleep. Her mind was racing, recalling the evening she had spent with Bill. Even in the shower, while the water rained down over her, she wrapped her arms around herself and pretended she was whirling around the dance floor in Bill's arms.

Jo arrived shortly after nine. Sally only opened the door a little way at first; she was still very annoyed with her friend.

"Hello, Sally," Jo waved a small white handkerchief. "I'm really sorry about last night. I hope you've forgiven me." She had spent the night wrestling with her conscience. She knew exactly what she would say if anyone tried telling *her* what to do. "Look, I've brought you a tape and the flyers I mentioned." She held up some papers and a small audiotape.

Sally opened the door a little wider. "I was really angry with you last night Jo, but we've been friends for a long time now, so I won't say anymore about it – except I'm seeing Bill this morning and I don't want anymore phone calls checking up on what time I get back." She paused. "Is that understood?"

"Yes. I promise," said Jo meekly. "I simply think you should…" She stopped when she saw Sally glaring at her. "Yes. I promise," she repeated.

"Right, now that's settled, perhaps you would like some coffee." Sally invited Jo into her home. She was glad the air had been cleared. It wasn't in her nature to stay annoyed with anyone for very long.

Bill arose early. Not wanting to oversleep, he had set his alarm for seven o'clock. Though it was late when he had finally dozed off, he hadn't slept well. Once he was dressed, he telephoned his mother. "How's Joey?" he asked.

"He's fine Bill. Don't worry about him. He's looking forward to the birthday party this afternoon," said Anne. "How are you, son? Is everything alright? You're phoning very early. Joey isn't up yet."

"Everything's okay, Mum. I want to get down to some work, that's all," replied Bill, uneasily. He felt guilty at lying to his mother. However he had decided not to mention Sally for the time being. If the relationship didn't work out after all, it would only give her further cause for concern.

"You work too hard Bill. I wish you would slow down and relax."

"I'm fine, Mum. Stop worrying. Tell me, what time is your train on Friday?" said Bill, changing the subject.

"It's not until two-thirty which means I've plenty of time in the morning to get organised," said Anne. "I think we should arrive there shortly before eight. Jack is meeting us at the station."

Bill smiled to himself. He knew how his mother hated being rushed when going on a trip. She liked to check everything at least three times for fear of forgetting something.

"Are you coming over on Thursday night or Friday morning?" she added.

"I don't know yet. I'll see how the work load is," replied Bill. "I'd better get on now. Tell Joey I send my love and I hope he has a good time at the party."

"I will son, and take care." 'That firm is working him too hard,' Anne thought, as she went back into the kitchen. She wished he would listen to his father and try to get out more.

"Would you like another coffee?" Sally asked, looking at the clock.

"Have you got time? I don't want to make you late."

"There's plenty of time. Bill isn't due for a while yet. Besides I'm ready. I just need my jacket," replied Sally going through to the kitchen. She looked out of the window. The sun was shining brightly this morning, but because of the hard frost the night before she knew she would need to wrap up well. It was likely to be even colder at the coast.

"Yes, you'll need something warm." Jo had followed Sally into the kitchen. "It looks nice through the window, but I can tell you it's very cold outside."

Sally studied Jo, as she poured the coffee. Her friend wasn't unattractive. She was slim and quite intelligent – well she was intelligent most of the time, so why didn't she get herself a nice boyfriend? It certainly wasn't because she was shy. On the contrary, Jo was very outgoing. Perhaps if she let her dark hair grow a little, instead of that short spiky style she favoured and dressed in something even a touch more feminine, anything, other than those camouflage trousers...

"I wish I could afford a place of my own." Jo interrupted her thoughts. "There still aren't any vacancies on the campus, I checked again yesterday." She sighed. "I guess I'll have to continue living with my parents for a while yet."

"Well I wouldn't have this place if it weren't for my father. He insisted on buying it for me. But I must admit it's very nice to have a place to call my own."

"All I have to call my own is my telephone." Jo laughed. Her parents had insisted on her having a telephone of her own, when she started mounting up large bills.

Suddenly the doorbell rang. Sally jumped. She glanced at the clock. It was only ten fifteen. "That must be Bill," she gushed He's early."

Jo couldn't help noticing the glow of excitement on Sally's face. "I'd better go." She put down her cup.

"No, it's all right. I expect you'd like to meet him, but please behave yourself," Sally warned, as she went to open the door.

"I promise I'll be good."

"I'm sorry, I'm a little early," said Bill, when Sally opened the door. Unable to wait any longer, he had already driven around the block twice.

"That's all right Bill. Come in and meet my friend Jo." Despite her friend's assurances, Sally couldn't help feeling a little anxious as she made the introductions.

"I'm pleased to meet you," said Bill.

Sally was relieved when Jo replied, "It's nice meeting you. Sally has told me so much about you."

Surprisingly, Jo was actually bowled over by Bill. For the moment, her feminist principles were completely forgotten and she could see why Sally had taken such a liking to him.

"Would you like some coffee Bill?" Sally asked.

"No thank you. I had some before I left." He had actually drunk gallons of the stuff, in an effort to kill time. He turned back to Jo. "Sally tells me you're both doing the same course. Are you enjoying it?"

"Yes, very much, I'm looking forward to passing the exams and getting down to working with children. Sally says you have a child."

Sally frowned, wondering what Jo might say next. But she needn't have worried as she continued sweetly, "She says he's a lovely little boy of four. That's such a lovely age. Full of mischief and questions."

"Yes he is, full of both." Bill hoped Jo wouldn't enquire what sort of questions his son asked.

"Well, I must be going. I've a lot of studying to catch up on. I'm not as far ahead as Sally." Jo rose to her feet. "It's been a pleasure to meet you."

Bill stood up and shook her hand. "I hope we'll meet again sometime," he said.

"I'm sure we will," said Jo going towards the door.

"I'll see Jo out, Bill. I'll only be a minute." Sally led her friend to the front door.

"He's very nice, Sally," said Jo, opening the door. "I hope it works out for you, I mean that. He's just your type. I'm sorry I was so stubborn and I promise no more phone calls or nasty remarks."

"Thank you, Jo. I really do like him."

"It's a lot more than that Sally," said Jo, thoughtfully. "You give yourself away every time you look at him. Your whole face glows. Well I'll be off. Have a nice day, as they say."

Sally went back to find Bill looking out of the window. "I'm ready. I just need to fetch my jacket." She disappeared into the bedroom and returned a few minutes later. "We can go now."

Bill bent down and kissed her lightly on the cheek. "Come on then. Let's go."

Once we get going, the car will soon warm up again," said Bill, as he started the engine.

"It's a beautiful day," said Sally, happily. "It's a good day for going on a brisk walk to blow away all the cobwebs. I hope you're prepared to walk along the beach. You can't go to the seaside without going onto the sands."

"As long as you don't expect me to swim in the sea," laughed Bill. "It's far too cold for that."

"I'll let you off today. However, when it's warmer there'll be no excuse." Sally tried to sound stern, but her laughter gave her away.

"If you come with me when it's warmer, then I promise I'll swim in the sea." Bill hoped Sally would still be with him when the weather turned milder.

It wasn't long before they reached the coast. During the summer months finding a parking space could be difficult, but out of season when the shops and the fairground were closed, there was never a problem. Sally leapt out of the car and ran across to the promenade. She looked down onto the beach.

"I'll race you to the rocks." She had already seen a slope leading down to the sands below and dashed off before she had finished speaking. Bill chased after her. They ran down the slope and onto the beach. They were both out of breath when they reached the rocks.

"I won," said Sally laughing.

"You cheated," said Bill. "You didn't wait for me." He placed his arm around her shoulders and pulled her to him. Her lips looked so inviting, he felt the urge to kiss her, but didn't dare. "We were supposed to start together."

"I'm a woman so I get a head start." Sally grinned. "It's in the rules."

"What rules?" Bill laughed. "We didn't discuss any rules."

As they walked along the beach, Sally teased him about winning the race. "You're out of condition because you sit at a desk all day and don't get enough exercise."

"You could be right." He had to admit it was good being out here today. Most of his weekends were spent working at home in between seeing to Joey. He should do this more often.

They continued walking along the beach and were so engrossed in each other that neither of them noticed someone watching them from further along the sands.

"If I didn't know better, I would say that was Bill over there." Rachel lifted the binoculars to her eyes to take a closer look. "It *is* Bill… and… if I'm not mistaken… he's with a woman."

"Quick let me see!" Colin grabbed the binoculars from his wife. "Well I'll be blowed. He did it then, he asked her out." he murmured. Though he had made the suggestion, he was most surprised Bill had gone through with it, knowing how shy he was.

"You're right, Rachel, It is Bill. Come on, let's go over and say hello."

"Do you think we should?" she asked, hesitating. "He's with someone and may not want us to intrude."

"Of course we should. Come on, it'll be fine." As he spoke, he grabbed Rachel's arm and pulled her across the sands. He wasn't going to miss an opportunity to meet Bill's new lady friend.

"Hello there. Fancy meeting you here," said Colin.

"Hello Colin, Rachel. I would like to introduce you to Sally," said Bill removing his arm from around her shoulders. "What're you doing here? I thought Rachel's parents were coming for the weekend."

"Yes, but they suggested we might like to get out on our own, while they looked after the kids, so we took the opportunity," Colin replied. "We have two young children, a boy and a girl," he added for Sally's benefit.

"Colin, I feel hungry," said Rachel. "Shall we go to the café we saw up on the promenade? I think it's the only one open today."

"Okay," said Colin. He turned to Bill and Sally. "Would you like to join us?"

"Are you hungry, Sally?" Bill asked. He had to admit he was feeling quite peckish himself. He had put it down to the fresh air, forgetting he hadn't eaten anything that morning.

"Yes, I am." she laughed. "I didn't have any breakfast."

"That settles it then. Lead on, Colin," said Bill.

They made their way over to the promenade. Rachel and Sally followed a little way behind the two men.

"I do hope we aren't intruding," said Rachel, still a little concerned they may have butted in.

"Not at all, it's nice meeting some of Bill's friends."

"Have you known Bill long?" Rachel was surprised he had never mentioned Sally before.

"Not long, only since Wednesday. I'm standing in for Mrs Miller at the nursery, while she is off with 'flu."

"Well you must have made quite an impression on Bill. He hasn't taken anyone out since his wife died three years ago. Has he told you anything about her?"

"No," said Sally. "And I haven't asked."

"It was all very sad. A car accident. It's a miracle Joey wasn't in the car at the time. Julie was with her parents; her father was driving. It was thought he had a heart attack at the wheel. The car spun out of control and smashed into a stone bridge. All three were killed instantly. Fortunately Bill was working from home that day otherwise Joey would have been in the car as well."

A shiver ran down Rachel's back, as she recalled the look of horror on Bill's face when she and Colin had tried to comfort him. "I'm sorry, Sally. I have no idea why I'm telling you all this. Let's change the subject."

As they walked across the beach, Rachel couldn't help noticing how Sally kept looking up ahead towards Bill. She didn't seem to want to take her eyes off him.

Meanwhile, Colin was talking to Bill about Sally. "You did it then, you took my advice and asked her out."

"Yes," replied Bill. He didn't mention how he had nearly been put off by the phone call from Jo. "I took her to The Showboat last night. We had such a wonderful evening and totally lost track of time. It was almost two when I took her home."

"She seems to be a nice girl," said Colin. "And very attractive."

"Yes she is," said Bill. He turned and smiled at Sally. "Last night she looked so beautiful. Every head turned when we walked into the restaurant."

Colin hadn't failed to notice the tone in Bill's voice softened, when he spoke of Sally. "You like her a great deal don't you?" he said softly, looking behind to make sure the ladies couldn't overhear.

Bill hesitated, then against his better judgement, added, "I'm in love with her Colin. I think I knew it the first moment I saw her."

"Does she know?"

"No, I don't think so. Well, I haven't said anything to her – you won't say anything will you?" he added hastily. "Not even to Rachel. I know what you're like. You'd probably make some joke of it, saying, pass the salt please, Sally, and by the way, do you know Bill's madly in love with you?"

"Surely I'm not as bad as that… am I?" Colin asked, holding up his hands in mock horror.

"You can be at times," said Bill. "Promise me Colin; don't make me regret telling you."

"Alright. I promise I won't say a word," said Colin, grinning. "But why don't you simply tell her how you feel?"

"Look at her Colin," replied Bill. "She's only a kid. I'm afraid, if I get heavy, she may be frightened off. After all, I only met her on Wednesday. She doesn't really know me."

Colin looked away and smiled to himself. He had never known Bill to 'get heavy' with anyone. He simply wouldn't know how. He wasn't that type of person.

"You don't know her either. Yet you say you love her," he said.

"I know enough," said Bill quietly.

"I've got an idea," said Colin. "Why don't you ask her to the firm's dinner dance next Thursday?"

"You're determined I should go to the Christmas Dance, aren't you?" Bill replied, smiling. "I'll think about it."

"Don't stop to think about it. Go for it, while you're on a roll. Ah, here we are." Colin opened the door to the café.

Looking at his friend, Bill wished for the umpteenth time he could be a bit more like him. He knew Colin wouldn't hesitate for a minute if he saw something he wanted. A few years ago when he first met Rachel, he went all out to get her, despite the fact she already had a steady boyfriend.

"Remember Colin. Please, not a word. Not even to Rachel. Promise me."

"Can't I just whisper in Sally's ear?" Colin teased. "I'll be very discreet and simply say how passionately in love you are with her and does she feel the same way about you." However, seeing the anxious look on Bill's face, he stopped joking. "Don't worry, my lips are sealed. I promise I won't say a word."

Relieved, Bill smiled his thanks and held open the door, allowing Sally and Rachel to enter the café first. A delicious smell of bacon and eggs met them when they walked in.

"Something smells good. Bacon and eggs for me I think. What about the rest of you?" Colin asked, rubbing his hands together.

They all agreed on bacon and eggs and placed their order.

"We didn't expect to find anywhere open at this time of the year," said Bill to the café owner, a jolly looking middle-aged lady.

"Oh, I open at weekends, if the weather's fine. There's always someone around needing a hot cup of tea or some soup to warm them up."

When the bacon and eggs arrived everyone ate hungrily.

"That was good," said Colin, wiping a slice of bread around his plate. "The best I've had in a long time. But now I think we'll have to get back and rescue Rachel's parents from our two monsters. We'll leave you to enjoy the rest of your day in peace."

Colin insisted the meal was his treat, when Bill opened his wallet. "We've encroached on your day, so we'll pay." Once outside, he grinned and gave Bill a broad wink, as they said their goodbyes.

"I hope she doesn't leave him." Colin was watching Bill and Sally walk hand in hand towards the lighthouse at the far end of the long beach. "They look so good together and he really needs someone."

"Sally won't leave him," said Rachel, confidently. "She's besotted with him."

"Are you sure? Did she say so?" Colin was surprised.

"She didn't have to." Rachel grinned at her husband. "She couldn't keep her eyes off him." She shook her head. "Oh sure, Sally was talking and listening to me, but it was Bill she was looking at. She's in love with him and he probably doesn't know it." She sighed. "No. Bill will be the one who ends that relationship."

"I don't think so," said Colin, not wanting to break a confidence with his friend. "But if he did, he'd be a fool. She's got to be the best thing that's happened to him in a long while." He felt a little easier knowing Sally wasn't simply leading Bill on, he deserved better than that.

"Didn't you know about her?" Rachel was curious. "Bill usually confides in you doesn't he?"

Not wanting to deliberately lie to his wife, Colin chose his words carefully. "Yes, Bill does confide in me to some extent, but he still keeps a lot to himself." He paused. "However, I must admit he did seem a little distracted last Thursday."

Sally and Bill drew close to the lighthouse. It wasn't used as a beacon anymore, during the summer months it was open as a museum, and a tourist attraction.

"I like your friends," said Sally. "They care a great deal about you."

"Yes. They were there when I needed them. I've known Colin a long time; we met at university. He's also my right hand man at the office."

"Rachel is very nice. She's very friendly and I found her easy to talk to." Sally paused. "I love her blonde hair. I used to wish I had been born blonde. I did think of dying it at one time."

"You have beautiful hair," replied Bill. "It suits you just as it is."

"Thank you." Sally paused, thinking back to what Bill had said a few moments ago. "It must be good to know you have friends you can rely on." She didn't really have anyone on her side, except perhaps, Jo. But even she wasn't what you would call a very sympathetic listener. "Come on; let's work off some of those bacon and eggs. I'll race you to the red flag over there," she added, not wanting to dwell on Jo for too long.

Sally started to run across the sands with Bill following close behind. They reached the flag together. "It's a tie!" she laughed.

"You did it again," Bill grinned. "You had a head start."

"I know. It's a woman's prerogative," Sally replied, her face glowing with excitement.

Bill put his arms around Sally's waist and pulled her to him. He gazed down at her, desperately wanting to kiss her. But she looked so young and innocent, he held back. She might think he was about to take advantage of her on this lonely stretch of beach and never want to see him again. Instead he took a deep breath and, grasping her hand, they continued to walk towards the lighthouse.

At last they reached the narrow causeway, which led across to the small island where the lighthouse stood. The tide was out, so they were able to take the short walk across.

"I find it very sad." Sally looked up at the lighthouse.

"What is it you find so sad?" Bill followed her gaze.

"That this lighthouse, which was once used as a beacon to save lives by steering ships away from the rocks, is now only used as a tourist attraction. It seems to have lost its dignity; its real purpose in life."

"I never thought of it like that," said Bill.

"When I was child, my parents used to bring me here. We climbed to the top and the lighthouse keeper showed us the lamp. The beam could be seen for miles." She paused, deep in thought. When she spoke again, she sounded more cheerful. "Do you know there are one hundred and thirty seven stairs to the top? I counted them once on the way up and then again on the way down, just to be sure."

"No, I didn't know, I can't remember ever going to the top, but I suppose I must have done at sometime. We could come back during the summer when it's open and climb to the top if you like." He laughed, "All one hundred and thirty seven steps."

"Oh Bill, can we? I'd love it." She took his arm. "Then we could go out onto the balcony and look down at the people on the rocks below. They look so small from up there, rather like ants. You can also make out the white dome of the ballroom across the bay, although I'm not sure what it's used for now. There is also a fun fair behind the building. What fun we all had. Isn't it a shame we have to grow up and leave it all behind?"

Bill watched Sally as she spoke. He loved how her large brown eyes sparkled when she was excited. If only this day could…

She interrupted his thoughts. "We used to go into the small café over there. My parents would have tea, while my brothers and I had lemonade or ice cream." Her face clouded a little, as she thought back over the years, but she brightened again. "We could bring Joey; he would love it up there."

"Yes. He'd like that," said Bill, surprised, yet delighted she had thought of his son.

They picked their way over the rocks around to the back of the lighthouse and looked across the treacherous rocks and out to sea.

"I think we ought to be getting back," said Bill. "It looks as though the tide is turning. I don't think we'd be very comfortable spending the next three or four hours here, it's turning colder."

"Yes, you're right," said Sally. "Several years ago, when the lighthouse keepers worked here, they often had to row people back ashore after they'd been caught by the tide."

"Now, there's no one here but us," said Bill, looking around.

Holding hands, they made their way back along the beach towards where they had left the car.

"Would you like a coffee or something before we drive back? I see the café is still open," said Bill.

"Yes please," replied Sally. "It'll help to warm us up."

"What time do you close?" he asked the cafe owner, as he ordered two mugs of coffee.

"Oh, I hang around until everyone has gone home," she replied. "I'll be closing very shortly now, but don't rush away, I still have some clearing up to do."

"I've had a lovely day, Bill" Sally sipped her coffee. "Everything has been perfect."

"I'm glad you enjoyed it. I did too. I'd normally have been working at home today. Now I know what I've been missing," said Bill.

"You work too hard. Jane told me you had a very demanding job."

"And what else did Mrs Miller say about me?" Bill hoped she hadn't been discussing him with Sally.

"Oh, nothing at all. Jane would never discuss the personal lives of the parents with anyone. She simply told me you were sometimes a little late collecting Joey because of your job, that's all. She was briefing me on what I needed to know about the children."

Bill was relieved. He still had a nagging doubt Sally might have only agreed to accompany him because she felt sorry for him. He changed the subject. "Drink up then. I think we'd better go and let this good lady get off home."

Bill was quiet as they made their way across to the car park. He didn't want to go back yet. This might be his last day with Sally. She may not want to meet him again. However, darkness was beginning to fall and already it was getting colder. He couldn't drive around the county all evening simply to keep Sally near him. Suddenly he had an idea.

"Perhaps we could find a restaurant that might be able to squeeze in two more people tonight? I know it's very short notice, being Christmas time and all, but we could try." He paused, wondering whether she may have had enough of his company already and wanted to call it a day. "What do you think, Sally?"

"Oh yes please, Bill. That would be wonderful."

Sally desperately hoped they would find a restaurant somewhere. Anywhere would do, even the local chip shop, so long as she didn't have to leave him. Until he suggested the restaurant, she had been a little afraid he might be tiring of her, as he had been so silent after leaving the café.

However, as Bill said, with Christmas barely a week away, she knew most places would be fully booked.

Driving back towards the town, they began to look out for restaurants. They tried two without success. The third was locked up, though the tables were laid out ready for the evening sitting. By the time they reached the fourth, an Italian restaurant called Luigi's, they were beginning to have doubts of getting in anywhere.

Bill walked over to the door. Inside he could see a man and woman checking the tables in readiness for that evening. He knocked on the door and the man came over to unlock it.

"I know it's a bit late in the day, but would you have a table for two for tonight?"

The man shook his head. "I'm very sorry. We're fully booked this evening."

Glancing at Bill, the woman then turned her attention towards Sally, still sitting in the car. 'They are lovers. Such a pretty girl and a handsome man,' she thought.

She called across at her husband and said something to him in Italian. Her husband turned towards the window and smiled.

"You are right Anna, what am I thinking?" He smacked his forehead with the palm of his hand and turned back to Bill. "My wife is reminding me of what it is like to be young and in love. We usually keep two tables free for passers-by. You can have one of them. Tonight, we will keep only one."

"Thank you," said Bill shaking the man by the hand. "Thank you very much." He walked over to the woman and bent down and kissed her on the cheek.

"Thank you so much," he said, softly. "You don't know what this means to me."

She looked delighted and touched the spot on her cheek where he had kissed her. Such a lovely man, she decided they must do something special for him and his young lady.

Bill left the restaurant and told Sally the good news. Glancing across towards the couple, she waved. He looked at the clock on the dashboard. "It's four-thirty now. It'll be nearly five o'clock by the time I drop you off. If I pick you up at seven, will that be alright?"

"That'll be fine Bill," said Sally. "I'll be ready and waiting."

"Don't bother to get out of the car Bill. You can go straight off," said Sally when they reached her flat. She put her arms around his neck and kissed him. "Thank you for a lovely day."

"It's not over yet Sally," said Bill, delighted at her gesture. "See you later." He waited until Sally had disappeared into her flat before driving off. He couldn't believe his good luck, these were the best two days he'd had in a long time.

Sally ran a bath and soaked the warm, scented water. She thought of how they had spent the day. It had been rather nice bumping into Bill's friends. Both Colin and Rachel had been very friendly towards her. And then there was the trip to the lighthouse and how it had stirred up the sweet memories of her childhood.

At more than one point during the day, Sally had felt sure Bill was going to kiss her. She wondered why he had held back. It was probably because of his shyness. If only she had responded – let him know she wanted him to kiss her, perhaps then he would have gone ahead. But she was shy, too. Besides, there was always the chance she had imagined it and he hadn't been going to kiss her at all. She would have felt very foolish, reaching up to press her lips on his, only for him to turn away. She thought of her friend Jo. Whenever she wanted something, she didn't hesitate. She reached out and took it. But then she wasn't Jo.

Sally suddenly realised the water in the bath was getting cold. How long had she been lying here? She quickly washed her hair and climbed out of the bath. After looking through her wardrobe twice and trying on a few things, she finally decided to wear a blue cocktail dress. Though it was a little old now, it still looked fashionable. Besides, she couldn't wear the black dress two nights in a row, so the blue dress would have to do.

She decided to do her hair similar to the way she had worn it the night before. Bill seemed to like it. She applied her makeup quickly and by the time the doorbell rang she was ready.

Bill complimented her on her appearance. Once again the young girl had disappeared and a sophisticated young lady had appeared in her place. He bent down and kissed her before helping her on with her coat. But it was the sort of kiss he could have greeted his mother with and he felt annoyed at having so little confidence in himself. Why couldn't he be more like Colin?

It took about half an hour to reach the restaurant. Luigi was waiting and led them to their table. His wife had decorated it with flowers and candles. Luigi lit the candles and left a menu saying he would personally take their order. He and his wife had discussed the young couple after Bill had left the restaurant earlier. Anna had taken a liking to him, especially after he kissed her. With his dark hair, trim waistline and charming manners, he had reminded her so much of their lovely son, still living in Italy. She wanted things to be right for him and his girlfriend.

Luigi came over with a bottle of champagne. "On the house!" When Bill tried to object, Luigi silenced him with a wave of his hand. "No, no. It is a gift. We insist," he pointed over to his wife in the corner. She was busy with some other diners but she smiled and nodded across to them.

"Thank you," said Bill, "You're so kind, I don't know what to say."

"You say nothing," said Luigi, filling their glasses. "There is an old saying, you sip your champagne and then you kiss your young lady."

Bill looked across at Sally. She nodded. She had never heard of this either, but it sounded a wonderful idea. They took a sip of the champagne and then Bill leant across and kissed Sally on the cheek.

However Luigi was having none of that. He sighed. "No! No! No! You take her in your arms and you kiss her – really kiss her. A beautiful woman is meant to be kissed in a warm embrace."

Bill looked at Luigi and then at Sally. He knew Luigi wouldn't let him off easily. Besides he didn't really want to be let off at all, it was the excuse he needed. But how would Sally feel about it?

He stood up and held out his hand to Sally. As she rose to her feet, he took her in his arms and kissed her as though there was no tomorrow. Everything he felt for her, he poured into that one kiss. How he had longed to do this all last evening and again today on the beach. It had taken this Italian to help him do it and he wasn't going to let the moment be wasted.

It felt wonderful to hold Sally so close and he didn't want to let her go. He knew the other diners were watching them, but at that moment he didn't care. He could have held her forever. Finally releasing her, Bill raised his glass and nodded towards Luigi before taking a sip. Behind him, the other diners clapped and cheered.

Sally hadn't believed Bill would go through with it, but she was delighted he had. Sipping her champagne, she wished they could dine at Luigi's every night, if it meant Bill would kiss her like that.

There wasn't a dance floor here, so Bill contented himself with looking at Sally and holding her hand across the table between courses.

The champagne went straight to Sally's head. She hadn't eaten anything since the bacon and eggs at lunchtime. Bill wasn't drinking too much because of having to drive, so she had most of it herself.

Luigi and his wife were very attentive during the evening. They wanted everything to be exactly right for this lovely young couple. Both Sally and Bill were sorry when the time came for them to leave. He went across to the small desk to pay Luigi for the meal. "Thank you for a lovely evening. You and your wife have been so kind to us," he said.

"It has been our pleasure. It's not often such a handsome young couple come into our restaurant. We hope you will both be very happy together."

"I'm not sure our relationship has gone that far," said Bill.

"Believe me, it has. My wife knows about these things," Luigi tapped his nose. "She's always right."

Bill desperately hoped she was. He helped Sally with her coat and after saying goodbye to Luigi and his wife they left the restaurant.

"What a lovely couple," said Sally as they drove back towards the town.

"Yes they are," said Bill. "We must go there again soon." He paused. "Would you like to come back to my house for coffee? There're no strings attached," he added hastily. "I'm not trying… I promise I'll take you home before midnight, or earlier if you say so".

"That would be nice Bill," replied Sally. "I think I need another coffee after all the champagne. Did you notice how the bottle never seemed to empty?"

"Yes." Bill smiled. "I did notice. But I think Luigi had something to do with that."

It wasn't long before they reached Bill's home, a large detached house standing in its own grounds on the outskirts of the town. After making the coffee, Bill sat on the sofa next to Sally and placed his arm around her. She lay her head on his shoulder.

"I've had a wonderful day Bill, truly wonderful."

"Yes, so have I. We must do it again sometime."

Sally sat up and drank some of her coffee. "I need this to clear my head." She giggled. "I've definitely had too much to drink. I'll probably have a headache in the morning."

They chatted while drinking their coffee and the time flew by. Bill looked at his watch, he was sorry to see it was already well after midnight. It was time to take Sally home. How he wished she didn't have to go. Even if they were to sit on the sofa all night the way they were now, would be enough. It was wonderful having her near him. However, when he had invited her back for coffee and said there were no strings attached, he meant it. He had promised to take her home before midnight, to now suggest she should stay the night, even to sit talking, was out of the question. She might misunderstand his intentions and feel unable to trust him ever again. He certainly didn't want that. The only option open to him was to take her home and hope she would go out with him again sometime. Perhaps even tomorrow – or was that too soon? He would ask her as he drove her home.

"Sally." Reluctantly, Bill removed his arm from around her shoulders. "I hate to say this, but it's time I took you home. I'll get our coats." He went out into the hall.

Not wanting the day to end, Sally didn't move. She knew Bill was not the sort who would invite her back for coffee, merely to lure her into his bed. But for one brief moment, she found herself wishing he were.

No! What was she thinking? Of course she didn't really mean that. If he were that sort of character, he wouldn't be the same person she felt so much in love with. Bill was a perfect gentleman. He had promised to take her home and she knew he would, no matter how he felt about her.

She was now very sure he had feelings for her; the kiss at Luigi's had told her that. The way he had held her, not letting her go, surely no one could possibly put so much passion into one single kiss without it meaning something. Even now, the thought of that moment sent tingles down her spine.

She didn't want him to take her home. Not now. Not ever. What she wanted was for him to take her in his arms, to kiss her and make love to her. She caught her breath at the mere thought of how much she wanted him. Oh my God, how she wanted him. She sighed. Yet it wasn't going to happen, not tonight anyway. Not unless… not unless she did something about it. But could she? Dare she tell him she wanted to spend the night with him? Would she be able to find the words? And if she found the nerve and the words, would he think she was a brazen hussy?

These questions and more were buzzing around in her mind when Bill came back into the room. He held out his hand to help her up from the sofa, but was alarmed when she didn't even look up at him.

"Is everything all right Sally? Have I done something to upset you?" He looked at his watch. "Have I kept you here too long?"

She didn't answer, and continued to look down at the floor instead.

Bill swallowed hard and a wave of panic swept over him. Perhaps she didn't want to see him again and was finding it difficult to tell him. Oh please, please don't let it be that. A pit formed in his stomach as he recalled how desperate he had felt when Jo telephoned the nursery and he thought it was a boyfriend. But this time it was much worse. By now he had spent some time in Sally's company. He had held her in his arms; he had kissed her for God's sake. How could he lose her now?

Thrusting the coats to one side, he slumped down beside her. He yearned to put his arms around her and hold her tight, but would that be the right thing to do? Believing not, he took her hand. "Sally, please tell me what's wrong. I'm sorry if I've hurt you." He paused, swallowing hard again to move the lump in his throat. "Don't you want to see me again?"

She gripped his hand tightly and her breathing became more rapid. "Bill…" She hesitated; trying to muster up the courage to tell him what was on her mind.

However, by now Bill feared the worst and fought back the tears forming in his eyes. He had known all along she might find him too old or too dull.

"It's all right, Sally," he said, not wanting to prolong her agony. "You don't need to say anymore, I understand. I'll take you home." He began to stand up, but she gripped his arm and held him back.

"No Bill, I don't think you do understand. "I… I don't want to go home… I want to spend the night… with you." She looked away, embarrassed at her boldness. She had never done anything so daring in her life. Even shouting at Jo couldn't be compared to this. What must he think of her?

Unable to speak, he put his arms around her and held her tight. "Oh, Sally, darling," he said at last. "I'd love you to stay, but are you really sure? You've had rather a lot to drink and might not realise what you are saying. I don't want you doing anything you'll regret tomorrow. You could wake up in the morning hating me. I couldn't bear to lose you."

Sally shook her head. She had never been surer of anything in her life. "Yes, I'm sure Bill. It may be the champagne giving me the courage to say it, but it *is* what I want." She laughed nervously, feeling even more embarrassed.

Pulling her to him, Bill kissed her exactly as he had in the restaurant, earlier in the evening.

"Can I get you something? Perhaps you would like some more coffee?" He didn't want to rush her. Afraid she may regret it later, he wanted to give her the chance to change her mind. He wouldn't really be upset if she did. It was just so good to know that she wanted to be with him.

"Nothing Bill, thank you. I'm fine, really I am." She smiled at him. She knew he was concerned for her, but this was what she wanted – what they both wanted.

Rising to his feet, Bill stretched out his hand towards her and led her upstairs. She trembled, as they entered the bedroom and he put his arms around her.

"Sally, you really don't have to do this. I can still take you home and see you again tomorrow."

"I'm all right, I don't want to go home," she replied. "It's just… I'm shy… I… What I mean is, I have never…" She broke off.

Bill looked at her. "You mean you're a…?"

"Yes, I am." She interrupted.

He pulled her close to him. "Oh Sally." He suddenly felt very nervous. "I had no idea." He hesitated. His heart was pounding. "Are you absolutely certain you want it to be me who…?"

She put a finger to his lips. "Yes, Bill, I'm certain."

"I'll leave you alone to get undressed." Bill showed her the adjoining bathroom, still very unsure he should be doing this.

"There're plenty of towels and bath robes in the cupboard. Help yourself to anything you need. I'll use the bathroom across the hall and will join you later. But Sally… please don't be afraid to tell me if you change your mind."

Closing the bedroom door behind him, Bill walked slowly downstairs. He poured himself a large brandy and drank it down quickly before pouring another. This one he took upstairs. Walking past the bedroom door he paused; he could hear Sally in the shower.

Once in the bathroom he undressed, pausing only to sip at the brandy. He took a warm shower and put on a bathrobe. He was about to go downstairs for another drink, but thought better of it. Instead, he sat on the edge of the bath, wondering whether he had given Sally enough time.

Finally, going into the bedroom he found her lying in bed. Her long hair lay loose on the pillow and the duvet was pulled up high, covering the roundness of her breasts. Filled with desire, he yearned to go to her, yet he held back, when a feeling of guilt swept over him. Was he taking advantage of her? She was so young and innocent, tonight should be for someone she really loves.

Walking across the room, he sat down on the edge of the bed. "Are you really sure about this, Sally? If you've had second thoughts, it's okay. Just tell me and I'll sleep in another room. I swear I won't touch you. You can lock the door if you want to." He pointed towards the key in the lock.

"No, don't go, Bill," she whispered. "I love you. Come to bed with me." She instinctively averted her eyes, as he dropped his robe to the floor, revealing his lean, naked body. Lifting the covers, he slid into bed beside her.

Later that night Sally couldn't sleep. Locked in Bill's arms she lay awake with the events of the last two days racing through her mind. She recalled everything they had said and done, right up until Bill had made love to her. She had never known anything so wonderful, even the very thought of his touch, sent waves of passion throughout her body. Yes, she had been nervous – scared was probably a more accurate word. Yet Bill had been so patient, so kind and gentle, her fears had disappeared within a few minutes.

She knew he had been nervous, too. She had seen it in his eyes when she told him this was her first time. She gazed at him, as he lay sleeping. I love you, Bill Roberts. I love you so much. She wished time would stand still – that she might lie here in his arms forever. She wanted this moment to last until the end of time.

Looking towards to the window, the twinkling stars caught her eye. They looked even more beautiful than the evening before and she recalled the wish she had made. But surely life was not like that. Wishes were only for children. Could this possibly be a dream? Would she wake in a few hours and find herself back in her flat with Jo banging on the door?

Bill stirred and pulled her closer to him. From that moment, she knew this was no dream. Perhaps there was some kind of magic after all. Maybe the magic of Christmas was for grown-ups, as well as for children, especially for those who really looked for it.

With this happy thought, Sally finally fell asleep.

Day Four

When Bill awoke, the winter sun was streaming through the window. For one brief moment, he was afraid Sally may have dressed and left. A wave of relief ran through him, when he found she was still by his side. Yet there was still a possibility that she might regret what had happened and never want to see him again. He quickly dismissed the thought; he couldn't bear to even consider it.

As she stirred, a wisp of hair fell across her face. When he reached out to move it, she opened her eyes.

"I'm sorry darling. I didn't mean to waken you." Bill put his arm around her and pulled her close.

Sally nestled herself beside him "Bill, I love you so much. I think I loved you from the first moment I saw you standing in the doorway of the nursery." She frowned. But you seemed to rush away when you collected Joey the following day. I thought you didn't like me."

"Didn't like you? Oh Sally, I loved you, too," he replied, "but I was afraid to tell you. I felt that someone as young and pretty as you would have lots of young men running after them. And then when Jo phoned, I thought my suspicions were correct."

For a moment she was puzzled, but then laughed when Bill went on to explain the misunderstanding. "It was Joey who unwittingly told me otherwise."

Despite their laughter, they both knew how close it had come to everything working out so very differently.

"Would you like some tea or coffee?" Bill asked. "Or even breakfast in bed? Say the word and I'll do whatever you want." He would like to have included making love again in his list of suggestions, but thought it best not to mention it. It might be too soon.

"Breakfast in bed sounds very nice… but later, thank you." Sally leant over and kissed him. "First, I would like you to make love to me all over again."

"When did I last show you how much I loved you?" Bill asked.

"Roughly about six or seven hours ago, but I'd love you to show me again."

He pulled her closer to him and began kissing her on her forehead, then on her mouth, and then continued very slowly down her long neck…

Later, Bill went downstairs and made coffee and toast for them both and took it up to the bedroom. Sally told him he was spoiling her. But he wanted to spoil her. He was so happy and in love, he would have done anything for her. It was nearly midday before they showered and dressed.

Bill gave Sally a tour of the house beginning with Joey's room, which was next door to his own. The room was full of toys and games, with a train set weaving its way between the legs of the bed. He went on to show her the other bedrooms. There were five in all, with the three larger ones having their own shower rooms.

"These rooms aren't used very often, only when my parents and my sister come to visit." He explained. "My mother usually cleans around properly for me when she's here as I don't get much time. She makes it an excuse to come, but I know Joey is the real reason."

Sally opened her mouth to say something, but Bill stopped her. "I know. I work too hard." They both laughed.

"How did you know what I was going to say?" Sally asked. But then she smiled. "Never mind, I guess I have mentioned it more than once.

He took her downstairs and into the large dining room. "I must say, we don't often use this room, Joey and I tend to eat in the kitchen."

He then led her to his study. The desk was piled high with files, still needing his attention. He closed the door quickly, not wanting her to notice the amount of work he brought home. He hadn't touched anything this weekend. Office work hadn't even entered his mind.

"And that's it. You've seen it all. The lounge you've already seen."

"It's a beautiful house, Bill. And so large, you must like plenty of space around you."

"Yes I do. However, the extra rooms are very useful when my family visit. My sister, Barbara and her husband, who now live in Scotland, visit regularly. I also have a sister, in Canada. I admit she doesn't get to England as often as she would like, but when she does, she and her husband stay here."

Changing the subject, he asked her what she would like to do that day.

"I'll leave it to you, Bill. Have you anything in mind?"

"Well, there's a little pub close by called The Bakers Arms. They do Sunday lunches," said Bill. "They don't take bookings. It's a first come, first served scenario. It'll probably be busy but you never know we might be lucky."

"That sounds like a good idea Bill, but I should like to pay for something. People tend to go Dutch these days."

Bill was horrified at the thought. "Oh no you won't, I don't believe in these modern ideas. I'm old fashioned. Besides, I'm a man. It's my prerogative. It's in the rules." He laughed

"Okay, okay. I give in." Sally held up her hands in mock horror. "But would you drop me off at my flat first? I think I need to change." She was wearing the cocktail dress she had worn the night before. "I may be a little overdressed for The Bakers Arms. If I'd known I was going to stay the night, I'd have brought a change of clothes." She grinned.

Bill was tempted to suggest she bring more clothes in case she stayed on another night, but thought better of it. "We can go now if you like. We'll stop and pick up some newspapers on the way. I don't bother to have any delivered. I'm usually too busy to read them."

"Bill. I know I've said this before, but I really do think you work too hard."

"My mother's always saying that," replied Bill.

"I think she's right." Sally recalled the mountain of files she had seen on the desk in the study before Bill had swiftly closed the door.

They set off for Sally's flat, only stopping to buy some newspapers on the way. When she opened her front door she found a note from Jo. Sally groaned inwardly. What could she want now? She had promised not to interfere anymore.

However, the note merely said there was to be another lecture, if Sally was interested. Jo had included the date and time. But Sally didn't feel in the mood for lectures at the moment. Life had suddenly become far too exciting.

"Come in Bill. It's a note from Jo about another lecture at the college on Wednesday. It seems she forgot to mention it yesterday." Sally stuffed the message into her pocket.

Sally showed Bill around her small flat. "The lounge, you saw yesterday." She sighed. "It's no where near your league, but it suits me very well."

"It's very comfortable. You have everything you need." Seeing the telephone on a small table reminded Bill he had forgotten to ring his son. "Could I use your phone, I usually speak to Joey every morning whenever he's away."

"Yes of course, help yourself. I'll leave you to it while I get changed."

Bill dialled the number. It was his mother who answered. "Hello Mum. Is everything okay?"

"Everything's fine. Joey had a good time at the party and wants to tell you all about it. He's been waiting for you to call. Is everything all right with you, son?" asked Anne.

Bill was tempted to say something about Sally. Yet he held back, still afraid that the relationship might end as quickly as it had begun. Perhaps he should wait a few days. So he simply said, "Yes Mum, everything's okay. I hope Joey isn't too much for you."

"Nonsense," said Anne. "We love having him here. You know, if you ever need a break, we'll have him any time."

"I know, Mum, but I really need him with me. He's all I have."

"Yes, son, I know. He's here now. I'll put him on." She handed the phone to Joey and went off to tell her husband, how much better Bill sounded this morning.

Joey told his daddy all about the party he had attended the day before and how he wanted one when he was five.

"Of course we'll have a party for you. We'll talk about it when you come home. You'll need to decide where you want to hold it, at home or at Nanna's house."

They talked a while longer before hanging up.

Sally left Bill alone while he was talking to his son. It was only after she heard him put down the receiver that she went back into the lounge.

"Is Joey all right? He must be missing you. He told me how much he loved you."

"Yes, we're very close," he replied, thoughtfully. It seemed his son had told Sally a great deal during the short time he was with her. Bill was delighted Joey had found himself able to confide in Sally. He didn't want him to grow up to be as shy and withdrawn like himself. However, he was beginning to be a little concerned at what his son had been telling her.

"I think I'm ready. Will I do?" Sally asked.

"You look wonderful, Sally." Bill thought she looked good in whatever she wore. "You always do."

Taking the chocolates Bill had given her on Friday night, she placed them into a large bag. "We can eat some of them later today." She didn't mention the bag also contained a change of clothes just in case he asked her to stay over again that night.

Arriving at the pub, they were delighted to find a table without having to wait too long. Finishing lunch, they left only to find the sun had disappeared and snow was beginning to fall.

"Your place or mine?" Bill asked. "I don't think we should risk driving anywhere today in case the snow gets too thick. We both have to go to work tomorrow or will Mrs Miller be back?"

"We'll go to your house," Sally replied. "It's much more comfortable than mine. And no, Jane won't be back for a few more days yet. When I spoke to her on Friday she sounded much better, but not well enough to return to the nursery."

Back at Bill's house, they quickly ran indoors. By now the snow was falling more heavily. He asked whether she would like to watch a DVD. "There're a few by the television, my mother brought them the last time she was here."

Choosing a film, Sally slipped it into the machine and they spent the afternoon watching the film and sipping wine. When it was over, Bill put on some music and asked Sally if she would like to dance. Moving gently with the music, she closed her eyes and imagined they were back at The Showboat.

As darkness fell, Sally went across to the window. "Bill come and see; your garden looks beautiful – almost like a Christmas card." The snow had continued to fall all afternoon and was quite deep now.

Joining her, Bill wrapped his arms around her and gazed out of the window. "Darling, if you want me to take you home we should get a move on. It seems this snow might be here to stay. Or…" He hesitated; wondering whether he should suggest her to stay. Would that be too…?

Sally was watching him closely. She guessed what was going through his mind – hers too. Perhaps she should help him out. "Or I could stay here tonight," she said, finishing the sentence for him. "But only if it's all right with you."

"Of course it is, darling." Bill smiled. Disappearing into the kitchen, he returned a few moments later with new bottle of wine. "Would you like another drink? Now we're not rushing off anywhere, perhaps we can relax a little."

"Yes please." Sally grinned. "But shall we take the bottle upstairs?" she added mischievously.

Day Five

After breakfast the following morning, Bill and Sally set out for work. There had been a thaw in the night so the roads weren't as treacherous as they had first thought. Dropping Sally off at the nursery, Bill stepped down from the car and gave her his card showing both his home and office number. "If you want to phone me at work please do, I'd love to hear from you during the day."

"Won't you be too busy Bill?" said Sally, looking down at the card. "You told me you had two important clients to see today. I wouldn't want to interrupt you at work."

"If things are tricky I'll say so, but please ring me. I don't know how I'll get through the day without at least hearing from you." He was finding it difficult to leave her for a minute, let alone the whole day.

"What time do you think you'll get away this evening?" she asked.

"Goodness knows. Where will you be? You can go to my house if you want to. I'll give you a key." Taking a key from his key ring, he handed it to her. "I'll leave the office as soon as possible. I postponed a few clients on Friday, but I'm not sure when my secretary fitted them in. I didn't wait to find out." He grinned. "I needed to get away early as I didn't want to risk being late to pick you up."

"Okay then, off you go. I'll phone you during the day when the little ones are quiet, but Bill, please tell me if it isn't convenient to talk."

He pulled Sally to him and kissed her. "This has got to last me all day." Climbing back into the car, he was about to pull away when he suddenly remembered the Christmas dance. "Sally, my firm hold a dinner dance every Christmas, would you like to go. It's at The Apollo Hotel this year. I must admit, I haven't been for the last few years, but I'd love to take you. Colin and Rachel will be there, so you'd know another couple."

"I'd love to go with you. When is it?"

"Thursday," answered Bill. "I'll order two tickets."

He drove to the office and as usual, he was the first to arrive. His desk was already piled high with files left by his staff on Friday afternoon. Alan had left the branch balance sheets on the top, together with a note saying he believed the clerk at the South Milford branch had made two errors. He added he had made the necessary corrections, but someone should check to make sure he was right.

Quickly checking through the figures, Bill found Alan had been right to alter the sheets. Should the figures have gone through the way they were, they would have been thousands of pounds out. He knew he would have spotted the mistake, as indeed would Colin, but there were others who might very easily have missed it. Alan had done well to find the error, especially as he was so new to the procedure. Bill found he had time to check one or two other things before the rest of the staff began to arrive.

When Colin arrived at the office he was tempted to rush straight through to Bill's office to ask how the rest of his weekend had gone. However, after a moment's thought, he decided against it. If his wife had been wrong about Sally and she had left Bill on Saturday afternoon, he would be in no mood to talk about it. Besides, he would be sending for him soon enough, there were some points they needed to discuss before the meeting scheduled for later that morning. All things considered, perhaps it would be best to leave it until then.

Shortly after nine o'clock, Miss Anderson went into Bill's office with his mail and a mug of coffee.

"Good morning, Mr Roberts, I've gone through your mail and there are two letters needing your urgent attention. I've put them on top of the pile."

"Thank you, Miss Anderson. Will you ask Alan to come into my office as soon as he arrives?"

"Yes of course, sir. I think he's here now. He's usually quite early. I'll send him in. Will there be anything else?"

"Yes. I would like you to order two tickets for the dinner on Thursday evening."

Miss Anderson, believing she hadn't heard right, didn't move. Mr Roberts never went to any of the firm's outings; let alone the Christmas dinner. "Two tickets, sir ... for the... Christmas dance?"

"Yes, Miss Anderson. Two tickets for the Christmas dance." He looked up from his mail. "Is there a problem?"

"No, sir, not at all, I'll see to it right away." Leaving the room, she met Alan in the corridor and informed him Mr Roberts wished to see him right away. On reaching her office, she telephoned personnel and ordered the tickets.

She was rather curious about the sudden change in Mr Roberts. Firstly, on Friday afternoon, he had cleared his desk and rushed away – now he was asking for tickets for the dance. She wondered whether she should say anything to Colin, but quickly dismissed the idea. It was her policy not to discuss her boss with anyone. She wasn't a *private* secretary for nothing!

Alan tapped on Bill's door. The sound was barely audible.

"You wanted to see me, sir?" asked Alan, quietly.

"Yes." Bill pointed at the papers on his desk. "It's about the figures you checked over on Friday. You did well. You were absolutely right about the errors. Well spotted. I'll ask Colin to make a note of it in your personal file."

"Thank you, sir." For a moment Alan felt elated. But then he recalled how long it had taken him to go through the figures. Surely no one could have possibly have missed the errors if they had spent so much time on them. "I should admit that it took me some while to check everything so thoroughly."

"It doesn't matter. You persevered and that's the main thing."

Alan left the office a happy man. At least Mr Roberts appreciated his work. The last boss he had worked for always took the credit for anything his staff did. Mr Roberts seemed to be very fair.

Bill asked Miss Anderson to send Colin in with the files he would need for his meeting.

"Here goes," Colin mumbled to himself, when he received the message. Going to Bill's office, he walked straight in. He didn't knock, he never did. He had known Bill far too long for such formalities. "Good morning. I have the files here all ready for you. I hope Mr Taylor isn't going to be too tough. I know he's asking for a lot more compensation than the top brass want to give. Personally, I think you'll have a fight on your hands."

Colin was rambling and he knew it. What he was saying was true enough, but he was simply trying to stay away from the subject of the weekend in case it hadn't ended too well for Bill. Most especially, as it had been his suggestion that he ask Sally out in the first place. However, his curiosity got the better of him and, unable to hold back any longer, he came right out and asked whether everything had gone well. "What I really want to know is, did you have a nice weekend?"

Bill didn't answer immediately. Too engrossed with the morning's mail, he hadn't really been listening. There was something, which had caught his eye – something that might help with his negotiations later in the morning. However, he did catch Colin's last remark. "Yes, of course I did. I had one of the most wonderful weekends of my life."

Colin heaved a sigh of relief. "I'm delighted for you Bill. I really am."

"We went to Luigi's on Saturday evening," Bill continued. "You must take Rachel there sometime. It's really very nice and we had a lovely evening. Then on Sunday, we had a pub lunch at the Baker's Arms. When we came out it was starting to snow, so we went back to my place and watched a DVD." He looked back down at the mail and ran a finger around his collar. He wasn't about to tell Colin they had spent a great deal of the weekend in bed.

However, Colin knew that sign. He guessed there was more to the weekend than Bill was saying and couldn't resist a quick dig at his friend.

"And then you simply took her home, did you?" He laughed as Bill shifted uncomfortably in his chair. "No! I didn't think so. It's little wonder you had a good weekend."

Anxious to change the subject, Bill looked up. "Are you and Rachel definitely going to the dance on Thursday? I've asked Sally and she'd like to go, but I told her you and Rachel are usually there."

"Yes, we'll be there. As I said, Rachel's bought a new dress for the occasion and it would be more than my life's worth to go back on my word now. My parents have agreed to take the children for a couple of days. That way we don't have to get up quite so early on Friday, although having said that, I've drawn the short straw, so I'll need to come into the office. We'd both like to meet Sally again. Rachel was very impressed; she thought her to be a really lovely young woman."

Just then Miss Anderson knocked and entered the office. "Mr Taylor is here with his company's chief accountant. They're waiting in my office."

"I don't envy you this," said Colin.

"Miss Anderson. They're very early. Tell them I'm with someone and offer them some tea, coffee – anything. I need a few minutes." Turning back to Colin, he continued. "I think I've found a way out of this. I've had two letters from a couple of small companies. They're having a few financial problems and are asking for an extension of at least six weeks on their delivery date. That would bring them into breach of contract. You phone one and get Alan to phone the other. Tell them I'm willing to give an extension of up to twelve weeks, if we can use their goods for another order. If they agree, I'll also allow them a £5000 discount on their orders."

"Why bother with the discounts? They'd probably agree anyway if they're desperate," Colin said.

"They're small companies and desperate at the moment. But they're growing fast. In a few years from now, I don't want our salesmen having to go cap in hand looking for an order because of something we did today. I want them to stay with us. When you've done that come back here and bring Alan with you. I want you both to sit in on the meeting. Mr Taylor has brought one of his staff with him, it's only right I should have some support."

"I agree, but why Alan? He doesn't know anything about Taylor Associates."

"I'm not expecting him to actually say anything Colin, but sitting in will be good experience for him. I gave him the branch figures on Friday as you weren't here and he did a good job. You were right in your assessments, he's very willing to learn and I think we should encourage him. And while we're on the subject, I would also like you to make a note to that effect on his file."

"Okay Bill. You're the boss."

"I do sometimes wonder about that." Bill grinned.

Colin and Alan returned to Bill's office saying both companies had readily agreed to the proposals. Bill phoned through to his secretary and asked her to show the clients to his office. She came through a few minutes later and introduced Mr Taylor of Taylor Associates and Mr Johnson, his chief accountant. She then turned back to Bill. "I take it you don't want any calls during the meeting, Mr Roberts."

"That's right, Miss Anderson, with the exception of Miss Hughes. If she calls, please put her straight through."

"Very well, Mr Roberts; only Miss Hughes." She looked across at Colin, who grinned and raised his eyebrows. This was the second time this morning, Mr Roberts had surprised her and it wasn't even ten o'clock yet.

Colin flashed Bill a cheeky grin and winked.

Bill coughed before turning to his clients. "Would you like any more coffee?" When they both declined, he dismissed Miss Anderson. "Now, shall we get down to business? As you know we had a fire in the warehouse. It didn't spread too much, but unfortunately most of your stock was destroyed. However, I'm in a position to offer you more than half of your order and we could deliver before Friday."

"That's not good enough," replied Mr Taylor. "Your company's contract clearly states, if the order is not filled in the time agreed, compensation would be paid. Is that not so? You're not filling our order therefore we're seeking compensation."

"You're asking far too much," replied Bill. "Under the circumstances, we are not prepared to pay that kind of money."

"What circumstances? What are you talking about? I won't be treated in this manner. I may consider taking my business elsewhere. For heaven's sake, man, you're welching on your own contract. Haven't you read your company's penalty clause?" Mr Taylor was beginning to get angry. It seemed Mr Roberts wasn't taking them seriously.

Alan looked down at a copy of the contract. Mr Taylor was right. Mr Andrews, from Websters Legal Department, Bill Roberts, Mr Taylor and a Mr Amos, a member of his legal team, had all signed the penalty clause. It looked straightforward enough, hadn't Mr Roberts read it? It seemed his boss had slipped up.

Bill looked at Mr Taylor. "Of course I've read the penalty clause, I wrote it and our legal department cleared it. I suggest *you* didn't read it carefully enough before signing."

Mr Taylor looked at the contract again. Not seeing anything amiss, he shrugged his shoulders and handed it to his associate. What on earth was Mr Roberts getting at? Was he simply playing for time?

Mr Johnson gazed at the document for a few moments, before suddenly turning pale. "Oh dear."

"What is it?" asked Mr Taylor. He grabbed the document from his chief accountant and peered at it more closely. "What's going on?"

"It's the way it's worded. You see what you want to see," explained Mr Johnson. He pointed a one of the statements. "However, in a nutshell, what they are saying is, if they can offer us at least half the order, then no compensation need be paid." He looked up at Bill. "Very clever, Mr Roberts."

"Who in our Legal Department is responsible for this oversight?" Mr Taylor uttered. Now feeling extremely foolish, he thrust the contract back his accountant's hand. Whoever it was – he would certainly have a few words with him when he got back to the office.

Reading through the contract again, Alan gasped. "Brilliant, I didn't see that," he whispered to Colin.

Meanwhile, in Miss Anderson's office, the telephone shrilled. "Good morning, Mr Roberts' office, can I help you?"

"I would like to speak to Mr Roberts please," said Sally.

"I'm sorry, but he's in a very important meeting at the moment and isn't taking any calls. Who is it? Perhaps I can ask him call you back."

"It's Sa… Miss Hughes. It's all right. I'll call later." Sally felt a little in awe at the crisp tone of Bill's secretary.

"No… wait. Please hold the line Miss Hughes. I've been instructed to put you straight through." Ringing through to Bill's office, she told him she had Miss Hughes on the line.

"Put her through, please." Turning to his clients, Bill asked them to excuse him for a moment.

"Hello Sally."

"I'm sorry, I shouldn't have interrupted you. I could have called later. Are things very bad there?"

"No. As it happens I had a bit of luck this morning."

"Well I won't keep you, but I thought I'd tell you I've decided to go to your house tonight. I'll cook something for dinner." Sally paused. "I love you."

"I'll look forward to it. See you later. Oh, and by the way, darling. What I said last night still goes." Bill said good-bye before hanging up.

The four men in front of Bill looked at each other and raised their eyebrows. If Bill noticed, he didn't show it. He merely hung up the phone and, turning back to them, said. "Now, gentlemen, where were we?"

Sally was having a very quiet morning. The children all seemed to be on their best behaviour. After all, Santa was due very soon and if they weren't good he wouldn't call on them, or so their parents had told them.

Jane telephoned the nursery quite early. During the conversation, she asked whether Sally had enjoyed the weekend. Sally told her she had spent a very pleasant couple of days, but decided not to mention Bill's part in it.

"I won't be in this week Sally. I think it best if I stay away until after the holidays. I'm so very grateful you were able to stand in for me. It was lucky the college had officially closed for the holidays otherwise I wouldn't have been able to call on you. I don't know what I'd have done. Did you manage to get to the lecture the other night?"

"No," said Sally. "Something else came up, but my friend, Jo, taped it and took a few notes for me, so I'll be able to catch up."

"That's all right then. Well, I think that's all for now. I'll settle up with you when I see you. Call in on Friday if you can. You may find you aren't needed at the nursery. The parents all try to get the last day off work. Usually there's only Joey left, but he's away this year."

"Yes. Bi... err, Mr Roberts said Joey was now going to stay over at his grandmother's until Friday." Sally chewed her lip. She had very nearly slipped up again. Jane was sure to have noticed this time. "I'll call in to see you on Friday afternoon," she added quickly, trying to skim over her blunder.

"I'll look forward to it. See you then," said Jane. She didn't mention Sally's slip of the tongue.

After Jane hung up, Sally decided to phone Bill. She had made up her mind to go to his house that evening. It would save him driving around to her home looking for her. She could make a meal for the two them and then they could relax together. No doubt he would be tired after the two meetings he had spoken of.

She dialled his number and asked the switchboard for Mr Roberts' office. She was a little unnerved when his secretary answered. Miss Anderson sounded so efficient. However, it was Bill who had told her to call.

She asked to speak to Mr Roberts. It was obvious Bill had prepared his secretary for her call, as when she gave her name she was put straight through. Bill sounded pleased to hear her. She knew what he'd meant when he said, "What I said last night still goes." Last night, he'd told her he loved her. She wondered who else had been in the room with him. Perhaps Colin was there.

She had intended to ask Bill if the dance was formal dress. She didn't normally go out to expensive restaurants. However since meeting Bill she had found herself going to three dinners in the space of one week and was fast running out of evening wear. She knew the Apollo Hotel to be rather grand and she didn't really have the money to splash out on another dress.

It had crossed her mind to ask her father for a loan. She would make it clear it was only until Jane paid her on Friday. On the other hand, she didn't really want to tell her parents about Bill yet. She had a feeling they weren't going to be too happy about him being so much older than she was, let alone a widower with a young son. They had always been keen on her getting together with Peter Thompson, a local young man, who worked in her father's office. But she knew he wasn't the man for her and had always declined his invitations out. Bill would lend her the money in a flash, but he wouldn't want to take it back and it didn't seem right he should pay for her clothes.

Putting the problem out of her mind, she began to think about what she would cook for their evening meal and decided to go shopping once she had finished at the nursery. She would also take the time to call at her flat and look at her wardrobe. There may be something suitable for the dance on Thursday. In any case, she needed something to take back to Bill's house in case he asked her to stay the night again. Her mind drifted back to the weekend. How they had made love and then afterwards…

The voice of a child jolted her back to the present. She really must stop day-dreaming. Looking at her watch, she saw it was still too early for lunch and decided to read to them.

"Come on now, gather around me and I'll tell you a story. You can choose what you want me to read."

After talking to Sally, Bill turned to Mr Taylor. "Look, you've done business with Websters for a long time. We certainly don't want to lose your custom and I'm sure you've been more than happy with us. Under the circumstances, we know you're going to have to compensate some of your clients, but not all of them. Some orders you'll be able to fill. Others will probably be relieved at not having to take delivery right now. Only this morning I had two customers asking us for extensions on the terms of their contracts. How about if I autho-rise you £15,000 compensation and another £15,000 discount, for late delivery on the remainder of your order?"

Mr Taylor thought it through. He knew Bill didn't have to offer him anything. After all, they had signed the contract. No one had stood over them. He had sent the contract to their office, giving them plenty of time to examine it. But someone had fouled up and as sure as eggs were eggs, their head would roll when he got back to the office.

"Very well," he said at last. "But in future, we shall look at *your* contracts very carefully indeed." He stood up and leaned across the desk. "We shall continue to do business with Websters, Mr Roberts, but if you ever decide to change your position, see me first. I could do with people like you on my team. You can name your own figure." He leaned across Bill's desk. "And I really mean that," he added, before shaking hands. Nodding to Colin and Alan, he swept out of the office.

Mr Johnson turned to Bill. "He meant it you know. About the job, I mean. Mr Taylor never says anything he doesn't mean, you'll probably be hearing from him again." He winked. "Heaven help the legal office when he gets back." He shook Bill's hand and followed his boss out into the corridor.

"You did it Bill. You had him eating out of your hand. But why give him the money?" Colin asked.

"Because I didn't want him to lose face and I wanted to keep their custom. Their orders are worth millions. You know that. Besides, what I gave him was peanuts and he knows it. Now I think we'll have an early lunch. But before we go I want you, Alan, to check that the credit rating for Hindmarsh & Company is on the file ready for my next meeting. When you've done that, put the file in my secretary's office."

"Yes, sir, said Alan almost jumping to attention. He was very impressed with what he had just witnessed. Would he ever be so clever?

"Colin," continued Bill. "I need you to get onto Head of Sales. Ask him to instruct his staff not to promise any early deliveries at least until after January. We must get Taylor's order ready first otherwise we *will* have to pay compensation. Then there're the two firms we put off this morning. We'll need to get their orders ready next. In the meantime, I'll have a word with Mr Smithers. I'd like him to authorise some overtime in the New Year. After that I'll meet you both upstairs in the executive restaurant. Lunch is on me."

"Okay, chief. Anything you say." Colin left the office laughing

Bill picked up the phone and asked Miss Anderson to put him through to the Managing Director.

"Well done, Bill," said Mr Smithers, when Bill explained. "You got us out of a hole this time. It would have been very bad news if Taylor had stopped doing business with us. How many others would have followed? John Taylor has a great number of friends in the business world."

"Thank you," said Bill.

After a few pleasantries they hung up and Bill phoned Sally. "I'm missing you," he said, when she answered the phone. "What're you doing?"

"I'm reading the children a fairy story," she said. "Actually, while you're on the phone, what sort of a 'do' is this dance of yours?"

"It's evening dress. Why?" Then realising her dilemma he said, "If you need a new dress, I'll pay for it."

"No! I can't let you do that. I have some money of my own," she lied.

"Darling. Please let me do this for you."

"Bill..."

"Please; I want to." Bill interrupted. "We'll talk about it tonight. I'll have to go in a minute. I said I would meet Colin upstairs for lunch. If I'm not up there soon, he'll send out a search party. But I needed to hear your voice again and tell you how much I love you."

"I love you too, Bill. I keep daydreaming about the weekend. I'm missing you, but you better go. See you tonight."

While Bill was making his calls, Alan and Colin went to check on the file and make the phone call.

"That was absolutely brilliant. I didn't spot the clever wording in the penalty clause. Are they all the same?" Alan said.

"No," said Colin. "There's no need for them all to be the same. Some companies are quite small. They wouldn't try getting so much compensation. Usually the legal department work out such clauses, but Bill often decides what to put on the contracts of some of the large businesses. You can see why Websters pay him so much. No doubt he'll get a bonus for this, especially if the managing director gets wind Mr Taylor has offered him a job. But then he deserves it. He saved having to pay out a couple of million or so in compensation *and* the threat of Taylor's buying elsewhere in future. I wouldn't like his job."

"Have you ever put in for one of the top jobs in the branches, Colin?"

"No. That's not for me. Second in command is less of a headache. Bill won't be able to use the same clause again. Not on Taylor anyway. Now he'll have to spend time thinking of something else. I can do without that sort of hassle. I enjoy my home life too much. Bill takes mountains of work home most evenings. But you haven't seen anything yet, Alan. Wait until you see him do calculations in his head. That's his real forte, he never uses a calculator." He paused. "Well! I've never seen him use one all the years I've known him."

"Really?" Lost in admiration, Alan remained silent for a few moments. "Do you think he'll take up Mr Taylor's offer?" he said at last.

"No. I don't think so. He's too loyal to Websters." Colin paused. He didn't like the idea of Bill moving on and until Alan mentioned it, he had never even considered it. However, now he saw it as a possibility and it concerned him.

"At least I hope not," he added slowly. "This place wouldn't be the same without him, well not for me anyway." He quickly changed the subject. "Come on. Let's get on and then we'll go for some lunch."

"Colin, Mr Roberts did mean *both* of us should meet him for lunch, didn't he?" asked Alan, as they approached the general office. "I didn't think I would be allowed in the executive restaurant."

Colin stopped walking and looked at Alan. "You can eat in there if you've been invited by an executive, and you were." He hesitated. "You're not frightened of Bill, are you?" He laughed at the thought of anyone being afraid of Bill. "He's not an ogre you know."

"No, of course I'm not afraid of him," answered Alan, a little too hastily. "I simply thought that he might have only meant you."

Colin could tell Alan was apprehensive about something but decided not to push it at the moment. "No, he invited you as well so hurry up. Bill's paying so that means I'll be having fillet steak!"

"What would you like to drink, Bill?" Colin asked when they all met upstairs in the staff restaurant. "Something to celebrate your victory?"

"I think I'd better stick to one glass of wine if you don't mind. Otherwise I'm likely to fall asleep in the middle of my next meeting," replied Bill.

"I could say something here," said Colin, winking at him. He was referring to Bill's weekend with Sally and would love to tease him further. However with Alan there, he knew it would have to wait.

"Well don't!" Bill gave him a warning glance. "Right, what do you want for lunch? I suppose it'll be steak for you Colin. What about you Alan, do you want the same?"

After lunch, Bill went downstairs to prepare for his next meeting. He didn't think this one would be as difficult as he had first thought. The credit rating had finally arrived; it had taken weeks to come, which usually indicated there was cause for concern. However, everything was in order and he was able to send the representative on his way quite quickly. Now if he could get the rest of his mail sorted out, he might be able to catch up with some of the other business that had started to pile up during the day.

His mind kept going back to his weekend with Sally. Yet he knew he should be concentrating on his work. It had been good to hear her on the phone earlier in the morning. And he was pleased he had rung back. He knew he was behaving like a lovesick teenager, but he couldn't help it; he was feeling so happy. For the first time in his life, at the age of twenty-eight, he was experiencing what it felt like to be sixteen and in love and he was enjoying every minute.

He considered ringing her again. On the other hand, if he carried on with his work, he might be able to get away early. That wasn't usually the case. Sometimes he was here until seven. On one or two rare occasions, Mrs Miller had even taken Joey home with her. He then had to collect him from her house.

He worked steadily for the next two hours and, in spite of constant interruptions, he managed to get through a great deal of work. By the time he looked at his watch it was ten to five. He glanced at the large pile of files still needing his attention. Normally he would have stayed on to finish them, or even taken them home, but not tonight. Tonight all he wanted to do was to go home and be with Sally. He rang through to his secretary.

"Is there anything that can't wait until tomorrow?"

"No, sir. There's nothing really urgent. You don't have any appointments in the morning and only one in the afternoon. A Mr Dawson from Jefferson International," she replied. "They want to open an account with the Peterborough branch."

Only one appointment, things were looking up. "Well then Miss Anderson, I'm going home, and I suggest you do the same. Good night."

"Good night sir," she replied in amazement. She had never known Mr Roberts leave at this time. As far as she was aware, he was always the last to leave the building.

Bill went through to the finance office to see whether Colin had gone home but found him in his office talking to Alan. "Would you excuse me a minute Alan? I'd like a word with Colin."

"Yes of course, sir." Alan beat a hasty retreat back to his own desk.

"Colin, I'm off home now, but first I would like to cash a cheque from the safe." He wrote out a cheque for £1000 and asked Colin to cash it. It was company policy that no one changed cheques for themselves. Either Bill or Colin had to count out the money.

"You can do it Bill. The rule doesn't apply to you."

"No. I'd rather you did it, Colin. It's a rather large amount this time."

"It certainly is," said Colin, counting out the money.

Bill gazed through the glass panel in Colin's office. It gave a clear view of everyone who worked in the finance department. He glanced across to where Alan was sitting; he appeared to be reading one the files. "Colin, is everything all right with Alan? Is he happy here?"

"Yes, as far as I know. I don't think he's considering leaving, if that's what you mean. He was in here just now asking me to tell him a little more about Taylor Associates. I told him I would go through the file with him tomorrow. Why do you ask?"

Bill shrugged. "He always seems to rush away whenever I'm around. Even at lunch today he was very quiet. Do I frighten him?"

"No," answered Colin, thoughtfully. He was recalling his conversation with Alan earlier. "I don't think it's you he's afraid of. I think it's more likely to be your position, but he'll get over it. He's probably been listening to the gossip in the staff restaurant. I'll have a word with him tomorrow. He paused for a moment. "Bill, are you going to take up Mr Taylor's job offer?"

"No, of course not," said Bill. "I'm quite happy where I am. What makes you ask? Were you going to ask for my job?" He grinned, knowing very well Colin would hate his job.

"No thank you, not on your life. I was just wondering that's all. Mr Taylor's offering a great deal of money, I thought you might be tempted," Colin was relieved. He had given the matter a great deal of thought since Alan had mentioned it earlier and he had come to realise how much he would miss Bill. "Anyway, here's your money." He said, changing the subject. "I'm pleased to see you're getting away on time for a change." Giving a sly grin and a wink he added, "Have a nice evening."

"I intend to," said Bill smiling.

Sally was able to leave the nursery by four o' clock. After doing some shopping, she called at her flat and began to rummage through her wardrobe. She found a black velvet skirt and a white silk blouse. If it came to it, she could wear those for the dance. She put a few clothes into a small suitcase before setting off for Bill's house. After preparing the meal she went upstairs for a shower.

Later she went into Joey's room. She wanted to get the youngster something for Christmas but needed to know what he already had. Looking at his train set, she wondered if he might like another carriage. It seemed like a good idea. Looking at her watch, she saw it was a little after six and wondered how much longer Bill would be.

Back downstairs, she checked on the dinner and had started to set the table when she heard the car pull onto the drive. She poured them both a glass of wine and went to open the door. Bill came in and dropping his brief case to the floor, he put his arms around her and kissed her.

"Sally, I've been waiting all day to do that. I've missed you so much. I would have been here earlier if the traffic hadn't been so bad."

"I've missed you too Bill. Come on, I have a glass of wine poured out for you and dinner is almost ready. You spoilt me all weekend so I want to do something for you for a change. You can put your feet up and relax. Did you have a bad day at the office?"

"The day turned out much better than I thought. I had a couple of lucky breaks." He followed her through to the kitchen and picked up a glass of wine. "What would you like to do this evening?"

"I think I would like to stay here, unless you have anything else in mind."

"No Sally. That sounds good to me." He kissed her again.

Bill enjoyed his meal. Normally when he came home he had to start cooking something for Joey, no matter what sort of day he'd had at the office. He had forgotten what it felt like to have someone at home waiting for him.

"Now you sit there and tell me all about your day, while I clear away the dishes," said Sally.

"I'd rather forget about it, if you don't mind. Tell me what you've been doing at the nursery. I'll give you a hand while we talk."

"You will not. You must sit there and watch, it'll only take me a moment. You have a dishwasher, remember?" Sally laughed. "Your secretary sounded very efficient when I rang," she added, changing the subject.

"Yes. Miss Anderson is very efficient. Actually, she's quite young to have got so far. But she's a good secretary and a nice person. She's been with me for almost three years."

In the lounge, Sally sat on the sofa next to Bill. He put his arm around her. "Sally, darling, I meant what I said this afternoon. I want to buy you a dress for the dance."

"Bill I can't let you do that. It doesn't seem right somehow."

"Why ever not? What's the difference? I love you and I want to buy you things." He reached into his pocket and pulled out the cash he had asked Colin for earlier. He counted out £500 and handed it to her.

"Will that be enough? I don't know how much these things cost."

Sally looked horrified. "I couldn't possibly spend all that on one dress." She had been brought up to be very thrifty.

"Well then, take what you need." He held out the money and Sally took £100. However, he wasn't having that. "Even *I* know you'll need more than that. Look darling, take the money and get whatever you want. It's my treat."

"No. I wouldn't dream of spending all that on a dress."

"Take it," said Bill. "Please."

"Thank you Bill, but I'll bring you the change." Sally took the money reluctantly.

"Don't bother. Keep it and let me know if you need anymore," He suddenly remembered he hadn't phoned Joey. "I'd better go and ring my mother or I'll be in her bad books." He went to the phone and dialled the number. "Hello Mum," he said. "Is everything all right? I'm sorry I'm late in ringing. I've really been so busy at the office today."

"Don't worry son. Joey's fine. He's in bed now, but he sends his love. I told him you'd probably ring when he was asleep."

"I promise I'll ring him tomorrow morning. But while I'm talking to you, I was wondering if it would be alright if I came on Friday at about twelve or even a little later to pick up Joey. I've decided to go to the office dance with Colin and Rachel on Thursday evening."

"That'll be fine," said Anne. "I'm delighted you're going to the dance. Now you just need to find yourself a nice girl."

Bill laughed. "I haven't got time." He still didn't mention Sally.

"Well," Anne said, "I'll go and tell your father about the dance. He'll be delighted you've taken his advice and are going to get out more."

Bill went back into the lounge and sat down next to Sally. He put his arms around her and kissed her. "Sally. I have to talk to you about Joey," he said quietly.

"What's the matter Bill? Is he ill?" She sat up looking quite concerned.

"No. It's nothing like that. I'm picking him up on Friday." He paused. "How do you feel about that?"

"Bill, I know you have a son and how much you love him. I would never ask you to choose between us. I'll love you both. I like Joey very much and I'm sure we'll get on well together. I would like to be a mother to him, if you'll let me."

Bill sounded relieved, as he pulled her to him. "Of course I'll let you. I've never been so happy, Sally and I'm terrified of losing you."

"I've told you, Bill. I love you and everything about you. You won't lose me." She laughed. "You'll have to push me away kicking and screaming."

"I'll never push you away," he replied, holding her even more tightly.

"But seriously, Bill, how are we going to play this? I don't think it would be a good idea if Joey were to come home and find me here. He might think I've taken his place."

"I know. I must admit, I've been thinking about it myself. He thought for a few moments. "What're you doing for Christmas?"

"Well, I normally go to stay with my parents, but they're going to Tenerife this year. My brother, Tom's asked me to go to his house, but I'm not very keen. He keeps asking when I'm going to date his friend Peter. Why do you ask?"

"I was thinking. On Christmas morning I could talk to Joey about asking you over for lunch. Perhaps saying I'd bumped into you and you were going to be alone for Christmas. Does that sound very bad?"

"No, at least not very bad. Just a little bit bad," she laughed.

"The only problem is, how on earth am I going to manage for two whole days, without seeing you?" asked Bill. He paused. "And by the way, who is Peter?"

Sally laughed. "He's someone who lives near my parents and works in my father's business. My family have been trying to get me to date him, simply because he lives close by. But he's not my type."

Bill was a little concerned. "Is he younger than me?"

"He's a year older than me. Bill don't look so worried, my dating Peter is never going to happen. Let me get you another glass of wine."

He nodded and she went into the kitchen to get the bottle. When she came back, she poured them both a glass. Bill told her he was going to take his upstairs, while he soaked in the bath.

Later, when she went upstairs to refill his glass, she found him almost asleep. "You'll drown yourself if you aren't careful," she laughed. "I'm going to undress and get into bed."

By the time Bill came out of the bathroom, Sally was in bed reading a magazine. He climbed into bed beside her. "Do you really want to read that?" He reached across and kissed her.

"No, not really, but I thought you were tired," replied Sally laughing. "You were falling asleep when I looked in on you before."

"Perhaps I was, but I'll never be too tired for you, sweetheart." Taking the magazine from her, Bill dropped it to the floor, before switching off the light.

Later that night, as they lay in each other's arms Sally asked Bill if he had told his parents about her.

"No I haven't," said Bill. "Though I know my mother will be delighted to hear about you. And so will my sisters, especially Barbara, the one who's recently had a baby. We were quite close as children. Why do you ask?"

"No reason. I was just wondering," replied Sally.

"What about you, Sally? Have you told your parents about me?" she didn't answer. "I know they aren't going to be happy about their lovely young daughter living with a widower and his child," he continued. "Not with a perfectly respectable young man waiting in the wings."

"They'll be alright. I am over twenty-one. I do know what I want and it's not Peter Thompson." However, even as she spoke, Sally knew Bill was right. Her parents weren't going to like it and she really wasn't looking forward to telling them.

A vision of her parents pulling their daughter away from him flashed before Bill's eyes and he shuddered at the thought. His life had changed so much over the last few days; how would he cope if Sally were to be taken from him now.

"I might tell my mother tomorrow morning." Sally spoke quietly. "I should at least tell her I'm at the nursery. If she's been ringing my flat and getting no reply, she'll be worried about me." It was Bill's turn not to answer. "Don't worry Bill. I promise you, I'm not going to leave you."

However, Bill was very worried. Her parents might demand she return home. And then there was this Peter standing by – waiting for her. He spent a very restless night. This could be the end of their relationship

Day Six

The following morning, still tormented by the thought of Sally being torn from him by her parents, Bill washed and dressed in silence.

Sally knew she wouldn't leave Bill, no matter what her parents said, but how could she convince him of that? She was sorry she had told him how dominating they could be, or of even mentioning, Peter Thompson.

Arriving at the nursery Bill helped Sally from the car and pulling her to him, he kissed her. "Ring me anytime. I'll instruct Miss Anderson to put you through no matter what I'm doing. I'll try not to be too late this evening. I love you, Sally."

Sally told him she would speak to her mother once she had settled the children. "I've told you, darling, it'll be alright. I promise to ring you with the good news before eleven o'clock."

Holding her tightly, Bill kissed her again. Then without another word, he climbed back into the car and drove to the office. As usual he was the first to arrive and was able to get through some work before the rest of his staff came in.

Colin arrived shortly after nine and called into Bill's office. He was most concerned when he saw at how tense his friend was. "Is everything all right Bill?" he said, hardly daring to ask, but knew he must. "Nothing's gone wrong, has it? Between you and Sally, I mean."

"No. There's nothing wrong. Not yet anyway. Sally's going to tell her parents about me today and they aren't going to be thrilled, are they?"

Colin frowned and shook his head. He didn't understand.

"What I mean is, they aren't going to like their young daughter being involved with a twenty-eight year old man and a widower at that." Bill explained. "And when they hear I have a young son...a ready-made family so to speak...

It doesn't bear thinking about." He paused. "It seems Sally has led a rather sheltered life. Her parents have been very domineering – always telling her what she should do. They may tell her to leave me. I could go home tonight and find she's moved back with her parents – somewhere in… Oh God, I don't even know where they live. I may never see her again."

"Sally's over twenty-one Bill. She knows her own mind. Don't worry about it." Colin couldn't really see the problem. If his daughter were seeing a man like Bill, he would be thrilled she had picked someone, not only sensible and thoughtful, but also had a damn good job! However, knowing Bill would continue to worry, he tried to convince him. "If your mother told you not to see Sally again you wouldn't take any notice would you?"

"No. But then I haven't spent my entire life doing exactly what my parents told me. Sally has. That's the difference. She may not be able to help herself." He closed his eyes. "I'm going to lose her, aren't I?"

"The path of true love never runs smooth, you know," quoted Colin smiling, trying to ease the tension. However the expression on Bill's face told him he had failed miserably. "I'm sorry, Bill. That was thoughtless."

Miss Anderson came in with the mail and a mug of coffee. Bill knew he would have to start concentrating on his work, but he was going to find it very difficult.

"Miss Anderson. If Miss Hughes calls, please put her straight through. No matter where I am, find me and put her through. On no account are you to put her off. I want her put through immediately. Is that quite clear?" Bill's tone was rather sharp.

"Yes. Of course, sir." She looked a little hurt that Mr Roberts could even think she would put off one of his calls when he had particularly asked her not to. She always followed his instructions implicitly. Leaving the mail and coffee on his desk, she began to leave – her eyes brimming with tears.

Colin felt very uncomfortable. He had never heard Bill speak like that to anyone, let alone a woman. Looking down at the floor, he shifted from one foot to the other.

Bill glanced up at him. "I can't believe I just said that." He leapt to his feet and hurried across the room. "Miss Anderson, please wait. That was a really terrible thing to say and I apologise. I've no reason to believe you would ever do anything against my express wishes. My remarks were rude and totally out of order; please forgive me. I really don't know what I would do without you in this office."

"Of course, Mr Roberts, I know how much pressure you're under here in the office. Please think no more about it. If Miss Hughes calls, you can rest assured I'll put her straight through – no matter where you are."

After a further glance at Colin, she turned and went back to her own office. She was quite shaken by his outburst. She knew he had never raised his voice to anyone before. No matter what pressure he was under.

Bill looked back at Colin, who looked to about to say something.

"Don't say it, Colin." Bill held up his hands. "Just don't say a word; I really don't want to hear it."

"I was only going to say…"

"Well please don't." Bill's tone was sharp. "Can't you just go away and leave me alone? Don't you have any work to do? Because if not, believe me, I can give you plenty." As he spoke he swept his arm over the files heaped up on his desk.

"Yes I have plenty to do. I'm sorry. I'll go. I simply thought you might like some company. Give me a shout if you need me." Colin hurried out of the office.

Standing outside Bill's office collecting his thoughts, Colin heard a crash followed by another, almost like something being thrown to the floor. Feeling very concerned about his friend, he glanced back at the closed door. Never before had he seen him like this, not even after Julie's death.

He resisted the urge to go back into Bill's office, believing it would only make matters worse. He felt tempted to give Anne a ring, but then thought better of it. Bill wouldn't thank him for calling his mother. Besides what could she do – except worry? Perhaps he would phone Rachel, she might have a suggestion. Yes, that was a better idea. She'd know what to do. He was about to walk away when Bill opened his office door.

"Colin. I'm sorry, I shouldn't…" He broke off.

"It's okay Bill, I understand. I'll come back later." Glancing past Bill into the office Colin saw that most of the files, which only a few minutes ago had been neatly piled on the desk, were now strewn all over the floor. There were papers everywhere.

Bill nodded his thanks before closing the door.

Colin walked slowly down the corridor. He decided to have a few words with Miss Anderson; perhaps he could smooth things over a little. She must realise

Bill was not his usual self. He was almost at her door when he met Alan who was on his way to Bill's office with an armful of files. "Are those urgent?"

"They're the figures from the two branches. Mr Roberts usually wants them as soon as they come in… Is he in his office?" Alan's tone was one, which definitely said, 'I hope he's not.'

"Yes he is, but put them on my desk. I'll do them this morning. Bill's a little snowed under today." Colin pulled Alan away from the door as he spoke. He didn't want him interrupting Bill this morning. The mood he was in, he would frighten Alan off completely. "And if you have any problems today, come to me. Tell the others to do the same. I'll be back in my office in a few minutes and we'll go through the Taylor file together, but I need to have a word with Bill's secretary first."

"Okay. Anything you say," replied Alan, glancing at Bill's door.

He wondered what was wrong. From what he had heard, Mr Roberts was always snowed under. Something else must have happened this morning. That being the case, he most certainly didn't want to go in there.

Leaving Alan, Colin went into Miss Anderson's office. "Vera, can I have a few words?" He always called her by her Christian name. Making sure no one was behind him he closed the door.

"What can I do for you?" she asked, quietly.

Colin could tell she was still upset at Bill's outburst. "Be an angel and put all Bill's calls through to me this morning, unless of course they definitely won't talk to anyone else. Has he any meetings scheduled for this morning?"

"No," she said glancing at her diary. "There's only Mr Peterson this afternoon."

Colin was relieved. If it came to it, he would see the rep himself. He dreaded to think what would have happened if Bill had been due to see Taylor Associates this morning. "Look, Vera, forget what happened earlier. Suffice to say he's having a few problems at the moment. Even I've come out of his office with a flea in my ear. We both know he's not usually like this." Colin didn't want to say too much. He knew Bill would be furious if he were to discuss his private life with his secretary. He pointed towards the corridor. "I've advised Alan not to go into his office, which means I'm stuck with the branch finances, and you know how much I love those."

"Very well, Colin," said Miss Anderson, forcing a smile. "All calls to you. But be it on your head, if he's annoyed about it."

After his mumbled apology to Colin, Bill sat quietly in his office. He couldn't believe he had acted so badly, first towards his secretary and then his best friend. He knew he would soon make it up with Colin, but Miss Anderson, she was a different matter.

He had meant what he'd said. He couldn't do without her in the office. It was a nightmare when she went on holiday. Most of the temporary staff sent from the agency didn't have any commitment, while the girls from the typing pool spent most of the day filing their nails. He didn't know what he would do if she asked to be transferred to another department – which was her right if she found herself unable to work with her boss. He decided to send her some flowers and phoned a local florist to order a large bouquet to be delivered to her at the office as soon as possible. Having done that, he suddenly remembered he hadn't spoken to Joey for two days so he dialled his mother's number. He felt a little cheered when he heard his son's voice.

"Daddy," he said, excitedly. "Do you know there are only six days left until Christmas? There was a clown behind the door on my calendar this morning."

Bill smiled to himself. Joey was determined to give him a count down to Christmas.

Joey went on to tell him about all the things he had done in the last few days, making a special mention of the big Christmas tree in the shopping centre. "Can we have a Christmas tree Daddy?"

"Of course we can. If you want one," said Bill. "We'll go shopping for one on Friday when I pick you up. We could have some hamburgers or pizzas some-where. How does that sound to you?"

It sounded very good to Joey and when he finally put the phone down, he ran through to the kitchen to tell his nanna he was going to get a Christmas tree.

After talking to Joey, Bill tried to get on with some work, but his heart wasn't in it. He looked down at the invoices still scattered across the floor. Normally he would never throw them down like that; working with figures was something he loved and he always treated his paperwork with utmost respect. However, he had felt so bad at the thought of both losing Sally and shouting at Colin, he had swept them off the desk in a fit of rage.

The files stared defiantly up at him from the floor, as though reminding him they would be his only companions for the rest of his life. For one brief moment he was tempted to put every single one through the shredder. Yet he knew he couldn't do that. Instead, he left them lying where they were.

During the morning, the phone didn't ring very often, however when it did, he picked it up quickly hoping it would be Sally. But it never was. Twice he thought of giving her a ring, but then changed his mind, half afraid she might tell him something he didn't want to hear.

When Miss Anderson received the flowers, she went through to Bill's office to thank him. The florist had taken Bill at his word and had sent the most enormous bouquet. "They're beautiful," she told him. "But really, there was no need." However it was obvious she was quite overwhelmed by his gesture. She was horrified to see the invoices all over the floor and offered to sort them out.

"I err… had an accident. I'll deal with them later," he said. He remained in his office all morning and managed to get through some work, though his usual enthusiasm had deserted him. He was grateful there weren't many interruptions. Usually members of his staff were in and out all the time.

Eleven o'clock came and went. By now he was extremely worried. He rang through to his secretary to confirm the time of his meeting that afternoon. She told him three o'clock. He looked at the time, twelve-fifteen. He should have some lunch, but his stomach turned over at the thought of food. Instead, he began to sort out the files on the floor. He was also going to have to face Colin very shortly. He guessed his friend had been dealing with all the queries that morning. Even the branch figures hadn't landed on his desk.

The time dragged on and there was still no word from Sally. Bill looked at his watch. It was almost two o'clock. Again he picked up the phone to ring her, only to put it down again. She may not even be there. If Sally's parents had called at the nursery to drag her back to the family home, Mrs Miller would have been forced to return and he didn't feel up to talking to her at the moment. She would most likely be furious with him for causing all this trouble. What a mess it all was. However, Mrs Miller was the least of his problems at the moment. To have found someone like Sally, only to lose her after a few short days didn't bear thinking about.

Just then, there was knock on the door and Miss Anderson walked in. "The Managing Director would like to see you in his office right away sir."

"Very well, Miss Anderson." Bill tried to compose himself. This was the last thing he needed at the moment, but he knew he couldn't refuse. He would have to go upstairs to see Mr Smithers. "If anyone wants me you know where I am." He forced a smile, not daring to upset his secretary again.

Upstairs, the MD's secretary gave Bill a warm smile as he entered her office. "Go straight in, Mr Smithers is waiting for you."

The Managing Director was behind his desk, but came forward to greet Bill. "Hello, Bill, I won't keep you too long, I know how busy you are. However, I wanted you to know that we, that is, the directors… well, we all think you did a good job with Taylor Associates yesterday."

Mr Smithers went on to tell him how Mr Taylor had telephoned him personally, to congratulate him on all his staff, but most especially, Mr Roberts. "He sang your praises, Bill. I think he would like to poach you from us. He said as much during our conversation."

Mr Taylor had actually gone so far as to tell him he had offered Bill a position with his firm should he ever feel the need to leave Websters. And then Mr Smithers had also heard from another company director, how Taylor Associates had spent the previous afternoon making enquiries about Bill Roberts and had been very impressed with the feedback.

"I can assure you I'm not thinking of leaving Websters, sir. I'm very happy with my position here." Bill told him.

"I'm most relieved to hear it. Nevertheless, the directors believe a little bonus is called for. Call it a Christmas present." Mr Smithers handed Bill an envelope.

"There's really no need. I'm already very well paid for the work I do."

"Nonsense! Take it – buy yourself something. Buy your girlfriend something special for Christmas. You do have a girlfriend, don't you?" As he spoke, he pushed the envelope into Bill's jacket pocket.

'I hope I still have,' thought Bill miserably. He was silent for a moment, remembering he still hadn't heard from Sally. However, seeing Mr Smithers was waiting for a reply, he quickly said, "Yes, I have a girlfriend."

Just then the telephone rang. "I thought I said no calls Mrs Gray." Then, after a moment's pause Mr Smithers continued. "Oh, I see, hold on a minute. It's for you Bill, your secretary says it's very urgent."

Bill's heart missed a beat, as he looked across to where Mr Smithers was holding the telephone. He tried to move, but his feet seemed to be pinned to the floor. It was too late in the day for it to be Sally; it was more likely to be her father.

Mr Smithers, concerned at how pale Bill had turned, asked if he was feeling unwell. "Would you like me to take a message?"

"No! No thank you, Mr Smithers. I'm all right," answered Bill, hastily. "I'll take it." If Sally's father was about to accuse him of seducing his daughter, he certainly didn't want the MD taking the call.

Though dreading what he may hear, he somehow managed to drag himself across the room and took the phone from Mr Smithers. "I'm sorry about this, please excuse me a moment." Bill wished he was in the privacy of his own office. However there wasn't anything he could do about it now, so taking a deep breath, he said, "Hello… this is Bill Roberts."

Once the children had settled down with their drawing books, Sally decided to phone her mother. She really wanted to get this over as quickly as possible. However, just as was about to dial the number, the line went dead. She hung up the phone and then tried again, but there was still no dialling tone.

Sally began to panic. She had hoped to speak to her mother while her father was away at the office, but apart from that, she had also promised to ring Bill before eleven o'clock. After checking that the children were all busy drawing, she ran to the office further down the corridor.

"Excuse me," she said to the girl sitting by the small switchboard. "Could I possibly use your telephone? I can't get a dialling tone on mine."

"I'm sorry, dear, but all the telephones are down at the moment. We had a letter about it early last week. They're working on a new system and all the phones in this area will be off until three, or was it four? Anyway, it's going to make my job a lot easier. Your call – was it anything important?"

"Err… no. Nothing important," replied Sally, swallowing the lump in her throat. She went back to the nursery and stared out of the window. It was pouring with rain. She couldn't possibly drag the children out in weather like this to find a telephone in working order. Nor could she go and leave them all alone, that would be unforgivable. There was no telling how long she might be. No, there was nothing else for it; she would simply have to wait until the lines were restored.

The morning wore on. Fortunately the children were quite happy to sit and draw; she was far too agitated to play with them. She knew Bill would be going frantic and she kept checking the phone, hoping it might be working again. But of course it wasn't.

By one o'clock she was pacing the floor. She could tell the children were becoming a little restless. Tired of drawing, they all wanted to play a game. However, Sally was not in any mood for playing games and suggested they have a little nap first and play afterwards. Hopefully by then she would have everything sorted out.

About quarter to two, a sharp ring pierced the silence in the nursery. It was so unexpected, Sally nearly jumped out of her seat. Picking up the receiver, she heard a recorded message informing her that the telephone was now operating. She gave herself a few moments to calm down before dialling her parents' telephone number.

"Hello Mum. It's Sally," she said, when she heard her mother's voice.

"Hello, Sally dear, I've been trying to ring you all weekend. Where have you been? We were beginning to worry."

"I'm standing in for Mrs Miller at her nursery. She's gone down with 'flu. I'm quite enjoying it. It's good experience." Sally told her mother a few things about the children. She still wasn't sure how to approach the subject of Bill, despite having rehearsed the conversation in her mind all morning. In the end she blurted it straight out. "Mum. I've met someone. A man, I mean. He's really wonderful and I'm sure you'll like him when you meet him."

"Who is he dear? Someone from college?" Her mother, Margaret, flicked some dust from the hall table as she spoke.

"No. He's not from college." She paused for a moment. "He's a widower. He's twenty-eight and he's called Bill." There she'd said it. Now all she could do was to wait for her mother's reaction.

"A widower! Oh Sally, are you sure about this?" Margaret couldn't believe what she was hearing.

"Mum. I've never been surer of anything in my life. I love him."

"Love him. How do you know you love him?" Suddenly Margaret was struck with a terrible thought. "Oh Sally. You're not sleeping with him are you? I don't know what your father is going to say about all this." She felt faint, and sank into the chair by the hall table. Her unmarried daughter sleeping with a man, it was all too much. He must have seduced her, lured her to his bed and raped her. Margaret's imagination ran wild. Her lovely young daughter wouldn't have done this on her own accord. No, it must be this man's fault, who ever he is. "Please tell me you're not sleeping with him."

Sally hesitated. It wasn't any of her mother's business. However she decided to be honest. "Yes. I've slept with him," She spoke softly. "I told you. I love him. Please Mum, try to understand."

"Oh Sally. How could you do this to us?" Margaret still wasn't altogether convinced. "You know Peter still loves you, don't you? What's wrong with him? He's a nice boy and only about your age." Then as an afterthought she added. "And he hasn't been married."

"Mum. I don't love Peter. I never will. I love Bill and there's something else you should know. He has a four-year-old son, called Joey. He's so sweet."

Even though she was sitting down, Margaret held onto the telephone table for support. "Michael, thank goodness you're here," she called out to her husband, who had arrived home for a late lunch. "Come here quickly and speak to your daughter. She's got herself involved with a widower, and he has a four-year-old son. I can't make her see sense. I simply can't believe it. You must make her come home at once. She doesn't know what she's doing. This man has tricked her and…"

Michael took the phone from his wife. "Calm yourself Margaret. Let me deal with it." He lifted the receiver to his ear. "Now then, Sally. What's all this your mother's telling me? Say it isn't true."

"It's true, Dad. I really love him. Don't tell me you've forgotten what it feels like to be in love." In the background, she could hear the muffled voice of her mother; telling him Sally had slept with this man.

"Sally, what are you thinking of? I knew it was a mistake to let you go back there on your own. You should have stayed here and married Peter. We want you to come home at once. I'll come over this afternoon and pick you up. I'll ring Peter at the office, he'll come with me."

Sally hesitated. She had never disobeyed her father before. He usually had the final word and she had always respected that. But then she thought of Bill and how she would feel if she were never to see him again. She took a deep breath. "Dad, I wouldn't marry Peter if he was the last man on earth and please don't bother to come over, I'm not coming back with you." Though she was shaking, she tried to keep her voice calm and relaxed.

"You'll do as you're told," Michael yelled into the phone He wasn't used to his daughter defying him. "Who is this man? He's using you, Sally. Can't you see that? You don't know what you're doing. You have no idea how scheming men can be. We know what's best for you. You need us to look out for you. Have your cases ready, we'll be over there as soon as we can." He softened his tone a little, "You know Peter will be so pleased to see you again? He's always talking about you. Can't you see that you and he would be good together?"

Sally was furious. "Dad, you're not listening to me. I've told you, I'm not coming back. And whose fault is it if I don't know enough about men? No boy was ever allowed to get near me. You and my brothers saw to that. For once in your lives, let me be my own person and do what I want to do." She paused for a moment to get her breath back. "All my life I've done everything you and my brothers wanted. You all keep forgetting this is my life. From now on I'm going live it the way I want to. You can't run my life forever. Listen to yourself, Dad. You're even arranging a marriage for me. Next you'll be telling me how many children I should have. You've probably got it all worked out. Well forget it and don't bother to turn up at my flat I won't be there." She was so angry she slammed the phone down. She was trembling at speaking to her father in such a manner. Yet, it had to be said. Having found Bill, she was determined her parents weren't going to drag her away from him.

She looked around the room at the children. They had all awoken and were staring at her. Some had even started to cry. For a moment she had forgotten where she was and now she felt guilty at sounding so angry in front of them.

"It's all right children; I'm not cross with you." She went over to them. "Come on Jenny and Sue, dry your eyes. I'm sorry I made you cry, but it's all over now." She hugged them all in turn, but though they stopped crying, they still looked nervous. She was desperate to ring Bill, but it was important she should calm the children first.

"I think we should all have a sweetie from Mrs Miller's tin." As she walked across to the shelf where the tin was kept she was relieved to see the frightened look on the children's faces being replaced with smiles.

Her father stood at the other end of the line hardly able to believe his ears. The receiver was still in his hand. Repeating what Sally had said, he sat down on the stairs and asked where they had gone wrong. "We only wanted what was best for her," he said. "Did we really push her so hard into our way of thinking?"

Margaret was fanning her face with an advertisement for new kitchens, which had suddenly dropped through the letterbox. "Perhaps we did. Oh, I don't know. We were worried about her – being a girl, after the two boys. Maybe we were a little over protective."

They sat there for what seemed like an age. "She's over twenty-one," said her mother at last. "And she's right, it is her life and we are trying to live it for her. She could have moved out a few years ago. We must either accept this, or lose her altogether. And I for one don't want to lose her. We need to be there should things go wrong."

"What was the number she called from?" said Michael, finally pulling himself together. His wife was right. They didn't want to lose their only daughter. They were going to have to accept the fact she wasn't a little girl anymore. She was a grown woman, ready to make her own decisions.

"I don't know. She didn't give it," said Margaret. "She was speaking from Mrs Miller's nursery."

Michael dialled 1471 and pushed button three before thrusting the phone into his wife's hand. "You speak to her. I'm not exactly her favourite person at the moment. Say you'll meet her tomorrow at whatever time she likes. I'll run you there. Tell her we'll go along with it. Ask if it would be possible for you to meet this man. I'll leave you with her and drive off. She'll be more open with you."

When Sally answered the phone, she was surprised to hear her mother on the other end.

"Sally. Your father wants me to meet you tomorrow. Any time that's convenient to you and before you say anything, we'll try to understand and go along with what you want. Will it be possible for me to meet, err… Bill, is it?"

Sally couldn't believe it. "Mum. You've made me so happy," she said. "I'm usually stuck here until about four o'clock every day, though the parents are beginning to pick up their children a little earlier as it gets nearer to Christmas. We could meet for tea somewhere." She paused, thinking of somewhere suitable. "What about the Happy Kettle? It's quite close to the nursery. You could keep a table until I get there. I'll ask Bill if he'll be able to join us. However, he has a high-powered job so he may not be able to make it. He's an executive in the Finance Department at Websters International."

Michael, whose ear was pressed against the other side of the phone, was suitably impressed and nodded at Margaret, indicating he knew of the firm.

"At least he has a good job," he whispered. Until then, he had visualised Bill as someone out of work, with a ring through his nose.

"Good. We'll leave it at that then," uttered Margaret. She was still feeling a little faint at the thought of her daughter sleeping with a man before she was married. Putting down the receiver, she turned to her husband. "I think you should be there if there's a likelihood of Bill turning up."

"I may join you if he actually appears on the scene. Let's wait and see. We'll play it by ear. Meanwhile I'm going to take the rest of the afternoon off and pour myself a very large brandy, I need it!"

Sally checked the time. It was two-thirty. Quickly, she dialled the number of Websters and when connected, gave her name and asked to be put through to his office.

Miss Anderson answered in her usual efficient manner. "Mr Roberts is upstairs in a meeting with the Managing Director, but I'll put you straight through."

"Is that wise, Miss Anderson?" Sally was apprehensive. Perhaps she should call back.

"Believe me Miss Hughes, it would be most unwise of me not to!"

Sally heard the Managing Director telling Bill the call was for him. Then after what seemed like an age she heard Bill's voice.

"Hello… this is Bill Roberts."

"Bill, it's me, Sally. I'm sorry I'm so late in ringing, but the phones have been down all morning and…" She broke off. That wasn't important now. "Anyway, I've spoken to Mum and Dad. It's all right Bill. They were okay about it. Mum is coming to meet me tomorrow for tea at about four o'clock and she would like to meet you. I explained you might be tied up, so don't worry if you can't make it."

Bill gave a silent prayer of thanks. For a while he couldn't speak. He sat down on the corner of Mr Smithers' desk.

"Bill, darling, are you still there?" said Sally, anxiously.

"Yes sweetheart, I'm still here. I just didn't know what to say. I was so worried at not hearing from you."

He told her he would be there to meet her mother, one way or another. "Sally, darling I love you so much I can't wait to…" He stopped, suddenly seeing Mr

Smithers grinning at him. For the moment, he had totally forgotten where he was. "Sally, I'll call you back in a few minutes." He grinned sheepishly at the Managing Director, as he hung up the phone.

"Can I take it you've had some good news, Bill?" asked Mr Smithers, relieved the colour had returned to Bill's cheeks.

"Yes, I have. The very best."

"Well I won't keep you any longer, I expect you want to get back to your office. You've obviously got lots of things to do…" He smiled. "And most certainly lots of things to say to a special young lady."

Shaking with relief, Bill raced down the stairs two at a time. Miss Anderson was waiting for him with a message from Mr Peterson. He had called to say he was running late and wouldn't be able to come until four thirty. "I told him it would be alright, I hope I did the right thing. You haven't any other appointments this afternoon."

"Yes, Miss Anderson, that's perfectly all right," he replied. He went into his office and phoned Sally.

"What a nice surprise, darling," she said. "I didn't expect you to call back so quickly."

"I wanted to tell you how much I love you and wish I was with you right now."

"I wish you were too, darling," replied Sally, wistfully thinking of them in bed together the night before. Seeing the children were looking at her, she pulled herself back to the present. "Bill, I hope I didn't get you into any trouble when I called. Your secretary said you were with the Managing Director. I told her I could call later, but she was adamant she should put me through."

"It was fine, Mr Smithers didn't mind at all." A feeling of guilt swept over him for the second time, when he thought of how he had spoken to Miss Anderson and Colin.

"I'm thinking of doing some shopping when I get away from here this afternoon," said Sally. "I'll try not to be too late."

"Would you like me to meet you somewhere when you've finished shopping? We could try to get a pub meal," replied Bill.

"That would nice. I'll give you a ring on your mobile to let you know where I am. The town is likely to be busy so I'm not sure we'll get in anywhere. But we could try."

"Well I'd better go. I really need to have a word with Colin. I gave him a hard time this morning. Give me a ring when you're ready to be picked up. I love you, Sally."

Having already made his peace with his secretary, it was time to speak with Colin. He called him into his office. "I've heard from Sally. She's told her parents and they are fine with it. I don't suppose for one minute they're ecstatic about it, but at least they're accepting it. Her mother is coming to meet me tomorrow so I'll have to be on my best behaviour. What time is it?" He looked at his watch.

"Quarter to three, have you had lunch yet?"

Colin told him he hadn't had time to have lunch. He hadn't even had time to call Rachel. Bill wasn't indisposed very often, but it was on such days that Colin realised how much work his friend did. "I've been kept rather busy this morning."

"Thanks Colin. I guessed you'd stopped people coming in here. I owe you one." He suddenly turned very serious. "Look I'm really sorry about what I said to you earlier. I didn't mean a word of it. I know you have plenty of work of your own to do. It was wrong of me to take my problem out on you... and Miss Anderson. I hope you'll forgive me."

"It's okay Bill, I knew how concerned you were." Colin was delighted everything had worked out well for his friend. "And don't worry about your secretary. She showed me her flowers. She's over the moon with them."

"I was concerned she might want to move to another department. I couldn't do without her. Come on then. Let's go and have some lunch at the little restaurant around the corner. I've an appointment, but he can't come 'til four thirty."

As he spoke he put his hand into his jacket pocket and pulled out the envelope Mr Smithers had put there earlier. "I forgot all about this in the excitement, the MD gave it to me. I was with him when Sally telephoned."

He ripped it open and pulled out a cheque. He whistled and showed it to Colin. "Well now. Just you look at that." The cheque was made out for £20,000.

"Can I take it, lunch is on you?" Colin gasped.

"You most certainly can," replied Bill.

Sally was able to leave the nursery shortly after three o'clock. She made her way to the precinct in search of a dress for the dance on Thursday evening.

She wanted something really special, something that would make Bill proud to be with her. After looking in about half a dozen shops and trying on countless gowns she finally made a decision. She also found some matching shoes. Then she bought some Christmas presents for her parents and brothers, deciding to leave Joey and Bill's gifts until Friday or Saturday when she would have more time. After buying wrapping paper and labels, she checked the time and decided to ring Bill, he would be wondering what had happened to her.

Bill was waiting for her call. He had stayed at the office to get on with some of his work. It would cut down his workload for the following day. His secretary had informed him he had two appointments the next day. One was in the morning, which was no problem. However, the other was during the afternoon and had already been postponed from last Friday. "Three o'clock," his secretary had said.

Bill hoped the meeting wouldn't drag on too long. If it did, he would have to leave Colin to finish off. He wouldn't like that. Bill smiled to himself. Colin hated meetings with clients. When Sally finally called, he told her he would be there in ten minutes.

"What kept you? I've missed you." Bill put his arms around her and kissed her.

"I've missed you too, darling" she replied. "However, as any woman will tell you, shopping is a very serious business."

They both laughed, as he put her parcels into the boot of his car.

"Be careful with that one, Bill. It's my new dress."

"Am I allowed to take a peek?"

"I'll show you when we get back to your house," Sally replied. "Now then, where are we going to eat?"

"Well, I thought we could try The Bakers Arms first. You remember? It's the place we had Sunday lunch a few days ago."

"Okay. Let's go. I'm starving. I haven't had anything since this morning." She had been too worried at lunchtime to even think of eating – only managing to make sure the children had their lunch.

Although the pub was full, they didn't have long to wait for a table. During the meal Bill told Sally the reason for his large bonus.

"I've had bonus cheques before, but nothing like this. I think Mr Smithers was sure I'd take up Mr Taylor's offer."

"Would you?"

"No," replied Bill. "I'm happy enough where I am. The work does build up sometimes, but that's my own fault. I know I shouldn't take on so much. Colin says I'm too easy on the staff. He thinks I let them get away with too much and he's probably right. It didn't bother me too much before, however, with you to come home to, all that will change." He reached over and kissed her lightly on the cheek. "How's your day been?"

She told him about the phones being out until nearly two o'clock. "That's why I was so late in ringing you."

"How did your parents really take the news? You can tell me. I won't be upset. I know they probably weren't excited about the idea."

"Oh, they weren't too bad." Sally had no intention of hurting Bill with her parents' real reaction.

"Okay. We'll leave it at that." He guessed she wanted to spare his feelings. "If we've finished, I'll pay the bill then we'll go home. It's gone ten-thirty."

It wasn't long before they were back at Bill's house. Sally unpacked her purchases and hung her new dress on a hanger. She stepped back to take a better look at it. It was made of a red shiny material, with one wide strap, which went over one shoulder. It was a very slim fit and had hugged her trim figure perfectly when she had tried it on in the shop.

"Sally, it's beautiful," said Bill, as he walked into the bedroom. "You'll look a million dollars."

"It is lovely," Sally agreed. "And I couldn't resist these shoes to go with it. I've brought you some change though and I insist on paying you back even if it's in instalments." She handed him £200.

"I don't want you to pay me back and I don't want any change. Keep it. Buy yourself something else at the weekend." She was about to protest, but Bill held up his hand. "Please Sally. Keep it. I want you to have it."

"Thank you, Bill. You're so generous." She suddenly thought about Joey. "Bill, have you had time to buy a Christmas present for Joey?"

"Yes. I got some things for him the last time he was at my mother's. A small bike, a racing car and a few other odds and ends. They're all wrapped up and hidden in the loft, well out of sight."

"I was thinking about getting him another carriage for his train set. Do you think he'd like that?" asked Sally.

"Yes. I'm sure he would. He plays with it a lot. Well I'm going to take a shower and get into bed. It's been quite a day."

She spent some time looking at her dress before taking a shower. When she returned to the bedroom Bill was already in bed and she climbed in beside him. "I'm so happy." She snuggled up close to him.

He put his arms around her and kissed her. "Darling, I don't know what I'd have done if your parents had stopped me from seeing you."

"I told you I wouldn't let that happen. I love you far too much." She smiled. "Bill darling, would you do something for me?"

"Of course Sally sweetheart, anything. What is it?"

"Make love to me."

"Anytime," replied Bill, putting out the light.

Day Seven

It was only five in the morning when Sally awoke. She lay for a while, wondering what she would say to her mother when they met later in the day. Though her parents had agreed to go along with the idea of her seeing Bill, she knew they still weren't happy with the situation – particularly her father. He would look for the slightest fault and compare him with Peter. It wasn't fair! Bill was a good man. She must make him see that.

Glancing at Bill, she was tempted to wake him. But she knew how worried he had been yesterday, so why upset him all over again? Besides, he really needed to sleep. She climbed out of bed and went downstairs.

She made a pot of tea and began to rehearse what she would say to her mother. Truthfully, she would rather they weren't meeting, but on the other hand it was as well to get it over with. It was going to happen sooner or later. She hoped Bill would be able to get to the café. It would be good if her parents were able to see how happy they were together.

Though she was only supposed to be meeting her mother, Sally felt sure her father would be there, too. She couldn't imagine him missing the opportunity to meet his daughter's lover. Just then she heard the alarm ring upstairs. Seven o'clock already! How the time had flown.

She heard Bill call out for her. Having told him of her reluctance to get out of bed in the mornings, he had assumed she wasn't feeling well. "I'm fine," she called out, climbing the stairs. "I was just putting the kettle on."

"You haven't forgotten I'm meeting my mother today, have you?" Sally glanced at Bill, as she bit into her toast.

"No, I haven't forgotten. I'll really try to be there and I promise to be on my best behaviour."

"No Bill. You must be yourself. I want Mum to meet the real you and see the kind, gentle and generous man I fell in love with. Act the way you normally do. Say the things you'd normally say. Don't try to change, you're wonderful the way you are."

Bill laughed. "Do you really want to introduce your mother to a man who can't keep his hands off her daughter?"

"Well, they already know I've slept with you." Sally grinned broadly.

Bill groaned. "Oh Sally, you told them *that*?" He was now even more concerned at meeting Sally's mother.

"Mother asked me. However, I didn't say I was actually living here. She would have had a fit. Especially if she knew I only met you one week ago today."

"Only one week. I feel as though I've known you for ages Sally. You're so much a part of my life now."

"And you, mine," replied Sally. "But we'd better get a move on. We're going to be late for work."

Bill dropped Sally off at the nursery and kissed her goodbye. "I'll see you later," he said, before driving off. He hoped he would have time to stop to buy some chocolates for Sally's mother.

When he reached the office Colin was already there. "You're early this morning. Couldn't you sleep?"

"I thought you might like me to give you a hand to clear your desk. The Christmas holidays are looming and I know you'll want everything sorted before then." Colin knew Bill wanted to be away particularly early today but he didn't want to mention Sally's parents. His friend was concerned enough about the event, without him banging on about it.

"Thanks, Colin. I'd really appreciate your help."

Just then Miss Anderson walked into the room with the morning's mail. "Good morning Mr Roberts." Then seeing Colin standing there, she added. "Good morning Colin. You're early this morning."

Colin looked at Bill, then at Miss Anderson. "Not you as well, it sounds like a conspiracy. I *have* been in at this time before, you know." Seeing the grin on Bill's face, he added, "Okay, I know. Not often. Tomorrow I'll be here at my usual time, 9 am on the dot." He usually made a point of never arriving before the appointed time. "When you've got yourself sorted out, Bill, give me a shout."

"Thanks Colin. I will." He turned to his secretary. "What have you got for me this morning? Oh, and while I remember. Will you get my afternoon appointment on the phone? Mr Stevens isn't it? I've decided to ask if he can come a little earlier. I'll speak to him myself. You had to put him off last Friday, didn't you? I'd better talk to him this time."

"Very well," said Miss Anderson. "There's not too much in the mail this morning. I think everyone is winding down for Christmas."

"Then I think we must do the same don't you?" said Bill. "Don't make any appointments for me until after the holidays unless they're really urgent." Seeing the look of astonishment on her face, he explained. "Tomorrow is the firm's dinner dance, and on Friday I just want to call into the office before I go off to my mother's to pick up my son."

Miss Anderson was amazed. Mr Roberts always worked until the last possible moment no matter what the holiday was. He had even been known to see a client at five o'clock on Christmas Eve. Her boss had changed so much in the last week.

Bill looked through his mail. There was nothing too difficult there. With a bit of luck and Colin's help, he would get away in good time. His secretary rang through to say she had Mr Stevens on the line.

The representative was more than happy to call earlier in the afternoon.

"It will fit in with my own plans very nicely," he said.

Now Bill was sure he would be able to leave the office in good time to meet Sally and her mother.

At the nursery, most of the parents informed Sally they wouldn't need to bring their children on Friday, having been given the day off. Therefore it seemed more than likely she would also have the day free. This would give her time to make sure Bill's house was clear of her belongings before he brought Joey home. It wouldn't do to have him find a woman's clothes lying about the place. The youngster had such an inquisitive mind, Bill might have to spend all Christmas thinking of plausible answers. Just then the phone rang.

"Hello Sally, Jo here! I was wondering if you were going to make it to the lecture tonight. You did get my note, didn't you?"

Sally winced, she had forgotten all about it. "Oh Jo I can't tonight. My parents are coming up to town. I'm meeting my mother as soon as I can get away from here. I'm sorry, but to tell you the truth it had slipped my mind."

"Don't worry. I'll go on my own. I'll probably meet someone I know when I get there. Have you managed to do the assignment?"

Sally cringed. That was something else she had forgotten. "No. I haven't had time. But I'm a little ahead anyway, so it won't matter if I miss this one."

Jo sighed. "I don't think you're going to finish this course, are you? You don't seem to have your heart in it anymore." She paused for a moment. "Are you still seeing Bill?"

"Yes." Sally hesitated. "I love him, Jo. I don't suppose you'll be able to understand it, but I really love him. I hate it when we have to go to work in the mornings and I spend all day looking forward to seeing him again in the evenings. I yearn to be near to him every waking moment."

"I see," Jo said, slowly. "And what about you're sleeping moments?"

Sally hesitated, it would appear a little of the old Jo was trying to sneak back in. But she wasn't going to allow her to take over again. "Yes and those too, though I don't see what it has to do with you." Her tone was cold.

"Yes, you're right. It has nothing to do with me. I'm sorry." Jo kicked herself. Why did she have to say such things? Quickly changing the subject a little, she said. "Do you're parents know about him?"

"Yes. I told them about him yesterday." Sally softened her tone. "I'm sure you can imagine their reaction. Nevertheless, I told them how I felt and they said they'd try to understand. My mother is hoping to see Bill today, if he can make it. I hope he can, as I would like it all settled before they go off to Tenerife on Friday."

"Gosh yes. I'd forgotten they were going away for Christmas this year. It's a sort of second honeymoon, isn't it?" Jo paused. "What're you going to do over the holidays?"

"I'm going to Bill's house. I could have gone to my brother's but, as you can imagine, I'd rather be with Bill."

"I hate to bring this up again, but what about this course?" asked Jo.

"I don't know," replied Sally. "However, you're right. I have lost interest in it at the moment. Dare I ask you to tape the lecture again, just in case? I may get a chance to listen to the two tapes on Friday. I think I'll probably have the day free as the children's parents are going to be home, so they won't be bringing them to the nursery. Though having said that, I must do some more Christmas shopping and I promised to call in on Jane. Bill has to go to his mother's to pick up his son. Oh, and I'm going to Bill's firm's Dinner Dance at the Apollo Hotel tomorrow night. I'm quite looking forward to meeting some of his friends and colleagues."

"Your social calendar sounds full," Jo laughed. "Unlike mine. The pages in my diary are blank. Well don't worry, I'll tape the lecture for you and pick up any other information I can. However, you're going to have to make your mind up about the course or else you'll get left behind. Well, I'd better let you get on. Good luck with your mother this afternoon. Give her my love won't you? I'll push the tape through your letterbox if you're not in. Say hello to Bill for me. 'Bye for now."

"Goodbye Jo and thanks. I'll ring you soon." After hanging up the phone Sally checked the time. "I think we'll have our lunch now. We'll get it over with in case your parents come early again."

By twelve-thirty the children had eaten and were taking a nap. Sally thought about giving Bill a ring, but wondered if he might be too busy. She knew he had told his secretary to put her through regardless, but she hadn't anything new to tell him. All she really wanted was to hear his voice. While she was still thinking about it, the phone rang.

"Hello," said Bill. "I have a few minutes to spare so I thought I would ring my favourite girl." He was still feeling on cloud nine and wanted to talk to her all the time.

"Just how many girls have you, Bill Roberts?" Sally laughed.

"Only one, sweetheart. Only you," replied Bill. "I wanted to talk to you before my next appointment. I persuaded him to come in earlier and Colin has taken some of my load. He even came in early this morning to help me out. I don't think he'll do it again, though. Everyone has teased him about it. Anyway, hopefully I should get away from the office in good time. But I'll give you time to have a chat with your mother first. What time are you meeting her?"

"I can't remember if we said four or four-thirty. However knowing my mother, she'll get to the cafe at about two o'clock and sit with four cups of coffee to keep the table free." Sally laughed. "But, as it happens I think I'll be able to leave here at two-thirty, so she won't have to wait long."

"Okay Sally. I'll get there as soon as I can. The Happy Kettle isn't it?"

"Yes, that's right. And Bill, don't be surprised if Dad's there. I think he'll be too curious to stay away."

"Now you're really making me nervous." Bill ran a finger around his collar. "Especially after you told them… Well, you know what you told them. He might want to thump me."

"Well thump him back." Sally squealed with laughter.

"It's not funny, you know. Anyway I think I'd better go. Judging by the three lights flashing on this phone, Miss Anderson must have some calls waiting. I'll see you later, darling, 'bye."

Sally was right. By two-thirty all the children had gone home. She cleared away the toys and went out to the cloakroom to get her coat. After checking her lipstick, she locked up and went off to the café.

It was as she had predicted, her mother was already waiting for her. The only difference was there were two coffee cups on the table, not four. Margaret waved, as she entered the café. As Sally walked across to her she couldn't help noticing how strained she looked. She kissed her mother on the cheek. "Mum, are you feeling all right? You look a little off colour today."

"Yes, I'm fine. I'm getting over a cold that's all. Tell me, how're you getting on with the children? Are they being good?"

"Yes, the children are adorable." Sally looked at the coffee cups on the table. "Is the coffee still hot, or has it been there for an hour?"

"We'd better order some more. It's been here for quite a while and the waiter keeps asking if anyone is coming or not."

Sally called the waiter over and asked for two more coffees and a plate of cakes. "That should keep him quiet for a while. Bill is going to try to come. He's been juggling his appointments around this morning. You know Mother, he's very nervous about meeting you and Dad. By the way, where is Dad? I half expected him to be here."

"He may come in, if and when Bill turns up. He had a little business to see to while he was here in town."

Margaret hadn't failed to notice how well her daughter was looking and how her whole face glowed at the mere mention of Bill's name. It was plain Sally was in love, but she desperately hoped this man loved her in the same way and wasn't leading her on. "Tell me a little about Bill."

"What would you like to hear first?" asked Sally. "His kindness, his gentleness, his good looks, his generosity, his..."

"Hey there, slow down," Margaret interrupted. "I simply want to know whether he's taking care of you. Your father and I love you very much and we don't want you to get hurt."

"Mum, don't worry. He loves me. Actually, he worships me. You'll agree when you meet him. But tell me, how are you and Dad keeping these days? Is the business doing well? Are you getting through that large order? You remember? The one we celebrated the last time I was staying with you?" Margaret didn't answer. She looked down at her coffee cup. "Mum. What is it? What's wrong?" A note of fear had crept into Sally's voice.

"It all went horribly wrong." Margaret mumbled. "We started the order. Well, we got most of it done actually and then the company backed out. They said they wouldn't need the goods anymore as they themselves were in trouble. But they must have known before they placed the order."

She paused, while she fumbled in her bag for a handkerchief. "Sally, we can't find anyone else to take the stock; none of our regular customers anyway. Your brothers are frantic with worry. They have families and mortgages to contend with. Your father and I are only going away because the holiday is booked and paid for, but we won't really enjoy it. He said I wasn't to tell you all this, as you would worry. However, I was never able to keep a secret."

Sally listened, in horror. Thank goodness she hadn't asked her parents for the money to buy a new dress. "I can't believe it. Surely you had a contract with this company?" Bill had told her about what had happened in his office the previous Monday; otherwise she wouldn't have had a clue about contracts.

"Your father thought he could trust them, as we had done business with them before. They shook hands on the deal. We know now it was a stupid thing to do, but your father's always taken people at face value and up to now we haven't had any problems. But never again! Look where it's got us. You see we had to take out quite a large loan at the bank to cover us until the money came in, only now there won't be any money."

The waiter returned to see if everything was all right.

"Yes thank you," replied Sally. "We'll have two more coffees please." She wished Bill would come. He would give her some support, he knew about these things, whereas she didn't know what to say. Like her mother she didn't have a head for business.

"Come on Mum. I'm sure it'll all work out in the end. I know you're worried, but you have your holiday to look forward to. Try to enjoy it and the boys may have it sorted out when you come back." She didn't really feel too sure about that, but what else could she say?

The waiter came back with the coffees and put them on the table.

"Can you make it another please?"

Sally looked up quickly, recognising the voice. "Bill darling. You made it, I'm so glad."

Bill sat down next to Sally and put his arms around her and kissed her.

"Hello sweetheart." He turned to Margaret. "Hello Mrs Hughes. I'm Bill Roberts. I'm so pleased to meet you." He placed an extremely large box of chocolates on the table. "These are for you."

Margaret was quite taken aback. "Why, thank you. That's most kind."

Sally squeezed Bill's knee under the table and he turned to look at her. Thank you, she mouthed, without her mother noticing.

Margaret could see why her daughter had fallen for Bill. He was tall, good looking and thoughtful, too. "I'm pleased you were able to come. Sally told us you had a demanding job and may be too busy to join us today."

"Well it is like that sometimes. However, I was able to alter my schedule without too much trouble."

Just then Sally's father came in and sat down beside his wife.

"I'm Michael Hughes. And you must be Sally's young man."

"I'm pleased to meet you Mr Hughes." Bill wasn't sure what to expect from Sally's father. He ran a finger around his collar.

"I'm afraid we don't know very much about you. We only heard of your existence yesterday." Michael watched, as Bill place his arm around Sally.

"Bill brought me a present," said Margaret. "It was very thoughtful of him wasn't it?"

"Yes it was," replied Michael, his eyes never leaving Bill.

The waiter came over with Bill's coffee. "Thank you." Bill looked up. "Could we have another please?"

"Coming right up," said the waiter.

Bill turned back to Sally's father. "What would you like to know about me sir? I'll tell you anything you want to know."

"I want to know if you love my daughter and I mean really love her. I want the truth, mind you, not cock and bull story you think might please me. We love

Sally dearly and don't want her hurt. You must realise you weren't exactly what we had in mind for her. I don't mean you any disrespect, it's just that… well, to put it bluntly, we thought she would find someone her own age, someone who hadn't been married before. And…"

Sally felt Bill's grip tighten on her arm. She could tell he was feeling unnerved by her father's approach. But then, so was she. How could he be so aggressive? It wasn't fair. "Dad, don't…" she tried to interrupt,

"It's all right, Sally," said Bill, quietly. "Let your father finish."

"Well, I guess you get my drift," Michael shrugged. "We simply wondered what a man of your experience was doing with our young daughter. We believe you're using her until you find someone better. And we don't want her coming home broken hearted because you've had your fun and sent her packing. Now, what have you got to say?" He sat back in his seat.

"Well, sir, I can't do anything about my age, or the fact that I've been married before. But I'm certainly not a man of… experience, as you put it. My wife, Julie was the first woman in my life and since she died three years ago, I haven't so much as looked at another woman until now." Bill paused and glanced briefly at Sally before continuing. "Mr Hughes, the truth is I do love Sally. I loved her the first moment I saw her and I can promise you I'll never hurt her. If she ever comes back to you, it'll be because it's what she wants and I'll be the one who's left heartbroken. I'll never ever ask her to go." He pulled Sally closer as though he was terrified her father was going to drag her from him right there and then. "I'll share everything I have with her. I own my house. I have a good job and earn an excellent salary, well over £250,000, plus regular bonuses. Yesterday I was given a bonus cheque for £20,000. Sally can have it if she wants it. All she has to do is ask. Mr Hughes, I swear to you, I'll give her anything she wants. Please believe me, sir. I really do love her and I promise you both, I'll do everything I can to take care of her and make her happy. Just don't take her away from me."

Michael listened to Bill without making any attempt to interrupt. He looked at his wife. She nodded. She had taken a liking to this young man even before his reply to her husband. Then he turned to his daughter who hadn't taken her eyes off Bill during the whole of his speech. It was obvious she was totally besotted with him. Looking back at Bill, he had to admit, in spite of himself, he rather liked this man's honest approach.

"That's all I wanted to know," he said, his voice softening. "You know I had to ask. One day you'll do the same if you have a daughter. You both have our blessing. Oh, and one more thing, we couldn't take Sally away even if we wanted to. She made that very plain to us yesterday." He looked across at Sally and winked.

Bill couldn't believe it. He reached across the table and shook Michael's hand. "Thank you sir. If there's anything I can do for you, you only have to ask." He was so excited he pulled Sally to him and kissed her, almost taking her breath away. Margaret and Michael exchanged glances and smiled, but said nothing.

Bill looked back at Michael. "Oh! I'm sorry sir."

Sally had remained silent throughout Bill's statement, but now she said, "Bill, Dad's firm is in trouble."

Michael looked at his wife. "You told her, then?"

"I had to. She guessed something was wrong the moment she saw me."

"What's the problem, sir?" asked Bill. "Can I be of any help?"

Michael relayed to him exactly what Sally's mother had said earlier.

Bill thought for a few minutes.

"Well, it's a long shot, but I could check with our sales office. They may have been asked for that type of equipment recently. They often get asked for things we don't produce."

He took out his mobile phone and dialled the number of his firm and asked to speak to John Wilson, Head of the Sales Department, saying it was Bill Roberts.

"Hello, Bill. Nice job you did on Monday with Taylor's."

"Thank you, John." Bill then went on to ask him to check with his team as to whether they had been asked for the type of components Michael had mentioned.

Sally and her mother shut their eyes and crossed their fingers.

"I can answer that straight away," he said, "I was asked about two or three weeks ago. It was one of our regular customers. They had been let down by their usual supplier. Gone out of business, I think. I told them I didn't know of anyone, so I can't say whether they got fixed up or not."

"Who are they, and what's their number?" Picking up a paper napkin, Bill wrote down the information. "Thanks, John. I owe you one."

He then called the company in question and asked for Mr Swan, Head of the Purchasing Department saying who he was.

"What can I do for you?" asked a voice on the other end of the line. "Haven't you been paid for the last delivery?"

"Your finances are in order. However, I've heard you were looking for some components and wondered if you'd managed to find them," said Bill.

"No. Not yet. We're going to be in trouble if we don't get hold of some very soon."

"Hold on a minute. I think I have someone here who might be able to help you out." Bill covered the mouthpiece and handed the phone to Michael.

"They're a small company in the North East, Thomas and Sons. They're a good credit risk, or at least they are to us. But as you've never dealt with them, ask for half the money to be wired to your account now, and the rest cash on delivery."

Michael took the phone and after agreeing a price, he repeated what Bill had said about payment and gave Mr Swan his banking details. After he hung up, he turned to Bill.

"I don't know how to thank you. I have no idea what we'd have done."

"There's no need for thanks sir. I was pleased to be able to help," said Bill.

"Don't call me sir. My name is Michael. Do you mind if I borrow that thing and call my sons to tell them of the good news."

"Of course sir… err… Michael." Bill passed him the phone.

Tom sounded relieved when his father gave him the news. "You did it then. You found someone?"

"No. Sally's young man made a couple of phone calls and well, you know the rest. Here's what I want you to do." Michael gave his son some instructions about delivery. Tom told him when the first payment came in he would drive the goods there himself. Michael gave a few more instructions then hung up.

"Thanks again, Bill. You must let me give you something for helping us out like this."

Bill pulled Sally closer to him. "You've given me everything I want, Michael. Nothing else matters."

They spent the next hour or so chatting. Michael asked Bill about his job at Websters. He was very interested to know more about the man who had so suddenly come into his daughter's life.

"Would anyone like to go for a meal?" Bill asked. It was almost time for the coffee shop to close. "I know everywhere gets busy at this time of the year, but Sally and I have managed to get into The Bakers Arms a couple of times lately."

"We should really be getting back… But what the hell; come on, Margaret, let's go with them." Michael was enjoying his talk with Bill. He rarely met anyone so enthused about business and he was learning a great deal. "Our car is at the other end of the High Street. Can you give us a lift down there?"

Driving down the High Street, they picked up Michael's car, before setting off for the public house. Although it was early, the Baker's Arms was still quite busy, however they managed to find a table. Bill said he would go and get some drinks; Sally went with him. There was a queue at the bar, so it was some time before they were served.

Michael and Margaret watched them.

"Now we're on our own, tell me honestly, what do you really think of Bill?" Margaret said.

"I like him. I didn't think I would. In fact to be honest, I came here today determined not to like him. What I really wanted to do was to punch him on the nose. However he seems a nice young man and I like him a lot. He's seems right for Sally. What do you think?"

"I must admit I liked him straight off. It's easy to see why Sally has taken to him. I only wish they weren't sleeping together." Margaret still hadn't quite come to terms with that. "Mind you, I thought you were a little hard on him earlier." She grinned. "Though I noticed, you changed your mind once you learned of his business finance prowess."

While they were watching, they saw Bill slide his arm around Sally and pull her to him. He kissed her and then whispered something in her ear. Whatever it was, it appeared Sally agreed, as she smiled up at him and nodded her head vigorously.

Margaret glanced at her husband to see his reaction.

"What you say is true. Yet my main concern was whether he loved her," said Michael, thoughtfully. "He'd been married before and could simply have been using her. However, I believe he really does love her and that's what matters."

Bill and Sally returned with the drinks.

"Sorry about the wait. I picked these up from the bar." Bill handed a couple of menus over to Sally's parents. "The barman said someone would be over in few minutes to take our order."

After a lengthy business discussion during the meal, it became even more apparent to Michael exactly how clever Bill was.

"Are you ever going to stop talking business, Michael," said Margaret. "I'm sure Bill gets enough of that at the office."

"I don't mind." Bill smiled.

"There you are! He doesn't mind. Besides, it's not often I get to talk to someone so knowledgeable," said Michael. "However, you're right, Margaret, besides, we should be making a move. We have a long drive back."

"You can stay at my house if you like," said Bill. "There's plenty of room. Then you can drive back in daylight. I have a rather good Brandy at home."

"Well, if it wouldn't be putting you out," said Michael.

"Of course it wouldn't," said Bill.

Sally looked at Bill and bit her lip. She was thinking her parents would see her clothes in Bill's room. The evening has been such a success it was a shame to spoil it now. She had been thankful the subject of her sleeping arrangements hadn't come up during the evening. Still, Bill had asked them now, so she would have to make the best of it.

Bill saw Sally's anxious expression and guessed what she was thinking. Sorry, he mouthed when her parents weren't looking. She smiled. She knew he was only trying to be helpful.

Arriving at the house, Bill asked Sally to show her mother to the bedroom his parents usually used. Meanwhile, he went to pour some Brandy for Michael and himself. He was in the kitchen putting on a pot of coffee, when Sally and her mother, came downstairs.

"I like your young man Sally. I think he'll make you very happy."

"Oh Dad, you don't know what it means to me to hear you say that," replied Sally. "I was determined I wasn't going to give Bill up, no matter what you said, but it's so much nicer having your approval."

Before Michael could say anything further, Bill came into the room carrying a tray holding the coffee and cups. "Would either of you ladies like some Brandy?"

They both declined, saying coffee would be fine for them. After about hour Sally started to put the empty cups on the tray. "I think I'll have to go to bed," she said, yawning.

"I think we should all be getting to bed," said Margaret. "Sally looks exhausted."

"Sally, darling," said Bill. "Why don't you go up to bed? I'll clear up here. You can have my room, I'll sleep..."

"Where would my daughter be sleeping if we weren't here?" Michael interrupted. His eyes were fixed firmly on Bill.

Bill looked at Sally. She sat down beside him and slipped her hand in his. Turning back to her father, Bill ran a finger around his collar and took a deep breath. "With me, sir." His stomach turned over and he breathed deeply.

Sally's father looked at them both, before his face broke into a grin. "I thought that would be the case." He shrugged. "But I wanted to hear what you would say. I'm pleased you were honest and didn't take me to be a fool. Well then, let's leave things as they are, shall we? And my name is still Michael."

Bill had prepared himself for a tongue lashing at the very least. Maybe even a good thumping, but he hadn't been ready for that. He didn't quite know what to say. He looked at Sally who was equally surprised by her father's remark.

"Michael!" said Sally's mother. "What are you saying?"

"Well. We can't have them running back and forwards across the hall all night, it would ruin our sleep," he replied.

"Don't be so coarse," uttered Margaret. "I'm going to bed, if that's all right with everyone. I suddenly have a headache." She left the room holding her head.

Looking at Sally, Bill inclined his head towards the stairs, indicating she should go up to bed. She nodded.

"Good night, Dad and thanks." She kissed her father on the cheek and ran upstairs.

Bill turned to Michael. "If it will make Mrs Hughes happier, I'll sleep in another room."

"Nonsense." Michael grinned. "Tomorrow night, you'll be back in bed with my daughter and we all know it. Margaret will be fine. She'll put it out of her mind. Anything she's uncomfortable with, she puts out of her mind. She's always been a bit on the dramatic side, or perhaps old fashioned is the phrase I should use."

He suddenly became more serious. "Bill, I want you to know I like you a lot and I think you're right for Sally. I have to admit I was worried at first, you being older, and married before. That's why I was so hard on you this afternoon. I'm sorry about that, but I needed to satisfy myself you really loved her. I'm sure if you had been playing around with her, you would have told me to mind my own business and walked out." He laughed, "You might have even smacked me around the face. But for Sally's sake I was willing to take the chance. However you sat there and took the trouble to explain your situation and I appreciated it. I see you're a really nice young man and yes I'll say it again, I like you and I'm proud to welcome you into our family. To tell you the truth, I think Sally has done very well for herself."

Bill was delighted to hear it, but he was concerned Sally may not have told her parents about his son. "Michael, I don't know whether Sally mentioned it, but you need to know, I have a four-year-old son. He's spending a few days with my parents at the moment."

"Yes, she told us. And we welcome you both."

Bill was relieved. "Thank you Michael. You can't begin to imagine how apprehensive I was about meeting you today. However, I've really enjoyed it. We've had a great day."

"Now, Bill, I think we should get to bed. In the morning, you've got an office to run and I have to drive home. Leave everything. Margaret will clear up tomorrow."

Sally had been in the shower and was in bed by the time Bill came into the bedroom. "What did you say to Dad when I left the room?"

Bill told her how he had offered to sleep in another room if it would make her mother happier, but her father had said it wasn't necessary. He went through to have a shower and came back into the bedroom drying himself.

"What else did Dad say to you?"

"He told me he liked me very much." Bill smiled. "Can you believe it? He actually likes me."

"Of course he does, he wouldn't even have gone to the pub with us if he hadn't liked you. Come on, Bill, hurry up and get into bed. I want you to make love to me."

Bill glanced towards the bedroom door. "What about your father?"

"What about him?" Giving him a quizzical look, she then grinned. "Are you saying that you want to make love to my father? Bill, I have to tell you, I really don't think Dad likes you in *that* way."

"Don't be an idiot." Bill laughed. "You know what I mean. Your parents are only down the hall."

He threw a pillow at her and she squealed out with laughter.

"Sssh," He glanced nervously towards the door. "They'll hear you."

He still wasn't used to the fact Michael was allowing him to continue to see his daughter, never mind sleep with her. He had visions of him bursting in at any minute saying he had changed his mind. That being the case, he certainly didn't want him to find them in the process of making love.

Putting her hand over her mouth, Sally tried to stifle the sound of her laughter, but failed.

"Sally, please." Bill pleaded. "Any minute now your father is going to come in here to see what I'm doing to you."

"They'll both be asleep by now. Besides, you're not doing anything to me, that's the problem. Kiss me, Bill"

Bill bent over and kissed her. "Sally I don't think we should..." He broke off as she pulled him down to her. She kissed him again.

"Sally, please, not tonight. Your father is only..." But he didn't finish as her lips were on his again and she began to run her fingers slowly down his spine. He tried again. "Sally, I don't think this is... Oh, what the hell..." Not able to resist her any longer, he climbed into bed and switched out the light.

Meanwhile down the hall Michael had settled down in bed. Lying there he recalled part of the conversation with Sally the previous day. "Have you forgotten what it's like to be in love?" The words rang in his ears. He looked across at his wife. She was sound asleep. Margaret had been the only woman in his life. He had loved her from the moment he had set eyes on her. But things were different in those days. There had to be a period of courtship, an engagement and then, only then, could the word 'marriage' be mentioned.

Sex before marriage was forbidden or it certainly had been where he was concerned. However, over the years, attitudes had changed and he had always tried to keep up with the times. He had turned a blind eye to some of his sons' escapades, much to the annoyance of Margaret. However, although the boys had been a little fancy free, they had turned out to be fairly responsible and were now happily married.

With Sally though, it had been different. She was their daughter, their little girl and they had been so intent on keeping her that way, they had failed to notice she was growing up.

He suddenly heard Sally laughing, followed by Bill's voice telling her not to make so much noise. Then there was silence. He could guess what was happening now and here he was, condoning it. Looking at his wife again he smiled to himself. It was a good thing she was asleep. She wouldn't have approved at all.

Turning onto his side he put his arm around her and gently pulled her closer. 'No Sally, I haven't forgotten what it's like to be in love,' he thought, as he drifted off to sleep.

Day Eight

It was Sally who rose first the next morning. She would love to have lain a little longer, but decided she wouldn't embarrass her mother by coming downstairs at the same time as Bill. She washed the glasses and cups they had used the night before and set the table for breakfast. She also made a pot of coffee ready for whoever came down next. It turned out to be her father. He sat down beside her and she poured him some coffee.

"Did you sleep all right, Dad?"

"Yes, thank you." He grinned at her and winked. "Did you?"

The expression on his face told all. Sally's face turned the colour of beetroot. "You heard us then," she whispered.

"I heard you both laughing, that's all. Don't worry, your mother was asleep and didn't hear anything at all."

"I do love him you know."

Michael took his daughter's hand. "Yes I can see that. I also see he loves you. He can't keep his hands off you."

"He said you would say that," she replied.

They both laughed.

"But seriously Sally, I'm glad we're able to have this little talk on our own. "I've given a great deal of thought to what you said on the phone the other day."

"Dad, I'm sorry. I shouldn't..."

"Please Sally," Michael interrupted, "Let me finish. I need to say this. I now realise how right you were. Yes, we did dominate you, but we really meant well; we wanted to take care of you. We always thought Peter would be the one for you. However we were wrong and we know it now. I suppose we were being selfish. Peter lives close by and we thought if you and he got together, you'd be on our doorstep. But you're a gentle person and you need someone like Bill. I'm not saying any of this because Bill got the firm out of a mess yesterday. If I thought he wasn't right for you, I'd tell you so. You must know that."

"Yes I do," replied Sally. "I tried to tell you on the phone how wonderful he is. I loved him the first time I saw him. Yet I wasn't sure he would look at me twice." She paused. "Let's face it, Dad; he's a top executive in one of the largest companies in the world. He could have anyone he chooses." She looked at her father and smiled. "Yet he chose me – it's me he loves. I'm so happy I could burst."

Before her father could reply, Margaret appeared in the doorway. "I could hear voices, so I thought I'd better get up. I think I had too much to drink last night, I still have a headache."

"There are some pain killers in the cupboard. I'll get them for you." Sally handed them to her mother.

"You seem to be very familiar with this house Sally." But a warning glance from her husband told her to change the subject. "Perhaps you would pour me some coffee."

By the time Bill came down everyone was already having breakfast. He apologised for being late.

"It's all right. We know how it is with you young people." Michael grinned and winked at him.

Embarrassed, Bill ran a finger around his collar and gave Sally a look, which said, 'I told you he would hear us.'

"Michael!" Margaret was horrified at her husband's insensitivity.

Bill sat down next to Sally and put his arms around her and kissed her. "Good morning, darling."

Sally grinned at her father, recalling what he had said earlier about Bill not keeping his hands off her.

I hope you both slept well." Bill buttered himself some toast.

"Yes," said Michael. "We both went straight off to sleep and slept like logs." He saw no point in embarrassing Bill or Sally any further.

Sally smiled and nodded her thanks to her father,

Once they had finished breakfast, Sally and Bill got ready for work.

"Look, I'm sorry, but I'll have to go," Bill told Sally's parents. "I want to get finished on time today. We're going to our staff Christmas Dinner Dance tonight.

Sally, sweetheart, do you want to come with me or will your father drop you off at the nursery?"

Sally looked across at her father. He nodded. "Don't worry, Dad will drive me there. Try not to be too late tonight, darling,"

Bill went across to Sally's mother and kissed her on the cheek.

"It's been a pleasure to meet you Mrs Hughes."

He looked over at Michael. "If I can be of any help with the financial side of your business, be sure to let me know."

Michael walked over and shook him by the hand. "Thank you, son. I'll probably take you up on that in the New Year. We could certainly do with some good advice."

"Anytime," said Bill.

Sally walked to the front door with Bill to see him off.

"Where is the dinner being held?" asked her mother, when Sally came back into the kitchen.

Sally told her parents it was at The Apollo Hotel and that Bill had given her £500 to buy a dress. She also explained how he had told her to keep the change. Though her parents were amazed at his generosity, it only confirmed what Michael now already believed. Bill Roberts was the right man for his daughter.

Michael dropped his daughter off at the nursery school. "Goodbye Sally. Take care of yourself."

Sally hugged both her parents. "I'm so pleased you like Bill. Have a good holiday. Give me a ring when you get back." She gave them Bill's home number.

"Thank you for the Christmas presents Sally. We'll pass them on to your brothers and their families, as soon as we see them. I'm sorry we haven't got yours yet, but what with the worry of the business, Christmas was the last thing on our minds."

"Don't worry about it." Sally hugged her parents once more before they drove off. Going into the nursery, she set out the toys and games ready for the children arriving.

Bill arrived at the office only to find Colin already there. "Twice in one week Colin, this has to be a record."

Colin followed Bill into his office. "I'm only doing this to help you out. You want to get away at a decent time tonight, don't you?"

"Yes; thank you Colin. You've really been a great help to me this week."

"By the way, how did it go yesterday, or shouldn't I ask? You don't have to tell me if you'd rather not, but I don't see any black eyes this morning." Colin peered at his friend's face and grinned.

"Well, it was a little hair-raising at first. Her father gave me the third degree, pointing out my age and the fact I'd been married before. He even asked what a man of my experience wanted with his young daughter. I was quite taken aback. I wasn't sure what to say at first. What would you have said?"

"Damn cheek!" Colin exclaimed. "I'd have punched him on the nose." Though he was amused to think that anyone could believe Bill was a 'man of experience'.

"I couldn't do that, Colin. After all, he is Sally's father. Anyway everything is fine now. In the end he said he liked me and apologised for his abruptness. He even called me, 'son' before I left this morning, but I must say I wouldn't like to go through it again. I should have been more prepared. I'd already guessed they weren't happy about Sally's relationship with me, especially when she told them... err... Never mind, I won't go into that." He looked down at the desk and ran a finger around his collar.

"I can guess what she told them," said Colin, grinning. "She's probably the kind of girl who tells her parents everything."

"Yes... Well," Bill still felt uncomfortable. "Anyway, we all went out for a meal and they stayed over at my house for the night. They were still there when I left this morning."

"Stayed the night eh? That would put a stop to your hanky panky. Or did it?" said Colin. He laughed when, once again, Bill ran a finger around his collar. "Apparently not."

Bill was relieved when Miss Anderson walked into the office with the mail. He knew Colin wouldn't make any further remarks with his secretary in the room.

"Good morning, Mr Roberts," she said. Seeing Colin she added, "Twice in one week Colin? This is becoming a habit."

"Yes. Thank you, Vera. I've already been through all that once this morning." Colin raised his eyes to the ceiling.

Bill laughed. It was good to see Colin being the butt of a joke for a change. "What do you have for me today, Miss Anderson?"

"Only the mail at the moment and there isn't much. You have no appointments today, so far."

"Good," said Bill. "Let's keep it that way if possible. We all want to get away early tonight, don't we? I take it you're going to the dance Miss Anderson."

"Yes sir. I'm going with my boyfriend."

"I should be pleased to meet him," said Bill. "I'll tell him what an excellent secretary you are."

"I'll remind you of that, when my pay rise is due," she said, turning to leave the office.

"I didn't know she had a boyfriend," Bill said, once she was out of the room.

"Bill my friend. You know absolutely nothing about anything that goes on here unless it is in the best interests of Websters. Vera is saving up to get married and wants somewhere of their own as they don't want to live in with either of their parents."

"When is her pay rise due?" asked Bill.

"Not until next July I think. Anyway Bill. What do you want me to do first?"

Bill glanced at the pile of files lying on his desk. "Well. You can either take a few of these, or you can do the figures from the branches."

"Then if it's all the same to you, I'll take a few of these. The branch figures drive me mad. They're always in such a muddle. I'm sure someone in their finance offices must be capable of calculating the figures correctly. I really don't know how they got their jobs."

"Okay, I'll do them. I'm going to speak to both the branches about their figures after the holidays. Send Alan in with them as soon as they arrive. Oh, and one other thing Colin. I know its Christmas and all, but I don't want anyone fooling around too much until the work's done. After that they can do what they like. I know in the past, I've seen to anything they've left undone, but not today. If they want tomorrow off, they'll have to finish everything, and I mean *everything*, before they leave here today. Or I'll expect to see them here tomorrow morning. Tell them I mean it. If you have any problems, let me know and I'll speak to them myself."

"Right Bill, I'll talk to them, but I'm sure there won't be any problems," said Colin, picking up some of the files. He knew what Bill said was true. He had spent many a Christmas Eve finishing off work, which the staff had quite happily forgotten whilst merrymaking. "I'll get these done, then I'll come back to see if there's anything else I can help you with." He left Bill's office smiling. At last, thanks to Sally, Bill Roberts was getting a life.

Bill sat down and phoned Sally. "Did your parents get away all right?"

"Yes. No problems at all. Mum is looking forward to going to Tenerife now, thanks to you sorting their problem at the office."

"What time do you hope to get away today?" asked Bill.

"I shall be finished by twelve, so I'm going to do some cleaning at your house. Change the beds and see to anything else that needs doing. It should all be spick and span when you come home."

"You don't have to do that. I'll see to it."

"Oh, but I want to," replied Sally. "It'll be all nice for Joey coming back tomorrow." Her voice trailed off. She knew, after tomorrow morning, she wouldn't see either of them until Christmas Day. "I think I'd better go now, before the children start fighting." She felt like crying but didn't want Bill to know.

However, Bill had noticed the change in her voice, but he said nothing. He was feeling the same way. He didn't know how he was going to live through the next few days without seeing her. "Okay sweetheart. I'll let you go, see you later. Love you."

The morning ran quite smoothly with the staff working conscientiously until lunchtime. Alan took the branch figures into his boss's office. He felt a little less nervous about going in there now. Colin had made it clear to him that, in spite of what he had heard about other heads of departments, Bill's door was always open to *all* his staff. Not just the more senior. "Don't listen to all the rubbish spoken in the staff dining room," he had told him. "Bill is not like most of the other heads of departments. You'll find out for yourself in due course, but in the meantime take my word for it. If you ever feel you need to talk to him, simply check with his secretary to make sure he isn't with a client and then go on in. He always makes time for his staff."

Alan emerged from Bill's office feeling jubilant. Due to some glowing reports from Colin, Mr Roberts was going to give him a few straightforward accounts to take care of in the New Year. It was a step in the right direction. "I'll take the time to go through them with you myself." Bill had told him. Alan knew he was being given a chance to prove his worth and he wasn't going to waste it.

After lunch the staff was more relaxed. Like all the other departments, the workload had slowed down. By two o'clock many of them were starting to drift off home to prepare for the dance. Colin and Alan volunteered to stay behind in case something turned up at the last minute. Besides, Colin wanted to make sure Bill got away in good time.

Bill called his secretary into his office. He told her she could go and she needn't come in the next morning.

"If I need any typing done I'll persevere with a typist from the general office. There are usually two on duty during the last morning before the holiday." He handed her an envelope telling her it was a Christmas present.

"I think this may be of more use than the perfume I usually get for you."

She opened the envelope and took out a cheque for £500. "I can't accept this Mr Roberts. It's far too much."

"Yes you can," said Bill. "Please take it. Put it towards your new home."

"Thank you so much," she said, with tears in her eyes. She reached forward and kissed him on the cheek. "I don't know what to say," she said.

"Then don't say anything. Just go home and prepare for the dance."

She thanked him once more and left the office.

Bill sat down and telephoned his mother. He asked how she and his father were and then asked to speak to Joey.

"Before I put him on Bill, I have something to tell you. There's been a change of plan. Your sister telephoned to say something had gone wrong with the boiler and they can't get the parts until after New Year. They would like to spend Christmas and New Year here with us. Their house will be too cold for the new baby. I was wondering if you and Joey would like to come over for Christmas Lunch and stay overnight. I know we'll be a little cramped but we'd manage."

Bill's mind was racing. As things stood, he wasn't going to see Sally until Christmas Day. If he went to his mother's he wouldn't see her until well after Boxing Day. They might even want him to stay for New Year. He knew he couldn't wait *that* long. He had to do something.

"Mother I have a better idea. Why don't you all come to my house on Christmas Day and stay over? You know I have loads of room."

"Will you be able to cope, son? With Christmas lunch and all?"

"Mum, I can put a turkey in the oven and peel the vegetables. By then you'll all be there to give a hand."

"Okay then, we'll do that. I'll do the shopping for you and you can take it home tomorrow when you pick up Joey. I'll put him on now. See you tomorrow.

No need for you to rush though. Not now we haven't a train to catch. Enjoy the dance tonight."

"Hello Daddy. Only four days left to Christmas. I opened another little door on the calendar this morning and there was a fairy inside."

Bill was pleased to hear him. In spite of everything, he was missing his son and was looking forward to seeing him the next day. He was just sorry Sally wouldn't be there as well.

"Hello, son, I can hear how excited you are. We'll look for a Christmas tree tomorrow on the way home, like I promised. Then during the evening, we'll decorate it together. How does that sound?"

"It sounds great Daddy. Can we stop for pizzas as well?"

"Yes, of course we can," replied Bill.

After he had hung up, Bill sat thinking for a few moments. He hoped Joey would take to Sally. He knew they had got on well while he was at the nursery, but bringing her into their home was a different matter. There had only been the two of them for as long as Joey could remember. It might be difficult for him to see his father caring for someone else as well. His thoughts were interrupted as Colin came into his office. Alan waited in the doorway.

"Are you ready to go now, Bill? It's gone three o'clock. I don't think anything will turn up now. Besides the post room have gone, so there's no one to bring any work up anyway."

"Okay then. Let's go." Bill was anxious to get away himself.

"Thanks for hanging on Alan. You must want to get off to see your girlfriend. Are you going to the dance tonight?"

"Yes sir. I'm taking Judy, so I'll probably see you there."

"I'll buy you both a drink," said Bill. "Now you go off home, I want a few words with Colin." After saying goodbye, Alan left the room. "Colin. Would you and Rachel look out for Sally and me coming into the Apollo tonight? Sally doesn't know anyone else and it would be nice for her to see a couple of friendly faces near the door."

"No problem, Bill. We'll get some drinks and watch out for you. I'll even go into the dining room and switch the place cards around to make sure we're all sitting together."

"Thanks – that would be great. Oh, and one other thing, Colin. No wise cracks or embarrassing remarks in front of Sally." He paused. "About her and me, you know the kind of thing I mean. I don't want her embarrassed or upset."

"Of course not, I promise. Besides, Rachel would kill me."

"Well if she didn't, I would." Bill grinned.

"Is there anything else I should, or shouldn't do, *sir*?" asked Colin, clicking his heels and saluting.

"No, that's all," replied Bill. "You can stand at ease. By the way, how did the team take my remarks today?"

"They were okay about it, but I think they were surprised to hear you were going to the dance tonight."

As they made their way towards the lift, Bill laughed. "I expect they think I'm taking my mother."

Colin didn't answer. He had heard one or two of the men making those sorts of remarks when they thought he wasn't listening. But he wasn't about to tell Bill that. In fact he hadn't said anything to them either. Let them think what they like for the moment, but they were in for a surprise.

When Sally heard Bill pull up onto the drive, she went to open the door. He came in, picked her up and swung her around before kissing her. "I've missed you, Sally. You have no idea how much I'm going to miss you over the next few days."

She was also going to miss him and couldn't bear to talk about it. She changed the subject. "How did your day go?"

"Not bad at all." Bill told her Colin had been a big help, enabling him to get away as early as he did. He also told her he had given his secretary her Christmas present.

"What did you give her?"

"Well, I usually rush out at the last minute and buy her some perfume, but Colin told me she was saving up to get married, so I decided to give her a cheque for £500."

"That was very generous Bill. I'm sure she appreciated it."

"Yes she did."

Sally looked at him and laughed. "I hope she didn't appreciate it too much."

Bill pulled her closer to him. "Don't be an idiot. Besides she isn't my type." He went on to tell her his family had changed their plans and how they would all be at his house for Christmas Day.

"Will you manage all right?"

"Well, I'll have you to help me won't I?" said Bill, laughing. "You're coming anyway. I'll have to think of something to get you here earlier."

"This is getting too devious for me," said Sally. "I think I'll go and have a bath. I want to wash my hair and do my nails. What time do we need to leave here?"

"About seven o'clock should be okay," he replied, pouring himself a drink. "I just have this before I take a shower. A short while later, when he had washed and shaved, he strolled through to the bedroom and found Sally wearing a bathrobe. She had a towel wrapped around her head and was drying her finger nails with the hairdryer.

"Sally," he said. "You look beautiful."

She looked at herself in the mirror, before turning back to Bill. "What! Like this?"

He moved slowly across the room towards her.

"No Bill," she said. "I know that look. There isn't time. We'll be late."

"No we won't," said Bill, quietly. "There's plenty of time."

"Stay away." Laughing, Sally backed away from him. She knew if she allowed him to put his arms around her she wouldn't be able to resist him.

Pulling her to him, Bill kissed her gently, before guiding her towards the bed.

"Bill darling," said Sally, as they showered and dressed later. "The next time we're going anywhere, we must begin to get ready a little earlier."

Colin was feeling rather anxious about Bill and Sally. He had been into the dining room and switched the place seating cards around, much to the annoyance of the waiters. As the tables were set for six, he had also put Alan and Judy on their table. That should help Alan get to know Bill a little better, he thought, mischievously

The four of them were now standing in the reception area, keeping an eye on the door.

"Perhaps they've changed their minds," said Rachel.

"Well, they were definitely coming when I left him," said Colin. "He particularly asked me to look out for them."

"Isn't that Mr Roberts now?" said Alan.

"Yes." Colin breathed a sigh of relief. He was pleased Bill had come after all.

Bill and Sally walked through the doors together. She had felt a little nervous at meeting all Bill's colleagues in one go. But he had assured her Colin and Rachel would be looking out for them arriving and the four of them would be sitting together at dinner.

Colin and Rachel gasped when they saw Sally. The last time they had seen her, she had been bundled up in thick sweaters and heavy boots. Tonight they were seeing someone completely different. Her lovely red dress fitted her slim figure like a glove.

"She looks wonderful tonight," said Colin, when he finally found his voice.

"And look at her figure," added Rachel, enviously. She looked down at her more generous shape.

"There's nothing wrong with your figure, you'll always look beautiful to me," he replied, looking her up and down. She *was* looking good. She really suited the new dress she had bought. The shade of blue highlighted her lovely blue eyes, making them sparkle even more. "And might I add that you look gorgeous tonight?

"Thank you, Colin." Rachel smiled.

He looked around for Alan and Judy. "Come on let's all go over to meet Bill and Sally."

Bill introduced Sally to Alan and his young lady.

"This is Judy sir, Judy Monroe." Alan sounded nervous.

Lowering his voice, Colin told Bill the dinner tables were set for six, therefore he had added Alan and Judy to their table.

"Thanks Colin," said Bill. Turning back to Alan and Judy he said, "I gather you are joining us for dinner."

"Yes, sir. We seem to be on your table... there must have been a mistake." Alan coughed. He had no idea it was Colin who had switched the seating arrangements and was concerned Mr Roberts may not approve of sitting next to one of his junior staff. "I hope that's all right with you, sir. He wondered what on earth he would find to talk about to his boss. On the other hand, perhaps Mr Roberts and Colin would spend all evening chatting together and totally ignore him and Judy. Surely that would be even worse. "We could find another table if you would prefer," he ventured. Though at this late stage, it was probably impossible.

"There's no need. It's fine the way it is. Incidentally, tonight call me Bill."

"Thank you sir... I mean Bill." Alan grinned nervously. Perhaps the situation wasn't going to be as bad as he had first thought.

Bill asked Sally if she would like some champagne. "It's the management's treat."

"Yes please," Sally replied.

Bill and Colin went over to the table and poured six glasses.

"Bill. What on earth happened? Why were you so late? We were starting to worry. You left the office early enough."

Bill turned and looked across the room at Sally and smiled. Well... err... something came up." He ran a finger around his collar.

Colin followed Bill's gaze and gave a knowing nod. "Yes. I can see how easily that might have happened." However, noting Bill's warning look he added, "I know, Bill, not a word. I promise."

They went back to join their party. Quite a few other men had stopped to talk to the three ladies, but it was obvious it was Sally they were most interested in.

As Bill approached, he heard two members of his staff asking her whom she was with. "Actually, Miss Hughes is with me," he said, handing her a glass of champagne.

He handed another to Judy. The men were speechless. They mumbled their apologies and hurried off. "I enjoyed that." Bill laughed.

"So did I," Colin agreed. They were the same two men who had been making remarks about Bill that afternoon.

Just then Bill's secretary passed by, accompanied by a pleasant looking young man.

"Oh! Miss Anderson. I have someone I'd like you to meet. This is Miss Hughes. Sally, this is my long-suffering secretary, Miss Anderson. And I believe this must be her young man."

"I'm so pleased to meet you Miss Hughes. This is Tom, my boyfriend, well my fiancé now."

"I'm pleased to meet you both. And please, call me Sally."

"Thank you, Sally. My name is Vera. We'll probably see you all later. We're going for some champagne. Something cropped up and made us late."

Colin looked at Bill and grinned. "There's a lot of it about. It must be catching," he whispered. Then, seeing a frown spread across Bill's face, he quickly added, "I know, I know, not a word."

The gong rang out, informing everyone dinner was being served. Bill was grateful Colin had included Judy and Alan when he had rearranged the place settings. Sally seemed to be comfortable in their company. Also, Bill had taken rather a liking to Alan. He didn't seem boorish, unlike some of the other younger members of his staff. After dinner they found a table in the ballroom and Bill offered to get some drinks from the bar. "Alan, perhaps you would help me to carry them over?"

"Yes, sir." Alan leapt to his feet. But when Bill peered at him, he quickly rephrased it. "Yes Bill."

Taking everyone's order, they went over to the bar. "Alan, if you and Judy would prefer to join any one else, I quite understand. You don't *have* to sit with the boss all evening if there are some friends from the office you'd rather be with." Bill was concerned Alan may feel obliged to stay with them.

"If you don't mind… Bill. I'd rather we remained with you and Colin," he replied. "We're enjoying your company… unless of course, we're in the way." It had suddenly occurred to him that he might have been right earlier, and Bill may not want to sit with his junior all evening.

"No, Alan, you are most certainly not in the way. I simply didn't want you to feel obliged to sit with us, if you would rather be with your friends."

Back at the table, Sally told Bill they had spoken with Vera again. Apparently Tom had given her an engagement ring that evening, which was why they were late. It had been meant as a Christmas present, but thinking she might like to wear it for the dance, he had sprung the surprise early. Bill went back over to the bar and ordered a bottle of Champagne to be sent over to Vera and Tom's table with all of their compliments.

Sally put her arm around Bill. "You're so thoughtful."

The band started to play the first Waltz of the evening and Bill asked Sally if she would like to dance. They were the first couple onto the floor much to the astonishment of Colin and Rachel.

"They make a lovely couple." Rachel whispered to Colin. "But I'd never have believed Bill would be the first up to dance."

"No. Me neither," said Colin. "Are we going to let them get away with it then Rachel?" He made as if to stand up.

Rachel pulled him back into the chair. "Leave them. Let's watch. Somehow, I don't think anyone else will interrupt and we shouldn't either. It's wonderful to see Bill looking so happy for a change."

"Yes, you're right." Colin sat back in his chair.

"They look good together," said Alan.

"Yes, that's what Rachel and I were saying. It's about time, Bill enjoyed himself."

Alan looked puzzled.

"You probably know that Bill was once married," said Colin.

Alan nodded. "Yes. Someone mentioned it when I first started working at Websters."

"Well, three years ago his wife was killed in a car accident. Since then he's devoted himself to his work and his son, Joey, who was only one year old at the time. I know you're nervous of him, Alan, but when you get to know him properly, you'll find he's a really nice guy. He's thoughtful, sensitive, and generous to a fault. However his staff takes advantage of his good nature. You won't have noticed it yet, but in time you'll see how he stays behind to finish what they don't do. Normally he doesn't come to these dances. He sits there in that damn office on his own and finishes everyone's work. He could run the finance department on his own and some of this lot would let him, as long as they could pick up their pay cheques at the end of the month. To be fair, they aren't all the same. There are a few good blokes in the finance office, people Bill *can* rely on."

He nodded towards some men sitting together at the back of the ballroom. "There's Keith, Brian, John and Michael, for example. These are men Bill has employed since he was promoted, but there are other people he inherited from the previous head of department, who do as little as possible. Why do you think the management pay Bill the money they do? He earns…"

"Colin!" Rachel flashed him a warning look.

"No! Rachel's right, I can't disclose what he earns. Suffice to say they pay him a very large salary, because they can't afford to lose him. Besides, being head of the finance department at head office, he is also the financial executive of all the branches of Websters. However, they also gave him a cheque for £20,000 for the Taylor affair…"

"Colin! I think you've had too much to drink." Rachel snapped. She was both surprised and concerned to hear her husband talking like this. He didn't usually speak about Bill, while in company. "You've said enough. You of all people know Bill doesn't like his private life discussed."

"Yes, Rachel's probably right. Mind you, some of what I've said isn't exactly a secret. Nevertheless, I hope I can trust you to keep this conversion to yourself, Alan."

"Yes, of course I will, but £20,000 – you must be joking." He didn't earn that amount in a year.

"For goodness sake, Alan, the one thing I never joke about is money. Taylor wants him badly; he's even spoken to the MD about it. He's willing to pay Bill goodness knows how much if he moves over to them, but he won't budge. My guess is the Directors were still worried and gave him a bonus of twenty grand to keep him at Websters. But you know something? He would have stayed anyway. They may even give him another pay rise yet. It certainly wouldn't surprise me."

He paused. Rachel was glaring at him. He realised that he had gone too far – he shouldn't have told Alan about the cheque. Nevertheless he had said it now and there wasn't anything he could do about it. However, he felt confident Alan wouldn't repeat what had exchanged between them.

Avoiding her gaze, he continued with a much lighter note. "I would be extremely sorry if Bill took Taylor up on his offer. I thought about what you said the other day and I was more than a little concerned at the possibility of him not being at Websters. It wouldn't be the same for me, having someone else in his office. I don't know what I'd do if that were to happen."

He paused for a moment and looked across at the dance floor. "He met Sally recently and she's good for him. Look at them, Alan. They're devoted to each other. I've known Bill a long time now – long before Websters. We were at University together. And do you know, in all that time, I've never known him to be this happy."

While Colin was talking, Alan had been watching Sally and Bill on the dance floor. Colin was right. Nobody could deny they only had eyes for each other. Tonight he was seeing a different man to the one who worked in the office. At work he was ice cool. Nothing ever seemed to panic him. On Monday he had manoeuvred the firm out of a very tight spot through a cleverly worded contract. And yet he had still given Mr Taylor the opportunity to save face. He glanced around the room at some of his colleagues. What Colin said was true.

He had heard them say, Bill was like a machine. Yet he had never thought of him in that way. He simply saw him as a very clever man.

Clever enough to be in the position he was at his age and from what he had heard he had held the post for over six years now. He could only have been about twenty-two when he was promoted. Alan couldn't see himself being anywhere near a position like that in a year or two from now. In one corner he saw the two men who had tried to talk to Sally earlier. They were also watching Bill. It was easy to tell they were surprised at the man they were seeing tonight.

He looked back at Colin. "Yes, I had heard one or two things before, but you *can* trust me. I promise I'll never repeat any of our conversation." He could see Rachel was still annoyed with Colin for his outburst. "I give you my word I won't say anything to anyone."

Rachel smiled and nodded her thanks. She was relieved. She couldn't think what had come over Colin to talk about Bill like that.

The Waltz came to an end and Bill and Sally walked back to their table. I thought you might have joined us," said Bill.

"You didn't need anyone else up there," said Colin. "You were doing all right on your own."

At that moment the Managing Director approached the table. Would you introduce me to these young ladies?" Once the introductions were made, he asked Sally for a dance.

Bill watched them glide around the floor for a few minutes before turning to Colin. "Do we need some more drinks here?"

"It's my turn," said Colin.

"Don't be silly, put your money away. I'll get them," replied Bill.

But Colin wouldn't hear of it and went up to the bar. Alan went with him.

"Mine's a mineral water, Colin," called out Bill. "I've brought the car."

By the time they got back, the dance had ended and Mr Smithers was escorting Sally back across the dance floor. "You're a very lucky young man, Bill."

"You think I don't know that?" Bill smiled at Sally and put his arm around her. "She's the most wonderful thing that's happened to me in a long time."

Mr Smithers then asked Judy onto the dance floor. He felt it was his duty to mingle with as many of his staff and their partners as possible. When the band struck up the next dance, Bill and Sally took to the floor once more. This time however, many other members of staff joined them.

Later during the evening they were joined by the Chairman of the Company. "Don't stand up," he said, as the three men started to rise. "This is a social occasion." Pulling up a chair, he sat next to Bill.

Bill introduced Sally. "Rachel and Colin, you know. This is Alan Hurst, a new member of the finance team and his young lady Miss Judy Monroe."

The Chairman shook hands with them all. He then turned to Bill. "You're doing a first class job Bill. You know you're much appreciated here at Websters."

Colin looked at Alan. He didn't say anything, he simply pulled a face. Alan tried hard not to laugh.

"Thank you for your support, sir." Bill didn't know what else to say.

"Not at all. I want you to know, my door is always open. If you need to see me about anything at all, just come in." Colin made another face at Alan. "We're still trying to find men for the finance offices at the two latest branches," the Chairman continued. "However, so far there isn't anyone we feel we can trust to do the job properly. Believe me; we do understand how heavy this makes your workload. We'll be holding interviews again early in the New Year, so hopefully we'll be able to appoint someone then; especially as there are talks going on about opening another branch in the north and two in Europe. I feel we'll be faced with the same problem thrice over." He hesitated. "How would you feel about taking on the new northern branch as well? Naturally, it will only be until we can appoint someone."

Colin had been listening intently. He could see his friend was going to be lumbered again. There was no doubt Bill could do it. He knew that. Yet was it fair? Simply because he was very clever with figures didn't mean he should be continually be taken advantage of. If Bill weren't around they would have to employ whoever they could get.

"What are the chances of you finding men at the next batch of interviews sir?" Colin tried to take the attention away from Bill, giving him time to think before having to reply.

"It's difficult to say," replied the Chairman. "A few of them have good references, but, as with the other interviews, when you actually meet the candidates you realise they're not up to the job." He gave Bill a sly glance. Turning back to Colin he said. "I notice you haven't put in for one of the positions, Colin."

"No. It would mean moving house, and I don't particularly want to do that at the moment. Besides I enjoy being Bill's right hand man and I think he likes having me around; someone to bounce things off, so to speak."

Bill smiled to himself. It was probably the other way around. However it was true that he would miss Colin if he decided to move on. They worked well together.

The Chairman looked across at Alan. "How are you enjoying being with us at Websters?"

"I like the job very much," he replied. "And I know I can learn a great deal from Mr Roberts, sir."

Bill interrupted, telling the Chairman how Alan was doing very well and proving to be a worthwhile member of his team.

"Well done. Keep an eye on Bill. He'll keep you right and one of these days we may find you putting yourself forward for one of our senior posts. Well, I must get back to my lady wife. Think about what we were discussing Bill. You know we would make it well worth your while. I may give you a ring when you've had time to think it over. Are you in the office tomorrow morning?"

Bill told him he would be there, but only for a short while. The Chairman stood up and walked across the dance floor, only stopping to chat to Mr Smithers before going back to his table. Unlike the Managing Director, he was not the sort to mingle with the less senior members of staff.

"I don't believe it; the cheek of the man. Colin was indignant. "How can they ask you to do any more? He admits this is a social occasion and then asks you to take on more work next year. If I were you, I would tell…"

"Bill, you can't let them put on you like this," Sally interrupted. "Please darling, promise me if they don't appoint someone for one of the other branches next month you'll say no to taking on this new one. You can't look after four of them. No doubt they'll want you to take charge of the two in Europe, too. It's simply not right." She had listened very carefully to the Chairman and was worried Bill was going to be put upon even further.

"Okay sweetheart. I promise," said Bill. "No more than three at a time."

Colin nudged his wife's knee under the table. She looked at him and smiled. Yes. Sally was certainly good for Bill.

"Would you like to dance, Sally?" Colin asked. "You don't mind, do you, Bill?"

"No, of course not." He desperately hoped Colin wouldn't say anything embarrassing and gave him a look that said as much.

"You look lovely tonight, Sally. Mr Smithers is right. Bill is a lucky man," said Colin, once they were on the dance floor.

"I consider myself lucky to have met Bill. He is such a gentle and caring man."

"Yes he is," said Colin. "He always has been."

"You've known him a long time, haven't you?"

"Yes. It must be over ten years now. We met at university. He was very shy and I took him under my wing."

"And you still look out for him? He's still very shy."

"I try to," said Colin. "But I really think he's going to take more notice of you and I can't say I blame him."

When the dance ended, Colin escorted Sally back to her seat. Bill, who had been dancing with Rachael, gave him an enquiring glance.

"Not a word – honest," he whispered, before asking Judy if she would like to dance.

Bill asked Sally if she would like to meet some of the other members of his staff. He wanted to show her off. They walked across to the other side of the room where most of Bill's staff were sitting. After making the introductions, many of them asked Sally to dance.

"Bill I'm having a wonderful evening," she said, when they finally walked back to join their party.

"I am too. I haven't been to a staff dance for years and I'm really enjoying it, but that's mostly down to you."

They arrived back at their table to find quite a few more people had joined their party. Most of them were from the sales office and much the worse for drink. One suggested that someone should get in a round of drinks.

Alan stood up. "I think it's my turn." Taking their orders, he went across to the bar. Bill followed him over. Filling the order, the barman asked Alan for the amount owing, but Bill intervened, handing over the money.

"It's my turn," Alan protested.

"You aren't paying out for that lot Alan. After they've drunk this, you probably won't see them again until next Christmas. At least I have to deal with them. Besides, no one will know unless you tell them."

"Thanks, Bill." Alan was quite relieved. The amount had been a great deal higher than he had bargained for. His salary, as a junior member of staff, didn't run to such expensive bar bills, especially when you were saving to get married. Colin was right when he said Bill was very thoughtful and generous.

When they got back to the table they found Sally and Judy deep in conversation. "What are you both planning?" asked Bill.

"Nothing," answered Sally. "We simply seem to have something in common. Judy is planning to be a nursery nurse and I suggested she should have a word with Mrs Miller. She'll soon tell her if she thinks she is cut out for it. Jane never minces her words."

"No, she's put me in my place on many an occasion," said Bill. But she means well and I certainly couldn't have managed without her."

The evening passed over much too quickly and everyone was disappointed when the band announced it was time for the last Waltz. Bill led Sally onto the dance floor.

"I have had another wonderful evening Bill. This week has been the happiest of my life."

"It has been for me too, Sally."

When the dance was over, Bill put his arms around Sally and kissed her. "Sally, I love you so much. You can't imagine how I feel about not seeing you for the next few days."

"Don't let's talk about it now," said Sally. "Otherwise I'll cry and make a fool of myself in front of all your friends."

Bill kissed her again. They seemed to have forgotten they were standing in the middle of the now empty dance floor. "As soon as Joey accepts you, will you move in with me?"

"Yes, of course I will. I only hope it doesn't take too long." Sally glanced across the floor. "Come on, your friends are waiting."

The other four were standing watching them. Rachel slipped her hand into Colin's. "It's all working out for Bill isn't it? I've never seen him like this before, not even with Julie."

"Yes. It seems to be. They look as though they were made for each other. They still have one hurdle to jump though."

Looking at Colin, Rachel said one word: "Joey."

Colin nodded. "Say no more, they're coming over."

"Would you all like to come back to my place for another drink? I don't think you're going to get a taxi for a while yet. Not unless you booked one earlier."

As none of them had thought that far ahead, they all piled into Bill's car.

Back at the house, Bill poured a Brandy for them all.

"Have you been together very long," asked Sally, as she handed Alan and Judy their drinks.

"Eighteen months," replied Judy. "But we knew from the moment we met we were meant for each other." She looked towards Alan and he nodded.

"We want to get married," he said. "However, Judy is not yet twenty-one and her parents want us to wait until she is. Nowadays people tend to do what they like once they reach eighteen. But we thought we would respect their wishes. I'm only twenty-two myself so we have our whole lives ahead of us, but it's still very difficult."

"Do you have long to wait?" asked Colin.

"Eight months," said Judy. "I know it doesn't sound long, but the time is dragging for us."

Bill understood how they felt. It could take that long for Joey to accept Sally.

"Perhaps we should try to get a taxi," suggested Colin, after a while.

"I have a few telephone numbers by the phone in the hall." Bill showed Colin the list of numbers and went back into the lounge. "I've left him to it. Any problems and you can all stay here."

Colin came back a few minutes later and told them someone would be around very shortly. "It seems they have quietened down now. I'm not surprised, have you seen the time?"

They were amazed to find it was almost three-thirty in the morning. When the taxi arrived, Bill and Sally went to the door to see their guests leave.

Bill pulled some money from his pocket and handed it to Colin. "Take this for the taxi fare. It's likely to cost a bomb at this time of night."

"Don't be silly," said Colin. "I'll see to it."

"No take it. My treat."

"Thanks Bill. I'll see you at the office in the morning," said Colin, climbing into the taxi. He pushed the money into Alan's hand. "You have further to go than us. You pay the driver. Don't worry," he added as Alan began to protest. "It's Bill's treat. There's enough there to get us all to Timbuktu."

Bill and Sally went back into the house. "Bill. I've had a wonderful evening, but I'm so tired. Leave everything until the morning. I'll see to it then."

"Okay. You go to bed, sweetheart, I'll be up in a few minutes." Bill pulled the chairs back into position and carried the cups and glasses into the kitchen before going upstairs. Sally was already in bed.

"How are you going to get up in time to go into the office?" she asked. "You have to be up in a few hours."

"I'll be as bright as a button. You'll see," said Bill.

He undressed and went into the adjoining bathroom to clean his teeth.

"Sally, are you awake?" he asked on his return. There was no reply. Walking over to the bed, Bill found she was asleep. He pulled the covers up around her and kissed her gently. "Good night Sally, darling," he whispered.

Switching off the bedside light, he drifted off to sleep.

Day Nine

Sally spent a restless night and awoke early. Today was the day she had been dreading – today was the day she would be moving back to her own flat. Bill was still sleeping, so she crept downstairs to make some coffee.

Carrying her mug of coffee though into the lounge she, she sat down on the sofa. She stroked one of the cushions as her mind drifted back to last Saturday evening. That was when she had asked Bill if she could spend the night with him. Even now, she didn't know how she had plucked up the courage.

She sighed. Was it really only six days ago? It seemed longer; so much had happened since then. Her parents had met Bill. They had even stayed here for the night and had given them their blessing.

Sally smiled to herself, when she recalled her mother's reaction to her sleeping with Bill. But then she had always been the same – even with the boys. However, it was her father's attitude, which had surprised her the most. After interrogating Bill, he had accepted him with open arms. This last seven days had been the happiest in her life.

Now fighting back the tears, she hurried back into the kitchen. She shouldn't have gone into the lounge. She should have stayed in the kitchen. Glancing at the clock, she decided to take a shower and get dressed.

She had almost finished dressing, when the alarm clock by the bed started to ring.

"Sally. How long have you been up? Why didn't you wake me?"

"Not long," she lied. "I thought you needed to sleep for a while longer. You've a long day ahead of you. You're going into the office and then you have to drive over to pick up Joey, whereas I can sleep all afternoon if I need to."

She tried to sound casual, but her bottom lip quivered, giving away her true feelings.

"Don't go Sally. I'll think of something to tell Joey." Getting out of bed, Bill went across to her. "I don't want you to leave, I love you so much."

"No Bill. I love you too, but it has to be this way. Joey might hate me if he came back and found I had moved in while he was at his grandmother's." She gave him a tearful smile. "Come on, get dressed. I have some coffee on downstairs."

Putting his arms around her, Bill kissed her gently. "Come back to bed with me Sally."

"Darling. You'll be late for the office."

"Damn the office," he said, as he led her across to the bed.

Much later Bill showered and dressed. They had lain in each other's arms for nearly an hour, neither wanting the moment to end. Even though he had known it would be difficult to part from Sally, he hadn't reckoned on it being this hard. When he came downstairs he found her case at the front door.

"I was going to ask you to drop me at my flat, but it'll make you even more late. I'll get a taxi."

"Of course I'll take you home. You come before the office any time."

"Bill, promise me if the Chairman rings you about taking on the new branch, you'll say no."

"Of course I will Sally. I won't go back on my word."

Bill dropped Sally at her flat. He hugged and kissed her not wanting to let her go, but after promising to phone at the first opportunity, he drove on to the office. By the time he arrived he was nearly two hours late; Colin was waiting in his office.

"I'm sorry I'm late, Colin."

"Sleep in did you? Or did something come up again?" Colin grinned. He couldn't resist the opportunity to tease his friend.

"Yes. It was something like that." Bill smiled.

Colin couldn't help noticing that Bill didn't run a finger around his collar this time. However, before he could comment further, there was a knock on the door.

"Come in," called Bill.

When the door opened, it was Alan who walked into the office. "Mr Roberts, I've brought you your change from the taxi last night, sir." He held out forty-five pounds.

"Alan, don't tell me you've dragged yourself in here in this morning to give me forty-five quid. I didn't want any change. Keep it. Colin would have done."

Colin laughed. "Too right I would. You've got a lot more money than me."

"I can't do that, sir, it's not right," argued Alan. Forty-five pounds was a lot of money to him.

"Just keep it Alan. Don't argue," said Bill.

Before Alan could reply the telephone rang. Bill answered and was told the Chairman was on the line. "Put him through. He looked at Colin. "It's the Chairman," he whispered.

Colin nodded towards the door, enquiring whether they should leave. Bill shook his head and pointed to the two chairs on the other side of his desk.

"He hasn't wasted any time," Colin whispered to Alan.

"Good morning sir. What can I do for you?" although all three knew exactly why he had phoned.

"I was wondering whether you'd had time to think about what I said last night." The Chairman's voice boomed down the phone.

"Yes sir, I have." Bill could see Colin watching him very closely. "And I've come to the conclusion I can't take on the new branch, unless of course you're able to appoint someone next month for at least one of the other branches."

Colin couldn't believe his ears. He had been telling Bill for a long while now that he was taking on too much work. He had begged him to take things easier, all to no avail. And here Sally, that slip of a girl, had asked him to say no to any more work and he had agreed.

Last night Colin had heard Bill promise her he would refuse the chairman's request. Nevertheless he had wondered whether he would actually go through with it. He glanced across at Alan and gave a thumbs up sign; he was delighted his friend was at last beginning to see sense. 'Well done, Sally,' he thought.

He looked back at Bill in time to hear him say, "And a Merry Christmas to you and your wife sir," before hanging up the phone.

"Bill, I know what you said to Sally last night, and I was pleased to hear it. Yet I have to admit, I didn't think you'd go through with it."

"I promised her and I meant it," answered Bill. "Mind you, I could have done as they asked, it wouldn't have been a problem, except I don't want to spend as much time working any more, not now I have Sally at home. I don't suppose you know, but what I didn't have time to do here I took home. I often spent a few hours on the accounts after Joey had gone to bed."

"But I *do* know," said Colin quietly. "Why do you think Rachel and I were so worried about you? I knew about the amount of work you were taking home. You know if some of the others pulled their weight, it wouldn't be necessary. You let them get away with too much. It's usually their work you take home."

"Well not anymore," answered Bill. "I'm going to keep an eye on a certain few. Things are going to be very different around here from now on. Anyone found slacking will be out on their ear." He changed the subject. "Alan, as you're here, you might as well make yourself useful. Would you nip down to the post room and see if anything else has come in since the mail was brought round? And you Colin, perhaps you could see whether anything has been left on Miss Anderson's desk? I'll open this mail here. There may be something, which needs to be dealt with straight away. Not all firms are closed for three weeks over Christmas and New Year. Someone may need a reply before we return."

The two men left the office, leaving Bill to open his mail. There were two letters which needed replies. A quick look at their files and he was able to dictate a reply into his tape recorder. By the time the others came back, he had finished.

"The branches have sent summaries of their finances, sir," said Alan. "They say they're leaving the details until after the holidays. The only thing is there are masses of them and they haven't done any of the calculations. Do you want me to stay behind to do them?" He pulled a calculator from his pocket. "I know you want to get away, sir and I have a couple of hours to spare. I'm not meeting Judy until this afternoon."

Bill held out his hand and took the papers from Alan. "I'm definitely going to have words with these branches after the holiday." He sat down and ran a finger along each line, filling in an answer at the end. He then ran a finger up the page, adding both the two columns simultaneously and completed the total at the bottom. He did this on all the sheets and it only took him two or three minutes.

Alan's jaw dropped open. Even with a calculator it would have taken him well over two hours, to work out the figures, checking and double-checking. He looked at Colin who merely shrugged his shoulders and mouthed, 'Told you so.'

"How do you do that sir?" asked Alan, when Bill had finished. "Those figures run into millions of pounds."

"I honestly don't know," Bill replied. "It's something I've been able to do since I was very young."

"That's absolutely brilliant, sir" said Alan in awe.

"There's nothing on Vera's desk," said Colin, trying not to laugh at the expression of admiration on Alan's face. "I've also checked in the general office in case something had been left there. Everything's all finished, except for what Keith is working on. He went to the dentist yesterday so he thought he'd better come in this morning to clear his desk, though he's almost through now."

"Colin. When I said all the work had to be finished. I didn't mean… He's only working on the Bradford account isn't he? Tell him to leave it and go home. On the other hand, I'd better see him myself. You're likely to tell him he has to spend Christmas here. I'll take this tape to the general office at the same time. I want the letters typed up before I leave." Bill went off down the corridor leaving Colin and Alan in the office.

"I've just had an idea, Alan," said Colin, starting to laugh. "Why don't we go and have some fun watching Bill struggle with the typing pool? We can cheer him on. The girls there can be so awkward when you want something typed up in a hurry and Bill's absolutely hopeless at dealing with them. He may need some help – we don't want to see him come out with his tail between his legs, do we?"

"Do you think we should?" Alan was doubtful. "I really don't think it's such a good idea. Besides, we shouldn't be spying on him; he is the boss you know. Well my boss, anyway and he is also an executive of the company."

"Oh, come on Alan, it's Christmas, he'll see the joke."

"No, you go on your own. I really don't think I should be there, I'd rather wait here."

Colin took Alan's arm and pulled him out into the corridor. "Come on, don't be a spoil sport. And hurry up or we'll be too late and miss all the fun," He continued to pull on Alan's arm.

Alan felt very uneasy and protested all the way down to the general office. It was all right for Colin. Apart from being Bill's assistant, he was an old friend. Whereas he was only a member of his staff, and a very junior one at that! However Colin had a firm grip on his arm, so whether he liked it or not, he found himself being dragged along to the general office.

After telling Keith to go home, Bill went to the general office, where a young lady was painting her nails. "Miss Smith, I would like you to type these two letters and bring them to my office for signature please."

"Put the tape in the tray and I'll do them if I have time." She didn't look up.

Bill didn't move. "Miss Smith." He spoke slowly and deliberately. "Perhaps you didn't hear me. I would like you to type out these two letters to the best of your ability and bring them to my office for signature, preferably within the next ten minutes. Otherwise, I shall speak to Mrs Saunders, your supervisor, regarding your future with this firm."

Looking up sharply, she was horrified to see who it was. "I'm terribly sorry, Mr Roberts... sir. I didn't realise it was you. I'll do them straight away." She was well aware that one word from Mr Roberts and she would be seeking new employment. She took the tape from Bill just as Mrs Saunders came out of her office.

"Is there a problem here, Mr Roberts?" She frowned at Miss Smith. "Is this girl giving you any trouble?"

"No, Mrs Saunders. I think there was a misunderstanding, but it's sorted now. Is that not so, Miss Smith?"

"Yes sir. Ten minutes, you said?" She was grateful Bill hadn't said anything to Mrs Saunders. It was only two days ago that she had received a verbal warning about a similar incident. But she found the typing pool boring and so desperately wanted a job she could get her teeth into instead of only being a stand in when any of the secretaries were away. Besides, she hadn't realised someone of Mr Roberts' grade would be in today. Most of the other heads of departments left any unfinished work to their staff.

Back out in the corridor, Colin and Alan were waiting for him. "I thought you might need reinforcements to cope with the typist so I brought Alan along with me," laughed Colin. "I told him how you couldn't handle them and usually came out with your tail between your legs. However, today you came out on top. Ten out of ten don't you think, Alan?"

Feeling extremely uncomfortable, Alan didn't answer. He could tell by the expression forming on Bill's face that he wasn't amused. If only he had stayed in the office. Why had he allowed Colin to drag him down here? Though on reflection, he hadn't had any choice in the matter.

For a moment Bill was shocked into silence. He could only gape at the two men in turn. It was unbelievable that Colin would bring the most junior member of his staff to watch him being humiliated by a girl in the typing pool. "You told him, *what*?" Bill's tone was cold.

Colin stared at his friend. He couldn't believe he had done that. The moment the words left his lips, he realised he had done the wrong thing. He should never have involved Alan. If Bill had been unable to deal with Janet Smith he would have looked extremely foolish. He knew how Bill hated being made to look a fool in front of anyone, but most especially in the presence of his staff. In all the years he had known Bill, he had never done anything like it before. What on earth had made him bring Alan along? How could he have been so bloody stupid?

Colin swallowed hard. "I'm sorry Bill." He couldn't allow Alan to be blamed for this. He had to make it right. "Alan didn't want to come. I physically dragged him here. It was all my idea." Reaching out, he put his hand on Bill's shoulder in a gesture of friendship, hoping to smooth things over.

"Yes, I can believe that," snapped Bill, pulling away from Colin. He closed his eyes for a moment and shook his head, trying to keep his temper. "Mr Shaw! I'm absolutely furious with you and at this moment I wish just I..." He paused. "Oh just go away before I say something I'll regret. Both of you – just go!" he repeated, looking from one to the other.

Colin gulped. Bill never called him Mr Shaw unless they were with a client. He reached out again. "Bill, don't let's leave it like this. I'm really sorry."

Ignoring him, Bill started to walk back towards his office.

Colin tried again. "Bill, let's talk..."

Bill swung around and glared at him. "It's Mr Roberts, if you don't mind! And what is there to talk about? You've just embarrassed and humiliated me in front of..." He glanced at Alan. "For God's sake, I'd never have believed you would do anything like that to me!" What on earth were you thinking? Haven't you any respect at all for me or for my position in this firm? What the hell were you trying to prove? It makes me wonder what else you've done behind my back. I've absolutely nothing more to say to you – to either of you. Now just go and leave me alone." His eyes flashed wildly, while the words spilled out.

"Bill... Mr Roberts, you can't mean that," called out Colin. He was very worried. His friend had never been so angry with him before. "I swear to you, I've never ever done anything like this. It was the first time and I admit it was very stupid; I'm really sorry."

However, Bill paid no heed. Storming down the corridor, he disappeared into his office and slammed the door shut behind him. Colin was stunned into silence. He stared down at the floor. Was this the end of their friendship? Would anything ever be the same again?

Inside his office, Bill sank into his chair and slammed his fist down on his desk. Why on earth had Colin done that to him? If he had gone to the general office on his own and made the same remarks, they would have laughed it off together. Instead, he had brought Alan to show him how weak his boss was. How could he forgive Colin for that? At least there was a three-week holiday break. Hopefully, his temper might have cooled a little by the time they came back to work. He picked up one of the files and began to check the figures.

Meanwhile out in the corridor, Alan was the first the break the silence. Until then he hadn't dared to utter a word for fear of upsetting his boss even more. "Should I say... something to him? Would... an apology help? Or would it only... make matters worse?" His voice trembled as he spoke. He didn't really want to see Mr Roberts at the moment. On the other hand, he didn't want all this on his mind for the next three weeks. Then another thought struck him. Would he find a letter terminating his employment in the post tomorrow morning? His stomach lurched over and he leant against the wall for support.

Colin looked up at him. By now Alan was shaking from head to foot. "I really don't know. You could try. None of this is your fault."

Alan swallowed hard and walked down the corridor to Bill's office, with Colin following a little way behind. Outside the door, he glanced back at Colin and took a deep breath before knocking.

"Come in."

Alan opened the door slowly. "Mr Roberts... sir."

Bill looked up from his desk. "Oh! It's you! I thought it was the typist with my mail." He looked back down at his work. "I told you to go home. What is it you want?"

"Please...I'm... so sorry Mr Roberts, sir. I... I didn't..." he broke off. What could he say without making it worse for Colin? "I'm sorry, sir."

The tremble in Alan's voice made Bill look up again. The lad had turned deathly white and his legs looked like they might buckle under him at any moment.

"Mr Roberts," said Colin, having arrived at the door. "I'm responsible here, not Alan. It really wasn't his fault."

Bill looked back down at his desk and closed his eyes. Though still very angry, he knew Alan wasn't to blame and he couldn't let the episode spoil his Christmas and New Year break. Truthfully, Colin was right. A week ago he would have simply left the tape in Miss Smith's office and beat a hasty retreat. He would even have taken on the extra work the Chairman had spoken of – but not anymore. Since meeting Sally, his life had taken a different turn. Nevertheless, Colin was well aware of how he felt about his stupid pranks and shouldn't have played one of his silly jokes in front of Alan.

Taking a deep breath to quell his anger, Bill rose to his feet and walked around the desk. He placed his hand on Alan's shoulder. "It's all right." He forced a smile. "I overreacted. I understand how persuasive Colin can be." Glancing at Colin, he realised he couldn't stay angry with him for long; he had been too good a friend over the years. Besides he truly believed Colin had never done anything like this before. His remark had been made in fit of anger. "Okay, Colin. I know it's early in the day, but go and get that bottle of single malt whisky you think I don't know about. We could all do with a drink. Alan, come in and sit down while we're waiting." He could see that Alan was still shaking.

Alan heaved a sigh of relief as he slumped into a chair. In future, if Colin wanted to play any tricks on Mr Roberts he could leave him out of it and he would tell him so at the first opportunity. He had been getting on so well with his boss these last two days and didn't want it to go wrong now. He really admired Mr. Roberts and wanted to learn as much as he could from him.

"How did you know I had a bottle in my drawer?" asked Colin, when he finally arrived back with the whisky. He had spent a few minutes sitting in his chair, trying to regain his composure. Though he hadn't been quite as nervous as Alan, he'd certainly had the wind knocked out of his sails.

"There're a lot of things I know about," answered Bill. "I don't miss quite as much as you think."

"I suppose you'll want to drink to Websters, you usually do," said Colin.

"No! We'll drink to our future," replied Bill.

There was a knock on the door and Miss Smith walked in. "Here's your mail, Mr Roberts. I can only apologise for being so rude to you earlier. Thank you for not reporting me to Mrs Saunders."

"Apology accepted, Miss Smith. Would you like a drink? Colin is being generous with his whisky."

"I don't know if I'm allowed to," she answered.

"Of course you are." Bill poured her a glass of whisky.

Miss Smith went on to explain why she seemed so disinterested in her job. She told them how bored she was in the typing pool, as she was capable of so much more. "All I need is a chance to prove it. But most of the heads of departments would rather take on temporary staff from the agency."

"Well, Miss Smith," said Bill. "I hope I won't regret this, but if you're really serious about that and haven't managed to get yourself dismissed before my secretary goes on her two week Spring break, I'll give you your chance. I'll speak to Miss Anderson about giving you some instructions, as to what is required. However, when I put in my report at the end of the two weeks, I'll be totally honest. If you mess up, I'll say so."

Miss Smith was delighted and assured him she wouldn't let him down, repeating she simply needed a chance. After she had left the office, Bill signed his letters.

"Can I rely on one of you to take these out and post them? I need to get away now. There are some stamps in my secretary's office. Top drawer of her desk I think."

"I'll see to it, Mr Roberts – sir." Alan leapt to his feet. He was still trying to redeem himself with his boss.

"Thank you, Alan, as long as I'm not putting you out."

"Not at all, sir. If I go now, I'll probably catch the midday post. Is there anything else I can do for you, sir?"

"Yes, Alan, there is. You can stop calling me sir. I like you and I'd like to think we're friends. If we're in here, call me Bill. If we're in the finance office, call me Mr Roberts now and again, for appearances sake. But there's no need to call me sir. Save that for the MD or the Chairman."

"Thank you, sir... I mean Bill. You don't know what it means to me to have you think of me as a friend," gushed Alan.

"Right," said Bill, feeling a little embarrassed by Alan's enthusiasm. "Now take the mail and go home. And have a good Christmas. See you in the New Year."

"And the same to you," Alan replied, leaving the office. He was relieved there had been no further mention of the earlier episode.

"I'll be back in a minute Bill." Colin followed Alan out of the office and caught up with him in the corridor. "Don't you ever let Bill down will you Alan? He likes you; so don't use it as an excuse to leave your work for him to finish. As I said last night, most of them here pile work onto him, from the Chairman down. I can't do much about some of the others, but I won't sit back and let it happen from someone he considers a friend. Just you try it and you'll have me to deal with."

"Colin, I'd never do anything like that. I'm delighted he considers me a friend. I've never met anyone like him. I admire him a great deal. He's clever – very clever. Brilliant with figures, I can see why Mr Taylor wants him to join his firm. But he's so thoughtful as well." He recalled how Bill had paid his bar bill in the Apollo Hotel the previous evening. "I'm not like some of the others. I'll pull my weight and more. I want to learn and I'm hoping he'll teach me. No! You've nothing to worry about as far as I'm concerned. And that includes getting mixed up in your schemes. I want nothing more to do with your pranks or jokes. Don't you ever, ever involve me in anything like that again! That little stunt you pulled back there could have cost me my future here at Websters. For heavens sake, Colin, I was scared stiff. I honestly believed I was going to lose my job today. Mr Clark, head of invoicing recently got rid of one of his staff for a hell of a lot less than that and he isn't anywhere near being an executive."

He paused a moment to catch his breath. "It would have looked good on my CV, 'sacked from Websters International for trying to make the Financial Executive look an idiot'. After reading that, who'd employ me?" He prodded Colin's chest. "Go on answer me. Who on earth would give me a job with a reference like that? Have you any idea what a cutthroat business it is trying to get a good position in this economic climate? Luck was on my side when I got this one. I know for a fact, there were a lot of other well-qualified people being interviewed that day – people with good experience, but somehow I got lucky. And today, through you, I very nearly blew it. I would never have got a decent job again. So from now on…"

He stopped abruptly, suddenly remembering who he was talking to. After all, Colin was the assistant head of the department and shouldn't be spoken to in such a manner – not by a mere junior anyway. He bit his lip and began to apologise, "I'm sorry. I shouldn't have said…"

"No Alan," interrupted Colin. "You're quite right. I shouldn't have involved you. It was a really stupid thing to do and I'm the one who should be apologising. I don't know what came over me, but Bill wouldn't have sacked you." He paused for a moment, recalling how angry his friend had been. At least he didn't think he would. "No, he wouldn't have sacked you," he repeated, more to convince himself, rather than Alan. "He knew it was my fault. It was me he was really annoyed with, not you. You simply happened to be in the firing line. But he won't bear you a grudge; he's forgotten it. He wouldn't have called you his friend otherwise. Try to put it out of your mind and have a nice Christmas and New Year. What's your phone number? I may be in touch over the holiday."

They exchanged numbers and Colin was about to go back into Bill's office when he remembered something. "Oh and by the way, Alan, one other thing. For your information, luck had nothing to do with you getting the job here at Websters. Bill told me that he appointed you because he believed you were enthusiastic and had potential, therefore deserved a chance to prove yourself. In other words, he thought you were the best man for the job."

Colin returned to Bill's office feeling extremely guilty he had upset both Bill and Alan. Especially as Alan had thought he was going to lose his job. It was little wonder the lad had looked so worried.

"What was all that about?" asked Bill.

"Nothing. I wanted to wish him a Merry Christmas and apologise for earlier, that's all," mumbled Colin, sheepishly. "I shouldn't have involved him. He wanted nothing to do with it, but I dragged him along. I took his phone number. I thought I might get in touch with him over the holidays to try and make it up with him. You know you've made him a very happy man telling him you would like him as a friend? He looks on you as his hero; a role model."

"Don't be stupid," replied Bill. "He's simply very young and wants to go far. But I like him. He reminds me a great deal of myself. I told him I would give him some new accounts to look after once the holidays were over. I think he's up to it."

"Yes, I know. He came straight along to tell me yesterday." Colin grinned. "He was like a dog with two tails. Especially as you told him you would take him through them personally. I'm telling you, he really does see you as his hero. If you were a woman, I'd say he had a crush on you. You'll see I'm right when we get back after the holidays." He paused and shuffled his feet. "Seriously though, Bill, he was worried earlier on. He really thought he was going to lose his job."

"Did he say that?" asked Bill.

Colin nodded. "Yes – out there in the corridor. He said he was really scared. You wouldn't have fired him, would you? I couldn't have lived with myself if I'd caused him to lose his job."

"No, of course I wouldn't. It never even crossed my mind." He paused. "You, on the other hand…" He rocked his hand back and forth.

Colin's jaw dropped.

"Only kidding." Bill grinned, at the horrified expression on Colin's face. "However, I will say, I was really furious with you at the time."

"Yes! I picked up the vibes. Mr Roberts, indeed." Colin pulled a face. "What was that all about?"

Bill shrugged. "It got your attention."

"Too right it did!" Colin paused. "I'm really sorry about this morning, Bill; I just don't know what came over me." He hesitated and looked away. "There's something else I should tell you. I think I must have had too much to drink last night – I'd already had a few, while we were waiting for you and Sally. Anyway, I said some things to Alan about you. Nothing bad…" He hesitated. "I was simply telling him what a great guy you were. But…" His voice trailed off.

"But what?" Bill asked. "What else did you say?"

"I told him about the cheque you received from the board of directors." Colin looked down towards the floor and shuffled his feet again. "Rachel was furious and intervened. However, she brought it up again when we got home. I had to do some pretty fast talking to save myself from having to sleep in the spare room!" Thank God she had stopped him from quoting Bill's salary. "I have to say," he continued, "Alan swore he wouldn't ever mention it to anyone and I believe him, therefore I wasn't going to say anything to you."

"So why are you telling me now?"

"Because I don't want to have an axe hanging over my head! Should it ever become office gossip, you would know it could only have originated from me. At least now you know."

"I see." Bill paused. Fearing another outburst, Colin remained silent, while he waited for Bill to continue. "Alright, Colin." Bill heaved a sigh. "Like you say, I don't think Alan's the sort to spread it around." He grinned and raised his eyebrows. "The spare room, eh? You wouldn't have liked that." He punched Colin playfully on the arm, as he spoke. "Now let's forget the whole thing and get away. I have to drive through to my mother's to pick up Joey."

"Is Sally going with you?" asked Colin, relieved at the change of subject.

"No," replied Bill, quietly. "She moved out this morning. She didn't want Joey thinking I'd moved her in while he was away, but I'm really going to miss her. The house won't be the same without her."

Colin noticed the change in Bill's voice. "I'm sorry Bill. I didn't realise Joey was still unaware you and Sally had got together." He suddenly grinned at his friend. "It's little wonder you were late in this morning. Making the most of it were you – having a long lie in?"

Bill groaned. "Shall we simply say I had to drop Sally off at her flat and leave it at that? Now, will you go home and let me get away? Save the rest of the bottle for when we come back. If anything develops over the next three weeks, I'll give you and Rachel a ring."

"Okay, I'll go, and Bill, I can only repeat that I'm really sorry about the episode this morning, I promise it won't happen again. I still can't believe I involved Alan. He's made it plain he wants nothing more to do with my pranks. In fact he gave me a dressing down out there. But you have to laugh when you think of the look on his face."

"I've already accepted your apology, Colin, now forget it and go home to Rachel. She'll be waiting for you." Nevertheless, Bill couldn't help smiling, when he recalled Alan's expression.

Colin left the office laughing, while Bill picked up the phone and dialled Sally's number, however there was no reply. Checking his briefcase, he left the office.

That morning, Bill's mother went shopping. It was raining quite heavily, so she decided to leave Joey with her neighbour, Sue, who had a young boy of her own. Later, when she called to collect her grandson, she found Sue standing at the front door with her finger to her lips.

"I saw you coming through the gate," she whispered. "I've been listening to the children. They're talking about what mummies do. Come and hear for yourself."

"So far, mummies cook, wash dishes, wash clothes and sew," said Sue, leading the way to the sitting room. "We lead very dull lives, don't we?"

"What else do they do?" they heard Joey ask.

"My mummy hugs and kisses me all the time," volunteered Beth, who lived across the street."

"So does mine." David, Sue's son was speaking now. "And she hugs and kisses my daddy as well."

Sue grinned and turned a deep shade of pink.

"Does your mummy sleep with you?" asked Joey.

"No," said David. "She sleeps in the same bed as my daddy. But if I have a tummy ache she sleeps with me."

"My mummy sleeps with my daddy as well," said Beth.

At this point, Joe, who had remained silent until now, decided to join in the conversation, saying his mummy and daddy also slept in the same bed.

"I once went into mummy's bedroom to tell her I was feeling sick and she was kissing my daddy," said David. "And my daddy was lying on top…"

He got no further, as Sue had quickly decided it was time to break up the conversation. "What's going on in here?"

Anne followed her into the room.

"Joey has asked Santa for a mummy for Christmas and he wanted to know what mummies did," said David.

Tears formed in Sue's eyes, as she looked at Anne. "I feel so sorry for you all."

"It's alright," said Anne, laying her hand on Sue's arm. "I'll speak to his father. He'll be here shortly. I'll get him to have a word with Joey about asking so many questions."

"No," said Sue. "Leave it. There's no harm done. Your son has enough to worry about. Besides, children ask questions all the time."

"Joey certainly does," agreed Anne. "I'll take him home now. As I said, his father will be here to collect him soon and I want to give them some lunch before they drive back. Thanks very much for looking after him for me."

As soon as his father pulled up onto the drive, Joey ran out of the house to meet him, his arms outstretched. "Daddy, Daddy," he called out.

Bill picked up his son and hugged him. "I've missed you, Joey. It's so good to see you again. A week is a long time for me to be without you."

By then Anne had appeared at the door. She was delighted to find Bill looking so much better than when she had last seen him. In fact she thought he looked positively happy. "Hello son."

Bill walked across to his mother and gave her a hug. She was surprised. He hadn't done that for years. He wasn't usually so demonstrative, except with Joey. "Hello Mum. I hope Joey has been behaving himself."

"Joey has been no trouble at all. He never is." She was still taken aback by her son's behaviour. "Come on in. I've got some lunch ready for you. Your father's in the greenhouse, I'll give him a call."

John came into the kitchen and washed his hands. "How are you son? Still working hard?"

Bill went to greet his father. "Hello Dad. No. I've taken your advice and am starting to take things easy." He shook his father's hand and clapped him on the back.

His mother was even more astounded. He hadn't called his father, 'Dad', for a long time. Not since he was a small boy. It had always been Father. She widened her eyes for a second before looking away, not wanting Bill to see her reaction. "Come on into the dining room I've set the table in there today. It's good to see you in such high spirits, Bill. Are you really cutting down on your workload?"

"Well, let's just say I'm not taking on any more," answered Bill. "Joey, you come and sit next to me and tell me what you've been doing."

Joey told his father everything. All about the party, the Christmas tree in the town centre and all the toyshops he had been to. "And we went to see the trains two times." He was quite breathless with excitement. "Daddy, are we still going to get a Christmas tree today to take home?"

"Yes. We'll stop on the way home and get a tree and a hamburger or a pizza." Bill fell silent for a moment, thinking of the time they had gone for a pizza when Sally had been with them. If she were here now, it would be perfect. He glanced at Joey, hoping he wouldn't mention it at the moment.

Noticing her son had gone quiet, Anne asked him if everything was all right.

"Yes, Mum everything's fine. Don't worry." He reached out and took her hand. "You worry too much. You know that don't you?"

Anne was still struggling to take in the change in her son's behaviour. Only a week ago he had been so tense, it had frightened her.

"It's what mothers do," she said. "We worry about our children and our husbands all the time."

"I know," said Bill. "And I've given you cause to worry haven't I? But I'm really trying to be more relaxed. Will that make you happy and worry less?"

She smiled at him. "Well it would certainly be a start." She decided not to mention Joey's conversation with his friends. There was no need to upset Bill about that today. Besides, Sue was right, children ask questions all the time; it was all part of growing up. "I've been meaning to ask you, whether you enjoyed the dance last night?" She cocked her head on one side and grinned. "Surely there was a nice young lady who caught your eye?"

"Well, yes," answered Bill slowly. "There was one lady I rather liked, but she was spoken for." He felt a little guilty about the deception. He knew he should tell his parents about Sally. However, having waited this long, he might as well get Joey's reaction first.

They talked for a while longer, and after lunch John took Bill out into the greenhouse to show him what he was planning to grow next year. When they came back, Anne asked her son what time they should all come over on Christmas Day.

"Just come as soon as you're able," said Bill. "Don't worry, Joey and I will have the lunch ready. Well, almost ready. Isn't that right, son?"

"We will, Daddy," answered Joey, importantly.

"Well Mum, Dad, I think we'd better set off now. We're going shopping for a Christmas tree. Aren't we, Joey? Can we leave you with the dishes?"

"Go on, get off with you." She laughed. "I've done some shopping for you for Christmas. Turkey, stuffing, everything you'll need. I had to get a taxi home as your father was still at work."

"Thanks Mum. How much do I owe you and that includes the taxi fare?"

Bill loaded the shopping into the boot of his car and strapped Joey into the back seat. "Goodbye Mum." He hugged and kissed her. He then shook hands with his father and gave him a hug. "See you both on Christmas Day." Both he and Joey waved as he drove off.

"I don't know what's come over Bill," said Anne, as she watched the car disappear down the road, "but whatever it is, long may it last. It's wonderful to see him like this."

"I agree," said his father. "It's been a very long time since I've seen him looking so relaxed and happy."

Once Sally put her things away in her flat she decided to visit her friend Jane Miller. She had bought her a Christmas present and thought it would be a good time to take it to her. Afterwards, she would call on Jo. But first, she wanted to stop off at Bill's house and wash up the dishes they had left from last night and breakfast that morning.

Bill had said he would see to it when he and Joey arrived home, but she had a strong urge to go back to the house. She hurried for the bus, only stopping at a sweet shop on the way.

When she opened the front door of Bill's home, she was almost swept over as the memories of the past week flooded over her. For a moment, she held her breath, wishing she hadn't come. "Perhaps this wasn't such a good idea after all," she murmured. Though her voice was barely a whisper, it seemed to echo around the large entrance hall. She closed the door and made her way into the kitchen. She quickly washed the dishes and then went upstairs to check whether anything else needed doing.

In Joey's room, she wrote a brief note and left it on his bed, together with the purchase she had made at the sweet shop. In the bedroom she had shared with Bill, she wrote another note and left it on dressing table. After taking a fleeting glance around the bedroom, she ran downstairs and fled out of the house.

Jane was pleased to see her and wanted to know all about the children.

"Jane, you've phoned me nearly every day enquiring about the children." Sarah laughed. "They're fine. They've missed you, but they're looking forward to Christmas. There's nothing more to tell you."

"Have you heard any more about Joey?" Jane stared at Sally as she spoke.

"Why do you ask? How could I have heard anymore about Joey? He's still at his grandmother's, isn't he?"

Jane didn't answer. She merely sat in her chair; her eyes firmly fixed on Sally.

"You know, don't you?" said Sally, feeling uncomfortable under Jane's gaze. "About Bill and me, I mean."

"I had a vague idea, but I didn't know for certain until now. Is it serious?"

"Yes," whispered Sally. "Very serious. I love him so much, Jane. We're waiting for the right time to tell Joey. You're not annoyed, are you? I know you didn't employ me to date one of the parents. It just sort of happened."

"My dear, I'm delighted." Jane's eyes twinkled. "Mr Roberts is such a lovely man. He needs someone. And so do you, if you don't mind me saying so. You're both perfectly suited. I was worried about you ever finding the right person. Especially with your friend Josephine hanging around all the time. I know I shouldn't say this, but I felt she was dominating you and you're so easily led, Sally." She clasped her hands together. "I couldn't be more pleased."

"Yes, you're right. We are well suited. Even my father agreed with that." Sally paused. Jane was positively beaming. Could she have arranged for Sally to meet Bill by staying away from the nursery? No! She couldn't, she wouldn't. Jane had the flu' – didn't she? "How did you guess anyway?" she continued.

"Twice when we were talking on the phone, you called him Bill," Jane replied. "Or at least you started to before correcting yourself, you would never have called him by his Christian name unless you had met him on a more social occasion. I've known him a long time and even *I* seldom call him Bill. But then I'm rather old fashioned."

"I didn't think you'd noticed when you didn't say anything." Sally laughed. "But I suppose I should have known better, you seldom miss a thing. Our only problem now is how Joey will react. He may not like sharing his father with anyone."

"Children adapt to circumstances more easily than you think, especially when it's in their best interest. This would certainly be in Joey's best interest. He simply needs a little time to get used to you."

Sally stayed for another hour and then said she must leave as she was going on to visit Jo.

She spent an hour or so with her friend. Jo wanted to know all that had happened during the last week, especially the reaction of Sally's parents to Bill. But she was very careful not to be too personal. By the time Sally returned to her flat, she felt quite exhausted.

Joey chatted all the way back home. Bill smiled to himself, it was good having his son with him again. As they neared the town, Bill asked him what he wanted to do first. "Do you want to go to get the tree? Or do you want to have a pizza?"

Joey thought about it for a while and then said. "Tree first Daddy."

"Tree first Daddy, what?" said Bill.

"Please," Joey replied.

"That's better. Joey you must remember to say please and thank you. It's very important to be polite."

"I'll try, Daddy."

"Good. A tree it is," said Bill.

He parked the car outside a large Garden Centre. There were lots of trees, all different shapes and sizes. Joey wanted a one as big as the one he had seen in the town centre, but Bill patiently explained it wouldn't fit inside the house. Finally, they found one Joey liked and would easily go into the sitting room. "Now, Joey we'll go and get something to eat."

At Pizza House, Bill avoided using the table they had used when Sally had been with them. He was missing her already and decided he would ring her just as soon as Joey had gone to bed. They finished their meal and returned to the car.

"We'll go home now Joey and put up the tree. We have some decorations in the loft and if we need anymore we'll buy them tomorrow when we're out shopping."

Pulling onto the drive, Bill stared at the front door, half expecting Sally to come out to greet him. She didn't of course; she was back at her flat. After all, hadn't he dropped her there that very morning? Joey jolted him from his thoughts.

"Come on Daddy. Please can we get out of the car?"

"Yes of course, son."

Inside the house, Bill could see Sally wherever he looked. In the kitchen, where they'd had breakfast a few hours ago – in the sitting room, where only last night they had sat with their friends. Was it really only last night? It seemed a lifetime ago.

"We'll unpack this now and get it over with," he said, carrying Joey's suitcase upstairs to his bedroom.

Following behind, Joey looked at his pillow. There was a large chocolate Santa with a note at the side. Picking it up, he read the note out loud. "Welcome home, Joey, lots of love, from Daddy."

Bill took the note from Joey and read it for himself. Sally must have come back. Come to think of it, he couldn't recall seeing the dishes they had left in the sink.

"Thank you Daddy," said Joey.

Bill didn't reply. Not trusting himself to speak, he unpacked Joey's clothes.

"I'll hang up my jacket and then we'll get the tree out of the car."

He went into his bedroom. The smell of Sally's perfume hung in the air and he could almost feel her presence in the room. Walking over to the wardrobe, a small piece of paper on the dressing table caught his eye. He picked it up and read the words. *My darling Bill, I love you so much, Sally.*

He was about to put it down, when he saw something glinting on the floor. It was a ring. He remembered Sally wearing it at the dance the night before. She must have forgotten it.

Reading the note again, tears formed in his eyes and he clutched the ring tightly in his hand. But when he heard Joey coming into the room he stuffed both the ring and the note into his pocket and quickly wiped his eyes with the back of his hand.

"Can we please bring the tree in now Daddy?"

"Yes. Of course we can, son." He looked around the room again to make sure there weren't any other tell-tale signs lying around, before bending down to pick up his son. "Joey. You know I'll always love you, don't you? We'll always be together. No matter what happens, I'll always be there for you. Never forget that."

Joey put his arms around his father's neck. "I love you Daddy. I love Nanna and Granddad as well, but I love you best of all."

Blinking his eyes furiously to fight back the tears, Bill's voice shook with emotion as he hugged his son. "Come on then, let's go and get the Christmas tree out of the car."

Joey was excited, when they decorated the tree. It was the first time he'd had a Christmas tree – well, the first one he knew about anyway. Bill felt guilty when he saw how much pleasure his son was getting from something so simple.

He reflected on the last time they'd had a Christmas tree. It was the Christmas before Julie died. She had chosen the decorations, saying, "I know Joey isn't old enough to understand what it's all about, but I'm sure he'll be able to see the coloured lights."

Bill recalled how she had been right. Joey could see the lights. He had stared at them every time they were switched on. "I'm so sorry Julie," he murmured. "I should have done this a couple of years ago."

However Christmas had a habit of creeping up so suddenly. He was always busy at work right up until the very last minute, but not anymore. No longer would his work come between him and his son. Sally had made him realise what he had been missing. This last week had been so wonderful. Once away from the office, he hadn't given it another thought.

On other occasions when Joey was at his grandmother's, he would stay at the office until very late. Yet this week he couldn't wait to get away. He would still give Websters one hundred per cent while he was there, but after office hours... well from now on, his time was going to be spent with his family.

Joey interrupted his thoughts. "What goes on top of the tree, Daddy?"

"Let's see what we have in the box, shall we? There's a star, or there's a fairy. You choose Joey, and I'll hold you up so you can put it right at the very top."

"Can we try them both to see which one looks best?" asked Joey.

Bill held Joey up so he could put the fairy on the top and then the star. In the end he decided on the fairy.

"I'd like to tell Nanna about the tree," said Joey, excitedly.

Bill dialled the number for him and Joey told his grandmother all about how he had decorated the tree. "It looks so pretty when the lights are switched on. Just like the one beside the shops." But he added that she was going to have to wait right until Christmas Day to see it.

Later, when Joey was sound asleep in bed, Bill telephoned Sally. "Hello darling," he said, when she answered. "Sally, I'm missing you so much."

"I've missed you too Bill. I don't know how I'm going to last until Christmas Day." There was a long pause. "How is Joey?"

"He's fine. It's so good to have him home. We decorated a Christmas tree this evening. Oh Sally, he was so excited. You should have seen him. If only..." his voice trailed off.

She knew what he had been going to say and felt the same way. If only she could have been there, helping them both. She forced back the tears. "And your parents, are they both well? I expect they'll miss Joey."

"Yes, they will miss him. I think he's a bit of a handful, but my mother adores him and loves to have him there." He changed the subject abruptly. "Sally sweetheart, I'm going to have to tell Joey about us. I'm going to go crazy without you. I need you with me."

"Bill, wait, you mustn't – not yet. See how he takes to me being there at Christmas. Don't say anything too early. Leave it. He's only a little boy give him a chance. Please."

"Okay Sally. I'll try," said Bill.

After a long conversation they hung up. Bill sat by the phone for a while. It was going to be a very long weekend. He went upstairs, took a shower and got into bed. After tossing and turning for several hours, he finally dropped off to sleep.

Day Ten

"Daddy, Daddy. What are we going to do today?" Joey ran into his father's bedroom and leapt onto the bed.

"What would you like to do today, Joey?" Bill asked. He wondered what Sally would make of his son bouncing around on the bed first thing in the morning.

Rushing into his father's bedroom was something Joey had always done and Bill had never discouraged it. He wanted his son to know he was always there for him. However, in the past there had only been the two of them. But once Joey got used to the idea of Sally living here, she would be sleeping in here and she may not like being attacked in the mornings by a four-year-old monster.

"I don't know, Daddy. You choose something."

"We could go to the shops to get some more tinsel for the tree and perhaps a few decorations for the house. And then we could look for some presents for Nanna and Granddad."

Joey was quite excited at the idea. He ran back to his bedroom, and came back with his advent calendar.

"You can open the little door today Daddy."

"That's all right son. It's yours. You open it."

"We share it," said Joey. "I've opened lots of doors while I've been at Nanna's house. It's your turn today."

Bill opened the flap to reveal a teddy bear. "Only one more day left and that's yours. Then the next day is Christmas Day."

"I'm so excited for Christmas Day to come. Then Santa will have been."

Bill also wished for Christmas Day to come, but not for quite the same reason as his son. "Come on then. Let me get out of bed and we'll go into the bathroom and get showered."

Once they had dressed and breakfasted, they set out for the town centre.

Sally needed to do some shopping. There was still Bill's present to buy. She had no idea what to get for him; he seemed to have everything he needed. She planned to get Joey another carriage for his train set. Knowing how busy the shops would be later in the day she decided to make an early start.

Buying the train carriage for Joey was no problem, but choosing something for Bill was a different matter entirely. She knew she could always get him some cufflinks, but they seemed rather dreary. And then if she wanted to buy some with his initials on, would she get some with B. for Bill or W. for William?

Come to think of it, she had never heard anyone call him William. Even when he had first introduced himself to her, he had said Bill Roberts. Then she thought of the expensive after-shave and cologne she had seen in his bathroom. She wondered whether to buy him something like that.

It was while she was wandering gazing into a shop window that she saw his reflection I the glass. He was carrying Joey on his shoulders. Her first instinct was to rush over to them. However, she stopped herself in time. Looking around she saw a coffee shop behind her and quickly slipped inside.

Once seated, she looked across to where she had last seen them. They were still there. Bill appeared to be pointing at something on a poster. The waitress came over and Sally ordered some coffee. She was still watching them when someone from behind spoke to her. "Hello, Sally. Do you mind if I join you?"

Turning around, Sally found herself looking at Vera, Bill's secretary.

"Please do." She pointed towards a seat facing the opposite direction to where Bill and Joey were standing. She rather hoped Vera wouldn't notice them. No doubt she would think it strange that she didn't go out to see them.

"Did you enjoy the dance the other evening?" enquired Vera.

"Yes I did. It was nice meeting some of the people Bill works with."

"Have you known Mr Roberts long? Vera hesitated and bit her lip. "Perhaps you shouldn't answer that. It's really none of my business."

"Well I don't think it's a state secret." Sally grinned. "Only ten days."

"I'm sorry Sally. I really shouldn't have asked. I'd hate Mr Roberts to think I was prying into his private business. He never discusses his personal life at the office – except perhaps, with Colin. Let's talk about something else, shall we?"

"When are you getting married?" asked Sally.

"We haven't set a date yet. We're trying to find something we can afford to buy or failing that, something to rent. Unfortunately for us, property is so expensive in this area, even the rents are high. We would rather stay local if possible, as we both have jobs we enjoy. But if it comes to it, we'll have to move away."

The waitress returned with Sally's coffee and Vera ordered one for herself.

Sally didn't say anything; she was still watching Bill and Joey. They had started to move away from the poster and were now wandering off down the High Street.

"I'm sorry Vera I was miles away. You know, if things work out for Bill and me, my flat will be going up for sale. I don't know whether you would be interested, as it isn't very large. Actually, it's really quite small, but it does have two bedrooms. I might even be persuaded to rent it out. However, it really depends on what the future holds for me."

"If you don't mind me saying so, your future looked very certain on Thursday night," said Vera. "But you know best. Your flat sounds ideal and two bedrooms would be fine. We simply want to start off on our own; not living with either of our parents."

"I'll be in all this evening and tomorrow morning if you would like to look around it. Just call in, there's no need to ring," Sally told her.

After giving Vera her address, they left the coffee shop.

Sally went across to look at the poster Bill had been showing Joey. It was advertising a Carol Concert under the Christmas tree in the Town Square on Christmas Eve. Bill must be going to take Joey, thought Sally. I wish I was going with them.

Bill wasn't quite sure what to get Sally or his mother for Christmas. His father's present had been easy in comparison. Anything to do with gardening was always appreciated and Jack, his brother-in-law, was very much the same.

While passing a jeweller's he noticed a gold locket in the window. Perhaps his mother would like that, especially if he put a photograph of Joey inside. She loved anything to do with Joey.

"Come on Joey. Let's see if we can find a Christmas present for Nanna in here." He could tell Joey was becoming a little weary. "Then we'll go and have something to eat. How does that sound?"

Inside the shop, Bill asked to see the locket. "What do you think Joey? Would this be a nice present for Nanna? We'll go to the booth across the street and get your photo taken to put inside."

Joey nodded his head vigorously. Bill decided to buy it. He wondered if there was something he could get for Sally. He wanted something special. This was their first Christmas together and he wanted to mark the occasion. He looked at some of the necklaces but couldn't see anything he liked. It was when he saw a tray of rings that he thought of the perfect present – an engagement ring.

But what would she like? And then there was the size. Perhaps this wasn't going to be so easy after all. Then, quite suddenly, remembered the ring in his pocket. The one he had found on the bedroom floor only the night before. He looked again at the rings. One stood out above the rest.

It was beautiful, a large sapphire surrounded by diamonds. It was very expensive, but he was sure Sally would like it. He took the ring from his pocket and asked the jeweller if the one in the case was the same size. He hoped it was. It was too late to have it altered in time for Christmas.

However luck was on his side, the size was exactly right. He also saw a gold bracelet, which he knew would be ideal for his sister. After pointing it out to Joey, he decided to buy that too. Having paid for his three purchases he told Joey it was time to get something to eat.

Joey wanted a hamburger.

"You know Joey. Your nanna is going to get cross with me for letting you have too many hamburgers and pizzas." But in the end he gave in. "Alright, but tomorrow we must have something cooked at home."

"How can Nanna get cross with you? You're grown up," asked Joey.

"I'm still her son, just as you are my son," explained Bill. "I sometimes get cross with you, don't I?"

Joey thought about this for a moment. "You only get a little bit cross with me." He was quiet for a few minutes and then said. "If I had a mummy, would she get cross with me as well?"

Bill picked up his son and held him close. "She would only get a little cross if you were really naughty. But you wouldn't be naughty for your mummy would you? I'm sure you would be a good boy for her."

"I would try to be a good boy," said Joey.

After they had eaten, Bill took Joey to the photo booth. They had several photos taken in different poses. Some were of Joey by himself while others were of the two of them together.

"We'll choose which photo to put in the locket when we get home," said Bill.

Joey, however, was adamant a photo of both he and his father together should go into the locket. "Nanna would like that best of all."

Later that evening, after Joey had gone to bed, Bill phoned Sally. He told her how he and Joey had been out Christmas shopping. He didn't tell her what he had chosen for her, but he did say how much he was missing her.

Sally decided not to say she had seen him at the shopping centre, instead she told him about meeting his secretary in a coffee shop. "She's very pleasant. She told me she is looking for somewhere to live when they get married."

"If you move in here, they might be interested in your flat."

"Well, I wasn't going to mention it now, but I did suggest that to her, though I pointed out it was only a possibility."

"Sally, Joey is going to have to get used to you being around. I can't bear it here without you. I'm sure it won't take him long to get used to the idea."

They chattered on for a while longer, each one not wanting to end the conversation, but they both knew they couldn't talk all night. "Only one more day sweetheart, it won't be long now." Bill reminded her.

"I know Bill. But what happens then? Christmas night I have to come home. What excuse can you give to invite me back the next day?"

"I don't know Sally. Perhaps I won't need one, but if I do, I'll think of something. I promise." He simply had to – he couldn't go on like this for very much longer.

After they hung up, Bill went into the lounge and poured himself a brandy. He wondered what other people did in this situation. Perhaps they simply moved someone in and let the children adapt in their own time. However, would that work with Joey? He didn't want to hurt his son, but on the other hand, he had a life of his own and now Sally was part of it.

Going upstairs to his bedroom, he sat down of the edge of the bed. Sally's perfume still hung in the air his thoughts were filled with them laughing and making love on this very bed. Everywhere he looked he could see and feel Sally's presence. It was almost as though he could reach out and touch her. He knew he couldn't sleep in here again tonight. Last night was bad enough. Tonight seemed even worse. Back downstairs, he poured himself another drink and switched on the television. After another two drinks, he didn't remember anymore.

Day Eleven

"Daddy. Daddy. Where are you?" Joey screamed out.

Bill awoke with a start. The television was still on from the night before. It took him a few seconds to realise where he was and how he came to be lying on the sofa. Still screaming, Joey ran into the sitting room, but not seeing his father lying there, he ran out again.

Leaping to his feet, Bill ran into the hall. "What is it Joey? What's the matter?"

Joey ran towards his father. His arms outstretched. "I couldn't find you... I thought... you'd gone away... and left me." He was crying so hard he was finding it difficult to speak.

"Joey, I would never go anywhere and leave you on your own. You know that." Bill picked up his son and hugged him. "I was lying on the sofa. I couldn't sleep, so I came downstairs, that's all. I promise I'll never ever leave you by yourself. Come on now, dry those tears."

Though Joey stopped crying, he still clung to his father and Bill took him into the sitting room and sat him on his knee. When Joey had calmed down a little, Bill suggested they went upstairs to get dressed.

Joey giggled. "You are dressed, Daddy."

"So I am." Bill laughed. "But I've changed my mind, I think I'd like to wear something else."

"We have to open the last door on my calendar Daddy." Joey sounded a little more like his usual self. "Only one day left to Christmas."

"Yes, Joey," murmured Bill. "Only one day left."

Later in the morning, Bill answered the door to find Rachel and Colin on the step.

"Joey, Auntie Rachel and Uncle Colin are here."

Joey came running to the door to see them.

"Where is our favourite Godson?" asked Colin, as he lifted Joey into his arms. Bill led them through into the sitting room. "Sit down. I'll put some coffee on."

Colin handed Joey to Rachel. "I'll give your daddy a hand Joey. You tell Auntie Rachel what you've been doing since we saw you last." Out in the kitchen Colin told Bill they had simply called to see how he was. "Have you seen Sally since Friday morning?"

"No. I've spoken to her on the phone, but that's all." Bill put some water and coffee in the percolator and waited for some wisecrack from Colin about his last morning with Sally. However, as none came, he continued quietly. "I'm really missing her." He paused and looked away. "I couldn't even sleep in my bed last night. Everything reminds me of her. Especially her perfume, it's still lingering up there in the bedroom this morning. I spent last night on the sofa." He hesitated again. "I don't know why I'm telling you this. You, of all people, you'll probably remind me about it for months to come. However, I really need to talk to someone."

"No I won't Bill. Not a word, I promise," said Colin softly. He desperately wanted to make amends for his stupidity at the office on Friday. "You need to be able to talk to a friend and I'm here."

"Thanks Colin," said Bill. "I don't suppose there's anyone else I *would* tell. I haven't even told my parents about Sally yet."

"Why on earth not? Colin was surprised. "They'd be delighted to hear there was someone in your life again. Especially your mother, she worries herself sick about you and Joey." He stopped short of telling him how his mother rang him occasionally when she was particularly worried about her son.

"Yes. I know. However, I put off telling her at first because it might not have worked out and that would have made her even more concerned. Later, I decided it might be best to get Joey's reaction first. Anyway, she'll find out tomorrow, they're all coming over. I think I told you."

"Yes, you did. But please, Bill, no more sleeping on the sofa. That's not going to do you any good."

"You're right. I can't do that again. I woke up with such a fright this morning. Joey couldn't find me and was running around the house screaming. He thought I'd gone out and left him on his own. He's all right now, so don't say anything unless he mentions it. I'd rather he forgot about it. Incidentally, where're your two kids?"

"My parents are staying for Christmas, so they've given us the morning off."

They went back into the sitting room with the coffee. Rachel was reading a story to Joey.

"Coffee's ready," said Bill. "I think I have some cake somewhere. Joey, would you like some orange juice?"

"Yes," said Joey, adding, "Please," when he saw his father frown at him.

When Bill left the room, Rachel looked at Colin, mouthing the words 'how is he'. She didn't want Joey to hear them talking about his father. Colin lifted his hands and rocked them to and fro. Rachel sighed. She would like to talk to Bill herself, but was at a loss as to what to say. Besides, Colin was his best friend and even he couldn't help him. Except perhaps be there to listen when he needed someone to talk to.

By the time Bill came back with the cake and orange juice, Rachel had poured out the coffee. Joey was telling her about their trip to the shops the day before. He told her about the locket for his grandmother and the picture that was to go inside. He went on to tell them about the bracelet for his Auntie Babs. Bill hoped Joey wouldn't say anything about the ring. He would rather keep that quiet for the time being. As it happened, Joey didn't mention it. Perhaps, he hadn't seen him buy it.

"Look at our Christmas tree, Auntie Rachel. Daddy let me decorate it. Don't the lights look very pretty?"

"Yes, Joey, they do look pretty. And I especially like the fairy at the top. Did you put it up there?"

"Yes, I did." said Joey, proudly. He explained how his daddy had held him up high so he could reach the top.

Colin and Rachel stayed for about an hour before taking their leave. "I'll give you a ring over Christmas," Colin called out, as he was backing out of the drive. "Just to ask how things are." He stopped the car for a moment. "If you need us, don't hesitate to call. We'll come over anytime. We mean that."

"Thanks Colin, I'll remember."

Both Joey and Bill watched until the car turned the corner at the end of the road. "Auntie Rachel gave me a present," said Joey. "She said I had to wait until Christmas Day before I opened it so we put it under the Christmas tree."

"That was very kind of her," said Bill, suddenly remembering he had some presents upstairs for Colin's children. He had forgotten to take them into the office on Friday. "I hope you said thank you."

"Yes I did," answered Joey. "And she said I was a good boy and I had to take care of my daddy."

"Right then, son. Let's go and put those lamb chops in the oven for lunch." Taking Joey by the hand, Bill led him back indoors.

On the other side of town, Sally was also having a full morning. Vera and Tom called to look at her flat. She left them to look around on their own while she made some coffee.

"There's not much to see. It's small, but I've been very happy here," she said. "The neighbours are pleasant, but they go out to work, so we don't see a lot of each other. However, it's nice to know that if there's a problem we're here for each other."

Both Vera and Tom liked the flat and, over coffee, asked Sally to give them first refusal, should she want to sell it. Sally was delighted and promised to let them know when she was more certain of her plans.

Shortly afterwards, Vera and Tom left and Sally was alone once more.

After lunch, Bill took Joey to the Carol Concert in the town centre. Joey was delighted to see the enormous Christmas tree with its pretty coloured lights. Several choirs from the district had gathered to sing carols and a large crowd had turned out to hear them. Bill picked Joey up so he could see above the heads of all the people.

Many of the carols were old favourites. Joey didn't know the words, but he could read well enough to be able to follow them from the song sheets handed out earlier. The singing went on for about an hour, by which time most of the people were starting to feel cold.

"Shall we go somewhere for a hot drink," asked Bill.

"Yes please Daddy. Can I have a hot chocolate… please?" He wasn't sure if he needed to say another please. However, as his father thought it was an important word, he tagged one on the end anyway. Bill smiled to himself, but didn't say anything. Better too many than none at all.

They found a coffee shop close by and sat at a table by the window. Joey could still see the Christmas tree and all the people rushing about outside doing their last minute shopping. Bill glimpsed his secretary and her boy friend. Catching sight of Bill and Joey, she waved to them. Bill pointed them out to his son, explaining how the lady worked for him in the office.

"Does the man work for you as well?" Joey waved at them both.

"No," said Bill. "The man is her boyfriend. They love each other and will be getting married one day soon."

Vera and Tom gave a final wave before they moved off.

"And then will they live together like Nanna and Granddad?"

"Yes Joey. They will," said Bill wistfully. He wondered how long it would be before he and Sally could plan their wedding.

"Daddy, do you love anybody?" Joey had not forgotten his conversation with Miss Hughes when he was last at the nursery. He was still worried his father had no one to love him.

Bill was taken by surprise. "I love you Joey. You know that."

"Anybody else?"

"Well, Nanna and Granddad, of course" answered Bill. "And you ask too many questions."

"Yes I know. Miss Hughes told me I was inqui... inqui..." He broke off, not able to remember the word.

"Inquisitive, Joey. The word is inquisitive and Miss Hughes is right." He was pleased his son hadn't forgotten Sally. At least that was something.

"Does anybody love you, Daddy," said Joey. "I asked Miss Hughes but she didn't answer me, not properly anyway."

"Well I hope you love me Joey." Bill wanted to change the subject. "If you've finished your drink, shall we go home?"

"I've finished now, Daddy," said Joey.

"Come on then. Let's go." Setting off for home, Bill pondered over whether there was anything Joey hadn't said to Sally.

By seven o'clock Joey was so tired he couldn't keep his eyes open.

"Come on son, time for bed," said Bill. "I've kept you up too long. Especially as you didn't have a nap this afternoon." He took Joey upstairs, gave him a bath and put him to bed.

Joey put his arms around his father's neck and told him he loved him.

"You won't hide from me tomorrow morning will you?"

"No son. I won't hide from you. I promise. Tomorrow morning Santa will have been."

"Yes I know. And Nanna and Granddad and Auntie Babs and Uncle Jack are coming." Joey could say Barbara but always called her Babs like his father.

"Go to sleep Joey and tomorrow will soon be here," said Bill.

Going into his own bedroom, he looked around. There was still the faint smell of Sally's perfume. He went back downstairs and poured himself a drink. After about fifteen minutes he made sure Joey was asleep before telephoning Sally.

"Hello sweetheart," he said, when she answered. "I miss you."

"I miss you too. What have you been up to today?"

Bill told her Colin and Rachel had called to leave a Christmas present for Joey. He went on to tell her he and his son had spent the afternoon in town singing carols around the Christmas tree. Sally told Bill about Vera and Tom calling to view her flat.

"Just a minute Sally, I think I can hear Joey stirring." He went upstairs and peeped into Joey's room, but found him still sound asleep.

Passing his own bedroom on the way back he shuddered at the thought of him sleeping in there without Sally. Making his way downstairs, an idea formed in his mind.

"Sally," he said, picking up the phone. "Come over here, this evening… now. Get a taxi and come over. Joey is sound asleep. He was so tired I think he'll sleep right through the night. He seldom wakes up anyway."

"Do you mean it, Bill? Really mean it? What will you tell Joey tomorrow?"

"At the moment I haven't a clue. However, don't worry, I'll think of something. Please say you'll come. You'll have to get a taxi, though. I daren't leave Joey in the house alone. Not after this morning. I'll pay the driver when you get here." Bill quickly told her what had happened that morning.

"Bill, I wouldn't let you leave him anyway. I'll try a couple of cab companies and give you a ring back." She hung up.

Bill went through to the kitchen and put some wine in the fridge.

It wouldn't be easy getting a taxi at this time on Christmas Eve. He wondered what they would do if that was the case. The phone rang and he dashed out into the hall to pick it up, not wanting the noise to awaken Joey.

"Someone can pick me up in about half an hour on his way to another job." Sally's voice came down the line. "I'll go and sort out something to wear for tomorrow. You're parents are going to be there aren't they? I want to make a good impression."

"Sally, you'll make a good impression whatever you're wearing. They're going to love you, I simply know they will."

"I'll see you in a little while," she replied. "I hope we're doing the right thing. As far as Joey is concerned, I mean."

"See you soon," said Bill and hung up.

He spent the time placing Joey's presents around the Christmas tree and ate the mince pie Joey had insisted on leaving for Santa, making sure he left a few crumbs on the plate.

It was about an hour later when the taxi pulled up outside Bill's house. He went out to pay the fare. Sally said she would see to it, but Bill wouldn't hear of it. He gave the driver the money and an extra fifty-pounds for himself.

"Thanks mate," said the driver, unable to believe his luck. He reached out to shake Bill's hand. "Have a Merry Christmas."

I will now," said Bill. He picked Sally up and swung her around much to the amusement of one of his elderly neighbours who was out walking his dog.

"Good evening Mr Fraser. Merry Christmas to you," Bill called out.

"And the same to you, Bill," he replied, recalling how good it was to be young.

Bill carried Sally and her case into the house. Putting her down, he closed the door behind him. He pulled her to him and kissed her. "Sally I've missed you so much. I hope we don't have to go on like this for too long. I couldn't stand it."

"I've missed you too Bill. I don't know when I've felt so miserable."

"Have you eaten?" he asked, leading her through into the lounge.

"Yes," she replied. "Shortly before you rang."

"I've put some wine in the fridge. Would you like some or perhaps you would you like something else to drink?"

"Wine will be fine, thank you."

Bill disappeared into the kitchen and returned with the bottle and two glasses. "Joey is sound asleep and I think he'll sleep though the night." He poured two glasses of wine and handed one to Sally. "We'll have to be up early in the morning, he usually bursts into my bedroom as soon as he's awake."

"In that case," said Sally, taking a sip from her glass. "I think we should take this wine upstairs and have an early night, don't you?"

"I'm not going to argue with you, Sally." Bill smiled.

Creeping up the stairs, they went into the bedroom and Bill closed the door. He led Sally across to the bed and took the wine from her and placed it on the bedside table. Pulling her to him, he kissed her. "I love you so much," he said.

"I know you do, Bill. And I love you, too."

Bill could smell her perfume, the same perfume that had haunted him for the last two days. He began to unbutton her blouse and she undid his shirt and before long they both lay naked on the bed, locked in a passionate embrace.

"Would you like anymore wine Sally?" said Bill, a while later. "I'm afraid it's rather warm now though."

Sally held out her glass and Bill refilled it. He still had one arm tightly around her – almost as though he was afraid she would disappear.

"I'd better set the alarm," said Bill. "I think it would be best if we were downstairs when Joey gets up. He's usually bouncing around on my bed by about seven o'clock. Shall I make it for six?"

"Six o'clock!" she uttered. "It's still the middle of the night, but being here with you makes it worthwhile. All this cloak and dagger stuff makes me feel like someone at boarding school having a feast after lights out. You know, like the ones in the girl's magazines or comics?"

"I didn't read girl's magazines or comics," he laughed. "Come to think of it, I didn't read boy's magazines or comics either."

"What *did* you read then?" asked Sally.

"My head was always stuck in some maths text book. Or any book to do with figures. I enjoyed anything like that. Right from an early age I always had a head for figures. No one bothered me, so I was left alone."

"That is so sad." Sally sipped at her wine. "Everyone needs to have fun with friends sometimes. It allows you to let off steam occasionally."

"I know. That's why I don't want Joey to be like me. Yes, I want him to do well at school and I'll encourage him in any way I can. Already I can see that he is very intelligent for his age. But I also want him to enjoy being with people. I want him to be able to communicate with them without feeling awkward." He paused. "Like Colin, I suppose." He grinned. "Well – perhaps only a tiny bit like Colin. He can be very outrageous at times."

He went on to explain why he sent Joey to the nursery. "It would have been easier for me if I'd engaged a live in nanny. But when Mrs Miller said she would take Joey I didn't hesitate. She was the ideal solution. It meant he was going to meet other children. However, enough of that, I think you should get your beauty sleep. We have a long day ahead of us." Taking Sally's empty glass, he placed the covers around her, as she slid down the bed. Lying beside her, he reached out and switched off the light. "Good night, darling."

"What do you mean goodnight? I want you to make love to me again."

"Anything to oblige," Bill replied, snuggling down under the covers.

Day Twelve

The alarm rang out at six o'clock and Bill reached over quickly to switch it off. He didn't want to awaken Joey too early. Leaning across Sally, he asked whether she was awake.

"No!" She pulled the covers over her head.

Bill laughed. "Okay. I'll get dressed first. You can lie there for a while longer."

It wasn't long before he was dressed, shaved and ready to go downstairs.

"Sally," he said. "I'm going downstairs now. I'll put the coffee on."

He waited for a reply, but there was none. He bent over her. "Sally darling, you're still awake, aren't you?"

Sally poked her head out of the covers. "Yes, of course I'm awake." Reaching up, she put her arms around his neck and pulled him close to her. She kissed him. "You go downstairs. I won't be long."

"I don't know that I want to go now." He sat down on the bed and kissed her again.

"Go!" she said, pointing to the door. "There definitely isn't time this morning."

"Okay, I'll go," he replied laughing. "This time I agree with you."

Sally showered and dressed as quickly as possible. After having coffee and toast, she went through to the lounge carrying the present she had bought for Joey.

Bill followed her. "Sally. I have a present for you, but would you mind if I gave it to you later? After we all grew up and went our separate ways, we started exchanging our gifts after Christmas lunch. By then we were all together, except, of course for Sue, who had moved to Canada."

"That's a lovely idea Bill. I'll save your present until then too."

"Daddy, Daddy. Where are you?" Joey called from the upstairs landing. "It's Christmas Morning."

"I'm here son." Bill went out into the hall. "Wait a moment, I'll come and get your dressing gown for you."

Walking across to the Christmas tree, Sally knelt down and placed Joey's gift alongside the others. She stretched over to read what was written on a large parcel. '*To our favourite Godson. From Auntie Rachel and Uncle Colin.*' She hadn't realised they were his Godparents. But why wouldn't they be? As she understood it, they were Bill's oldest and dearest friends.

Her thoughts were interrupted when the door flew open and Joey rushed in. He stopped in his tracks when he saw Sally.

She held out her hand to him. "Hello Joey."

He stood there for a few moments, not saying a word. Sally panicked. What was wrong? The last time he had seen her, he had opened up and told her all sorts of things. Was he upset at seeing her in his house?

Suddenly Joey called out, "Daddy! Daddy! Come quick. Come and see what Santa has brought me. He got my letter, Daddy! He really got my letter and he's brought me a mummy… and it's Miss Hughes."

Bill arrived in the sitting room in time to see Joey run over to Sally and fling his arms around her neck. "Daddy, look, Santa has brought me a mummy," he cried out in joy.

"Joey," said Bill. "I don't think…"

Placing her finger over her lips she shook her head. If that was what Joey wanted to believe, then so be it. It could all be explained another time. "Come on Joey. Open your other presents. Your daddy and I will help you."

Bill couldn't believe his good fortune. At least Joey was pleased to see Sally, even if he did believe Santa had dropped her down the chimney.

Joey wouldn't let Sally out of his sight all morning. It was as though he believed his new mummy might disappear as quickly as she had arrived. He even wanted to help her and his father prepare the Christmas lunch. "Wait until I show Nanna what Santa brought me," he repeated, several times.

Bill was setting out the drinks in the sitting room when he heard a car pull onto the drive. Looking out, he saw his parents together with his sister and her family. Quietly, he let himself out the front door and hurried down the drive to meet them.

Stepping out of the car, Jack held out his hand and wished Bill a Merry Christmas. Bill shook hands, before turning to his mother who was still sitting in the back seat with Barbara.

"Mum, Dad, I have something to tell you… It's good news though," he added quickly, seeing a look of anxiety spreading across his mother's face. "Mum! I have a girlfriend."

Quickly jumping out of the car, Anne hugged her son. "Bill, I'm so pleased for you."

His father rushed around the car to shake his hand. "Son, this is wonderful news, I'm delighted for you."

"You sly devil." Barbara was still sitting in the car holding a carrycot containing her baby. She grinned at her brother. "Why didn't you tell us? Is it anyone we know?"

"No, Babs," Bill replied. "Her name is Sally – Sally Hughes. She's wonderful, she's beautiful and I love her, and she loves me." He turned back to his mother. "I'm sure you'll like her, Mum."

"Bill, if she's responsible for this change in you, then I like her already. But, Hughes, I know that name, don't I? Isn't she the girl who stood in at Joey's nursery school last week?"

"Yes that's her," said Bill. "She's here now. She came over to help with the lunch and Joey found her under the Christmas tree this morning. He thought Santa had brought him a mummy. He's very excited about it. Apparently he asked for one in a letter he wrote to Santa at nursery school." He hesitated. "However, there is one problem. Joey doesn't seem to like me touching Sally. If I hold her hand, he stares at me until I move away. He's done that all morning. We're both a bit upset about it."

"She must have been here pretty early this morning for Joey to find her under the Christmas tree." Barbara laughed. She was like Colin. She loved teasing her brother and had done so since they were children.

"Okay Babs, I'll come clean. She's been here all night. I called her over after Joey had gone to bed last night." He paused. "I suppose you might as well know, it'll probably come out anyway. She was here all last week. She only went home on Friday when Joey was due back. She didn't want him to think I had moved her in while he was away."

"That was thoughtful of her," said Anne. She sighed. "Come on. I want to meet this young lady."

"Go careful Mum," said Bill. "She's a bit shy."

"Shyness is something we all know plenty about," replied Anne, briskly. However, seeing the worried expression on her son's face she quickly added, "Don't worry Bill. It'll be all right. We'll all be on our best behaviour." She looked at her daughter. "Won't we Barbara?" She knew how Barbara loved to tease her brother.

Bill helped his sister out of the car. "You have a beautiful baby Babs. Mum said you'd called her, Wendy. That's a pretty name."

"Thank you Bill. We thought Wendy had a nice ring to it."

Stepping into the hall, they could hear Sally's voice through the kitchen door. "That's right sweetheart. You're being such a big help to me"

Bill showed his family into the sitting room and took their coats.

"Make yourselves comfortable. I'll bring Sally through."

The moment Bill had left the room, Anne turned to Barbara. "Even if this girl has two heads and a tail, I don't want you teasing your brother – especially not today. It's been a long time since I've seen him this happy, so I don't want you upsetting him with any foolish remarks. We all know he needs some good luck for a change."

"Your mother's right," said her father. "There's a time for joking and this isn't it."

Jack put his arm around his wife and nodded in agreement. "We wouldn't like it would we?"

"Okay Mum." Barbara grinned. "I won't tease my big brother… Well, not today anyway."

In the kitchen, Bill spoke to Joey. "Nanna's here. Go into the sitting room and say hello. I'll bring Sally."

"Oh Bill. I'm so nervous about meeting your family." Sally took off her apron.

"Not half as I was at meeting yours," laughed Bill. "How do you think I felt? As far as they were concerned, I was the wicked man who had lured their daughter to my bed, wasn't I? Come on, it'll be fine."

"Do I look alright?" Sally smoothed down her dress. "Is this dress okay? Should I have tied up my hair? Do you think they'll like me? Do…?"

"Sally you look absolutely wonderful and they'll love you," interrupted Bill. Taking her hand, he led her through to the sitting room. "Mum, Dad, I would like you to meet Sally."

Not knowing what to expect, they all turned to look at the young woman standing next to Bill. Barbara and her mother glanced at each other. They had both noticed that Sally was holding Bill's hand so tightly her knuckles had turned white.

Anne walked across to Sally and hugged her. "I'm so happy to meet you."

"And I'm pleased to meet you, Mrs Roberts." Sally felt relieved. Bill's mother seemed warm and friendly.

"Nanna, this is my new Mummy. Santa left her for me last night."

"Well Joey," said Anne. "I think you must have been a very good boy for Santa to leave you such a lovely present."

Bill introduced Sally to the rest of his family and then asked everyone what they would like to drink. He went into the kitchen to get some water for his father's whisky.

Barbara followed him. "Bill, she's beautiful." Unable to resist a little dig, she added, "What on earth can a lovely young woman like that see in you?"

"It must be my irresistible charm, little sister."

Barbara hugged her brother. "I'm so happy for you. I'm sure Joey will be okay."

"I hope so, Babs." Bill paused. "You know, I love her so much I couldn't live without her. If she were to leave me now… well, I don't know what I'd do. I can't tell you what it's been like without her these last few days." He hesitated. "Actually Barbara, while we're on our own, there's something I've been meaning to ask you for some time… If anything happened to me, you and Jack would take care of Joey, wouldn't you? I'll make sure you have enough money, so you'd never have to worry about finances. And then there's this house…"

"Of course we would take care of Joey." Barbara reached out and put her hand on her brother's arm. She felt a little uneasy at where this conversation was going. "Jack and I look on him as a son anyway. But you have your whole life ahead of you, Bill. Nothing is going to happen to you."

"No… No, of course not." replied Bill. "It's just something that's crossed my mind a couple of times, that's all." He shrugged his shoulders, "Come on, we'd better get back to the others."

Back in the sitting room Anne frowned at Barbara. She hoped she hadn't been teasing her brother. Bill sat down on the sofa next to Sally. He placed his arm around her shoulders, but removed it when he saw his son staring at him.

"Did you have a good journey down from the north, Jack?" asked Bill. "Was the traffic bad?"

"Not half as bad as it was coming here this morning. We were held up so many times," he replied. "We should have been here ages ago. I don't think I would like to live down here anymore. It takes so long to get anywhere."

"Where's Bess, Nanna?" asked Joey.

"Your friend, David, is looking after her," said Anne. "You know how she hates to travel in the car."

Joey nodded. He remembered when they went on a picnic once, Bess had howled all the way there and back and his granddad had been very cross about it.

After everyone had chatted for a while, Bill refilled everyone's glass. When he returned to his seat, he took Sally's hand in his, but pulled away when he saw Joey staring at him.

Sally stood up; she had tears in her eyes. "Excuse me, I'll go and check on the lunch." She hurried out of the room.

Bill was about to follow her, but his mother stopped him. "No, I'll go." In the kitchen, she saw Sally standing by the window and went across and put her arms around her.

"Mrs Roberts," said Sally. "I love your son very much. He's the most wonderful man I've ever met. We were hoping Joey would accept us being together, but he seems to hate me being near to Bill and I don't know what to do about it."

"It'll be alright," said Anne. "You'll see. Joey will come around."

"I hope so," said Sally, sadly. "I know it's not his fault. He's only a little boy and he doesn't understand." She paused for a few moments. "Mrs Roberts," she said eventually, "I think it would be best if I went home, at least for today. It's Christmas Day and my being here is spoiling it for everyone. I really can't let that happen, I know how much you've been looking forward to spending Christmas together. I've prepared the lunch and the table is all set in the dining room. You can take over now. You don't need me."

"Please, Sally, you can't go. Bill needs you," Anne pleaded. "Even I can see that it would break his heart if you leave now."

However, Sally hadn't heard. She was already making her way upstairs.

Anne hurried through to the sitting room. "Bill. You'd better come."

"What is it, Mum?" Bill asked when they were out in the hall. "What's happened? Is Sally ill?"

"Bill. There's no easy way to say this, Sally's going home. She's upstairs getting her things together."

The colour drained from Bill's face, as raced up the stairs two at a time. He found Sally sitting on the bed. She was crying.

"Sally, please don't go." He put his arms around her. "I love you, sweetheart. I need you."

"I'm sorry Bill, but I think it would be better if I went home. If I stay it will only spoil it for you all. I'll walk home; it's not too far. Besides, it'll give me time to think. I've told your mother lunch is all prepared. There's not much left for her to do."

"Time to think about what?" A pit formed in Bill's stomach. His whole world was caving in around him. "Sally, darling, please don't say you're leaving me."

Sally quickly looked up when she heard the note of anxiety in Bill's voice. She was shocked at how pale and worried he looked. "No Bill! No of course not. I couldn't leave you. I love you too much. I simply meant that perhaps there's another way of doing this. I could stay away until after the holidays. Then I'll ask Jane if I can help her out at the nursery, she's always telling me it would be good experience. It would give Joey more time to get to know me."

"And what do we do in the meantime?" asked Bill. "Say hello when I drop him off in the mornings and goodbye when I collect him at night? That could go on for months. Sally, I need you with me, I can't live without you."

"Well perhaps you could invite me for tea at weekends," she said. "Then Joey would get used to seeing me about the house."

"It could still take weeks, Sally." Bill felt even more miserable at the prospect. To have her call at the house, but not to be able to touch her, to kiss her, to make love to her…

"Bill, I think I should go now." Sally interrupted his thoughts. "You must get back to your family. You can't leave them sitting down there, they'll be wondering what's going on." As she spoke she began to stand up, but Bill pulled her back to him.

"Please Sally, please don't go."

"Bill, I don't want to go," she sobbed. "But I must. It's the only way. We knew that this might happen. We should have been more prepared. Please don't make it any harder for me than it already is. Between us we'll work something out, but now I must leave."

Meanwhile, downstairs Anne looked very distraught when she walked back into the sitting room. John asked her what was going on.

"Sally's leaving," she said.

Barbara looked up quickly. "Why? What's happened? Is there anything we can do?" She paused for a moment, before continuing without giving her mother a chance to reply. "Mum, if she goes, Bill may never get over it. Even I can see that. We've got to do something." She thought back to the conversation she'd had with her brother in the kitchen. What was it he had said – something about not being able to face living without Sally? He had asked her to promise to take care of Joey should anything happen to him. Was this the sort of situation he'd had in mind? It was all falling into place. Oh my God, if Sally left him now, what would he do? Barbara had never felt more concerned for her brother than she did at this moment. Her mother's voice jolted her back to the present.

"Of course we have to do something," snapped Anne, "But what?"

"What's the problem?" asked Bill's father.

"Sally's finding it difficult today," said Anne, pointing at Joey. "He doesn't seem to want Bill to be near to her."

Barbara nodded. She had noticed how Joey behaved whenever Bill and Sally were together.

Joey's face clouded and he started to cry. He had been listening to his grandmother and aunt talking and was very upset his lovely new mummy was going to leave him. "Nanna. She can't go away. She's my mummy. Santa brought her. Tell her, Nanna. Please tell her she can't go away."

"She can go if she wants to Joey," said Anne. "We can't stop her, but I don't think she really wants to go home. You know, Santa brought her for your daddy as well as for you. Mummies are there for daddies too." She paused for a moment desperately trying to think of what to say next. Suddenly remembered the conversation she had overheard on Friday morning. "Can you remember what your friends told you when you were asking them what mummies did?"

"Yes," said Joey. "They said their mummies looked after them and their daddies as well. They did the washing and the cooking for them."

"And what else did they say mummies did?" asked Anne.

Joey looked at her and thought for a minute. "They hugged them all the time, and hugged their daddies as well."

"That's right," said Anne.

"And they said their mummies slept in the same bed as their daddies," he continued. "And David said his mummy was in bed kissing his daddy and he was lying on…"

Anne interrupted before he could say anymore. "Yes… Well, we'll leave that bit for the moment."

Barbara looked at her mother and grinned. "What else did David say about his daddy?" she asked.

"Well Sally doesn't think you want her to hug and kiss your daddy," continued Anne, giving Barbara a warning frown. "She loves you both, exactly as a mummy should. However, she thinks you want her all to yourself and you don't want to share her with your daddy. That's why she's thinking of leaving you both."

"Steady on Anne," said her husband. "He's only a little boy. I really don't think you should…" He paused when Anne peered at him over the top of her glasses. "What do *you* think Joey? What do *you* want?" she continued.

Barbara went across to her father. "Dad, the situation is desperate. You know Mum wouldn't normally speak to Joey like this," she whispered. "However, right now we have to think about Bill."

Her father nodded and patted her hand. "I know. It's just that…" his voice trailed off as Joey started to speak again.

"I want her to love both of us, Nanna," he said. "I do want to share her with Daddy. We always share everything. I want her to stay here with both of us."

"Of course you do, sweetie," said Anne. "You want her to be a mummy exactly like the ones your friends have, don't you? Why else would you have asked them what their mummies did? So you see you mustn't get upset if your daddy wants to hold your mummy's hand, or hug her, like he does with you. It's what mummies and daddies do when they love each other."

Joey nodded. "I know Nanna and I wasn't upset. I want Daddy to love my mummy the way I do. I only looked at Daddy because I haven't seen him hug anyone else before."

Barbara looked at her mother. "All that worry for nothing."

Why don't you and I go upstairs now and tell her before she goes out to find another little boy to be a mummy to?" said Anne.

"Jack, look after Wendy. I'm going too." Not wanting to miss anything, Barbara thrust the baby into Jack's arms.

All three climbed the stairs. Still holding Sally tightly, Bill looked up as they came into the room. He was deathly white, but this time he kept his arms around Sally, even though his son was there. Barbara gasped. She had never seen her brother look so ill.

"Please Mum. Not now," Bill mumbled.

"Joey has something to say to you both – and I think you should listen," said Anne, before Bill could argue. She pushed Joey forward. "Go on Joey. Tell your mummy what you told me."

Walking over to the bed, Joey looked at Sally and his father. "Please Mummy. I don't want you to go away." Looking back at his grandmother, she smiled and waved him forward, encouraging him to continue. Joey turned back to Sally. "I want you to stay and love me and my daddy."

"I told Joey he shouldn't get upset if his daddy wanted to hug his mummy," said Anne. "And what did you tell me Joey?"

Joey looked at his father and Sally and repeated what he had said downstairs.

Sally looked first at Bill and then at Joey. Holding out her arms, she beckoned Joey to come to her. Lifting him onto her knee she said, "I love you Joey and I love your daddy. I was rather hoping we could all be happy together."

Looking at his father, Joey whispered. "Santa won't take her away from us will he Daddy?"

"No son. I don't think so. Not now," he replied, glancing at Sally.

She smiled at him and shook her head. "No, Joey. Santa won't take me away."

"Right," said Anne, briskly. "Barbara and I will take Joey downstairs. I'm sure he would like to help us finish the lunch. Bill, you take care of Sally. We'll give you a shout if you're not down when lunch is ready."

Anne took Joey's hand and led him to the door. "We'll go downstairs and leave your daddy and mummy alone for a little while. They'll come down when they're ready."

Barbara went across to Sally and gave her a hug. "Take as long as you like. There's plenty of time." She turned to her brother and winked. "I'll forget to put the potatoes in the oven." She went out, closing the door behind her.

"Sally. You gave me such a fright." Bill was still shaking but he looked a little less pale. "I was so afraid you were going to leave."

"Bill. I couldn't have stayed here today. I think it would have spoiled it for everyone. And to think it was all a terrible misunderstanding. We didn't handle it very well, did we?"

"No and it was my fault," said Bill. "I should have spoken to Joey and my mother about you before today."

Suddenly the telephone on the bedside table began to ring.

"Someone downstairs will get it." Bill didn't want to let go of Sally for fear she might change her mind and go home after all.

"Oh it's you, Colin." Anne's voice rang out from downstairs. "Merry Christmas to you, Rachel and the children. Yes everything is fine here." There was a pause, then, "Can I ask him to give you a ring back? He's upstairs with Sally at the moment." There was another pause, then. "Yes, I'll be sure to tell him. Give my love to your parents. Speak to you soon. 'Bye."

Bill groaned when he heard Anne put down the receiver. "Perhaps I should have taken the call after all. Colin is going to tease me about being upstairs with you. You know what he'll be thinking, don't you?"

"Well Bill, my darling," Sally grinned, as she undid his tie and unbuttoned his shirt. "Colin could be right."

"I really don't know how I'm going to face your family when we go downstairs." It was an hour or so later and Sally was getting dressed. "I've probably ruined their Christmas Day."

"No you haven't. Dad and Jack will be enjoying my Malt Whisky as we speak. And no doubt my mother and sister will be at the sherry or wine bottles."

Sally laughed. "Can you zip up my dress please?" Once Bill pulled up the zip, she turned to face him. "What do you think? Will I do?"

"Sally, sweetheart, I've told you before, you always look beautiful in anything you wear." He pulled her to him and kissed her.

"Come on. We'll go down together." He hesitated. "Oh, and by the way, don't mind my sister. She teases me like mad. Always has done. She's a bit like Colin; she loves to see me squirm. If she makes some remark about..." he inclined his head towards the bed. "Don't take any notice. It's me she's having a dig at."

"All right, Bill," said Sally, gripping his hand tightly. "Let's get this over with."

In the sitting room, it was as Bill had said. His father was refilling Jack's glass from a whisky bottle, while his mother and sister were both drinking sherry. Bill shot a grin at Sally.

"Sally. You look beautiful," said Barbara. "And what a gorgeous figure you have. I must say my big brother has good taste."

"Thank you," said Sally, gripping Bill's hand even tighter. "I must apologise for my behaviour earlier. I'm really sorry for upsetting you all."

"Forget it." Anne walked over to Sally and gave her a hug. "We all have. I'm sorry but lunch is running late. Barbara forgot to put the potatoes into the oven. I don't know what's wrong with the girl."

Bill looked at his sister and winked.

"Right Sally," he said, rubbing his hands together. "What do you want to drink?"

"A glass of white wine please." Sally looked around the room. "Where's Joey?"

"He went up to his room to play with his new carriage from you and the station he got from Colin and Rachel," said Barbara. "We told him under no circumstances was he to go into your room."

"We didn't hear him." Bill sounded surprised.

"I don't suppose you did." Barbara winked at her brother. "And I don't suppose you heard him racing around down here in his new pedal car either?"

Bill grinned at his sister and shook his head. "Not a thing," he said. "But would you really have expected us to?"

"No." Barbara noted how her brother didn't seem to be so easily embarrassed. Normally he would, at the very least, have run his finger around his collar.

"I'll go up and make sure he's okay." Sally went to the door. "I don't want him to think I'm cross with him."

As soon as Sally left the room, Anne spoke to her son. "Can we take it everything is alright now? We were all worried sick down here."

"Yes, thanks to you," said Bill. "I handled it badly though, didn't I? I should have spoken to Joey about her. You know if she'd gone, I'd have been devastated. My life has changed so much this last week. I even turned down the Chairman's request to take on the finances of another branch simply because she asked me to."

"If she has that sort of influence on you, then all I can say is, I want her to stay as much as you do." said Anne. "Bill, your father and I noticed the change in you on Friday. We even told Barbara and Jack about it when they arrived yesterday, but we didn't know the reason why. If you had only mentioned Sally earlier, I could have told you how Joey hadn't stopped talking about her all week. He told us how you all went to have a pizza together because you were late in picking him up. He really likes her…." She shrugged. "Never mind it's over now so we should forget it." Pausing, she glanced around at all the members of her family. "Truthfully, I'd rather this subject was never mentioned again. But most certainly, never in front of Sally."

They all nodded in agreement.

"There you both are," said Bill, as Sally and Joey came into the room. "We were wondering what had happened to you. Here's your wine Sally. Joey, would you like me to get you some juice?"

"Yes… please, Daddy," said Joey, remembering to add the please.

Somehow he had upset his father and new mummy once already this morning. He wasn't sure what he had done wrong, but he certainly didn't want to do it again.

"Bill, I nearly forgot," said Anne. "Colin rang. I said I would get you to call him back."

Bill glanced across at Sally. She was grinning at him. "Okay Mum," he said. "I'll ring him later. They'll probably be in the middle of lunch now."

"As we would be, if Barbara hadn't forgotten the potatoes," said Anne. "I'll go to check on them; hopefully we will be having lunch very soon."

"I'll come with you Mum," said Barbara standing up. She grinned at her brother before following her mother out of the room. About ten minutes later she came back and announced lunch was ready.

After lunch it was time to exchange their Christmas presents. Bill suddenly felt very nervous. Though he had planned to give Sally the engagement ring at the table, he had forgotten it would actually mean proposing to her in front of his whole family. Nevertheless, he would have to go through with it now. He went over to the small table in the corner and picked up the presents.

"These are for you," he said, handing out two parcels to his parents. "And these are for Barbara and Jack. The cheque is for Wendy. I didn't know what else to get for her. You can open an account in her name, or buy whatever she needs at the moment. I've made it out to you." Then he went across to his son "This is for you Joey." He had bought an extra gift for his son, not wanting him to feel left out.

When everyone had begun to open their presents, Bill went to Sally and bent down on one knee. He opened the small box, which held the engagement ring and almost whispered, "This is for you Sally, my darling. Will you marry me?" His hands trembled, as he waited for her reply.

No one had heard him propose to Sally, but they did hear her response. "Bill, of course I'll marry you," she squealed. Everyone looked up, as she took the ring from the box. "Oh Bill, it's the most beautiful ring I've ever seen. Thank you so much." She asked Bill to slide it onto her finger. It was a perfect fit. She put her arms around Bill's neck. "I love you so much."

"I love you too Sally." He kissed her.

"Let the poor girl come up for air, Bill," Barbara laughed.

"Sorry," said Bill laughing. "For a moment, I'd forgotten you were all here."

Anne was the first on her feet to congratulate the couple. She was so happy for her son, she laughed and cried at the same time. Sally had certainly brought him out of his shell. "Bill, Sally, I'm so pleased for you both." Tears streamed down her cheeks, as she hugged him. How she had longed for this moment.

Barbara was also delighted for her brother. She wanted to hug and congratulate him, but she held back, allowing her mother to speak to him first. Like her mother, she had worried about him ever meeting anyone after Julie died. He was such a shy person. Though she enjoyed teasing him and laughing at his embarrassment, she would never stand by and let anyone else do it – with the exception of Colin. She knew how Colin teased Bill. However, he had been a good friend to him for a long time and had always been there whenever her brother needed someone to talk to. Besides, he would never embarrass Bill in front of anyone else – she would most certainly have something to say if he did and Colin knew that. "I'm delighted for you, Bill – for you both," she said, hugging her brother when she finally got near him. "This is surely the best Christmas ever."

Turning her attention to Sally, Barbara hugged her. She could see how overwhelmed the young woman was by the fuss. Bill was right. Sally was shy. That had worried her at first. Did Bill really need someone as shy as himself? But now she could see how good Sally was for him.

She watched Bill place a protective arm around Sally's shoulder. She had never seen him do that with Julie. He had loved her of course, but he would never have been so demonstrative in front of his family. How long had he known this girl? A little more than a week and already Bill was a changed person. After all, he had even proposed to her in front of them all. "Sally, you're wonderful person and so perfect for Bill, and we all love you."

"Thank you, thank you all so much." Sally looked across towards Joey. He was sitting in his chair looking a little left out. "Come over here," she beckoned him. "Come and give Mummy a hug and see my new ring."

Joey rushed over to her and she hugged him tight. "Isn't it beautiful?" Sally showed him the ring.

"Yes," said Joey. "I was with Daddy when he bought it."

"I thought you hadn't noticed," said Bill, slightly bemused. "You didn't mention it to Uncle Colin, but you did tell him about Nanna and Auntie Babs' presents.

"But I didn't know who it was for," said Joey.

Picking up Joey, Sally gave him another hug. "I love you."

"I know," said Joey. "You told me before I went to my nanna's house. And you said you liked my daddy very much as well."

"Don't you ever forget anything?" Sally blushed.

"No, he doesn't." Anne laughed. "Well now, let me give everyone their presents."

Both Barbara and Anne apologised to Sally, for not having a gift for her. "We didn't know anything about you until this morning."

Sally told them not to worry. "I have all I want," she said, taking Bill's hand. "The only presents I have to give, are one for Bill, though it's not half as exciting as the one he's just given me and a small one for you Mrs Roberts."

"Please, my dear, you must call me Anne." She beamed.

"Bill and I will clear away and load the dishwasher. It's the very least we can do after this morning," said Sally, once all the presents were opened.

"There's no need, Sally. We can all give a hand," said Barbara. "And, can I please add that we've all forgotten about this morning."

"No, I insist." Sally pointed to the door. "You all go and have another drink. Bill and I will soon sort this lot out. Won't we, darling?"

"Anything you say sweetheart," said Bill. "I don't care what we do, as long as we're together. Joey, be a good boy and go with Nanna and Granddad. Play quietly with your toys while Mummy and I clear up, we'll be with you shortly."

Once everything was cleared away, Bill was reluctant to go back into the sitting room. Here in the kitchen, he had Sally all to himself. He put his arms around her and kissed her.

"Bill, tomorrow morning would you take me home so I can get some more clothes? I didn't bring very much with me yesterday."

"Off course I will. Just tell me when you want to go. Bring all you need. We'll load up the car." He grinned. "But you might like to bring a nightdress or pyjamas. Joey usually comes in and jumps on the bed first thing in the morning. I could speak to him about it if you like and ask him not to."

"No," said Sally quickly. "Let's not change anything. And Bill, for your information, I had a nightdress here all last week. But you never gave me a chance to put it on!"

There was a chuckle from the doorway. They turned and saw Barbara and Jack grinning at them.

Bill groaned. "I don't believe it," he murmured in Sally's ear.

"I'm sorry Bill. I didn't know anyone was listening."

"Don't worry, Sally." Barbara walked across to her. "I'm not going to say a thing. I don't want to upset my brother today; especially after he has given us such generous presents. We only came in to ask if you would look after Wendy for a few minutes. I'd ask Mum but she and Dad have fallen asleep in the sitting room. Jack and I want to sort out our luggage.

"Of course I'll look after Wendy." Sally took the baby from Barbara. "I'd be delighted."

"You take Wendy into the sitting room, while I go and give Colin a ring and get it over with," said Bill.

"What're you going to say to him?" Sally grinned.

"I'll deny everything," answered Bill, laughing.

"Merry Christmas, I believe you phoned earlier," said Bill when Colin answered the phone.

"Yes. It was only to ask if everything was all right, but your mother said you were both upstairs, so I guessed it was. Can't you leave the girl alone for five minutes?" Colin's laughter rippled down the phone.

"Colin, simply because we were upstairs doesn't mean... Oh, what the heck. You're right."

"I knew it, I just knew it." Colin laughed all the more. "You're a randy devil, Bill."

Bill smiled to himself. "Sally and I got engaged today. Would you all like to come over tomorrow afternoon and have a drink or two?"

"Congratulations Bill! I'm delighted to hear it. Rachel and I will definitely be there, but my parents may prefer to stay here and sleep it off. Mum's getting over a rather nasty cold. I'll ask them, though, and see what they say."

"I've had another thought – you said you had Alan's number," said Bill. "Give him a ring and ask if he and Judy would like to come over as well. And Colin, try not to make it sound like a command. They may have something else on."

"Okay. I'll ask him politely," said Colin. "But mark my words, he'll be over like a shot. He won't want to miss a chance like this. I told you, he sees you as his hero. See you tomorrow, and Bill, congratulations again. I know Rachel will be as pleased as I am."

"Thanks Colin. Come anytime after four."

Colin put down the receiver and told Rachel about the engagement and the invitation for drinks the next day.

"He's asked me to invite Alan and Judy. I'll do it now, otherwise we'll have a few more drinks and I'll more than likely forget. He may be at Judy's house of course and I don't have her number."

He dialled Alan's number. The phone rang for some time before Alan answered.

"Hello Alan. It's Colin. I was almost about to hang up. I thought you must be spending Christmas Day with Judy and her parents."

"I am," answered Alan. "But I forgot to take something over there and just popped back for it. What's up? Not a problem I hope."

"No, not at all. Bill asked me to give you a call. He and Sally got engaged today and he's invited us over to his house tomorrow for a few drinks. Can you and Judy make it? He did say to stress you don't have to go. His actual words were – it's not a command, only if you want to.'"

Alan didn't hesitate. "We'd love to go. We aren't doing anything special."

Colin smiled to himself. Even if they were, he would probably have cancelled it.

"Okay then, any time after four. And Alan, it's only a few drinks. Nothing formal. There's no need to dress up." Colin passed on Bill's address.

"Okay. See you there. Thanks for ringing, Colin."

"What did he say?" asked Rachel, when Colin put the phone down.

"They're going." Colin laughed. "I knew he would. If Bill asked him to fly to the moon in an air balloon, he'd do it."

"As bad as that, is it?" laughed Rachel. "But seriously I'm really pleased about the engagement. They're made for each other. Joey mustn't have been a problem after all. No doubt we'll hear all about it in time. Or at least you will."

"I quite agree. They are made for each other," said Colin. "And Rachel, for your information, Bill doesn't tell me everything, just nearly everything."

"What did Colin say?" asked Sally, when Bill came into the sitting room.

"He said I was a randy devil." Bill whispered, after checking his parents were still asleep and Joey was out of earshot,

Sally giggled. "I think he could be right. But I thought you were going to deny everything."

"I was, but he wouldn't have believed me."

"Your niece is beautiful, Bill and she hasn't made a sound," said Sally, gazing down at the infant.

"Did I hear you on the phone Bill?" Barbara came into the room.

"Yes, I returned Colin's call. I haven't got around to telling Sally yet, but I've asked him and his family over tomorrow afternoon for a drink. I thought we could celebrate our engagement." He looked at Sally, "I hope you don't mind, but I've asked him to speak to Alan and Judy. I thought they might like to join us. Is that alright?"

"Of course it is Bill," answered Sally. She looked at Barbara. "You're very lucky. You have a lovely baby. She's been very quiet." She handed Wendy back to Barbara.

"You won't be saying that later when she's crying in the night for a feed. We've taken the room on the other side of the hall, the one next to the bathroom. We thought the rest of you might not hear her so much there."

"Can I get you another drink?" asked Bill, looking at Jack's empty glass.

"Yes please," replied his father, who had awoken. "I'll have another whisky."

"You never miss a trick, Dad," Bill laughed.

The rest of the afternoon and evening passed over without any further mishaps. Anne telephoned her daughter, Susan, in Canada and they all took it in turn to speak to her. She was delighted to hear about Bill's engagement and congratulated him.

"I know we don't write to each other as often as we should. But Mum keeps me up to date with all the news. She told me about the extra work you've taken on and I've been so worried about you."

Bill promised he wouldn't be spending so much time at the office.

Susan then had a few words with Sally, saying how much she was looking forward to meeting her when she and her husband came to England the following year.

Afterwards, they all had tea and played some games with Joey until it was time for him to go to bed. Bill and Sally took him upstairs and read to him for a while, but he was so tired, it wasn't long before he was fast asleep.

Barbara and Jack were the next ones to go to bed. "I think we'll try to get some sleep before Wendy wakes up."

Bill's parents weren't long in following, leaving Bill and Sally on their own. "It's been quite a day." Sally looked at her engagement ring. "It could have all gone so horribly wrong. If your mother hadn't spoken to Joey and found out the truth, I would have left until after Christmas."

"Don't let's think about it. It all worked out in the end." Like his mother, Bill wanted to forget the whole episode. After all, it was his fault. He should have spoken to Joey about Sally. He shuddered when he thought back to the moment when Sally was going to leave.

"Come on," he said. "Let's go to bed. Tomorrow morning we'll get some of your things from the flat and after the holiday we'll sort out the rest. Have you decided what you want to do with your flat?"

"I told Vera she and Tom could have first refusal," said Sally getting up from the sofa. "I even suggested they might like to rent it if they couldn't afford to buy. At least it's somewhere they can call home. How would you feel about it? Would it affect your professional relationship with Vera if they were to buy my flat?"

"I don't see why it should," answered Bill. "She would be dealing with you. It's your flat and has nothing to do with me."

"Well, we'll see," said Sally. "I would make it very clear they would be dealing with me." She yawned. "Actually I'm tired myself. It's been a long day. Don't forget, we were up at six o'clock this morning."

They climbed the stairs as quietly as possible, not wanting to awaken Wendy. When Barbara and Jack retired for the night, they had looked very tired.

Undressing quickly, Sally found the nightdress she had brought over the Sunday before; Bill wore pyjamas.

Climbing into bed, Bill switched out the light and Sally snuggled up against him. "Bill darling, thank you for my wonderful Christmas present. I never dreamed I would ever have anything so beautiful, or someone so special." She kissed him.

Bill leaned across her. "Sweetheart, are you really feeling so very tired?"

"I was when I came to bed," she replied. "But not anymore." Bill kissed her gently and she giggled. "It was a waste of time putting on this night-dress."

Epilogue

Early the next morning the bedroom door flew open.

"Daddy, Daddy," said Joey, running into the room. He stopped abruptly when he saw Sally lying next to his father.

Bill took her hand under the covers and waited to see what his son would do next. Had he forgotten Sally was here?

"Mummy, Mummy," said Joey, jumping onto the bed. "It's morning. Wake up." Bill heaved a sigh of relief. He would hate to go through the trouble they'd had the day before.

Sally opened her eyes. "What time is it?"

"Seven-thirty," said Bill.

"Ugh! It's the middle of the night. Come on. Get into bed with us for half an hour. Don't make too much noise, Wendy may still be asleep."

Joey squeezed himself down the covers between his father and Sally.

"She's not." Barbara's voice came from the doorway. Joey had left the bedroom door wide open. His father's bedroom door was usually open and he didn't see why today should be any different. "She was crying so I took her downstairs in case she woke everyone. I came up because I heard Joey's voice."

Bill's mother appeared in the doorway. "Is everything alright? I heard Joey calling out." She saw Joey snuggled in the bed between Bill and Sally. "Oh, Sally, I'm sorry. For the moment I'd forgotten you were here." She looked quite embarrassed.

"Is there a problem?" Hearing everyone talking in the hallway, Bill's father had come along to see what the trouble was.

"Dad, Mum, Barbara. All we need now is Jack and then we'll all be in here."
Bill hoped Sally wasn't too embarrassed by all this. "We're in bed. Can't we
have any privacy?"

However, Sally burst out laughing. Bill looked at her and he started to laugh,
and in the end they were all laughing. Then when Jack appeared asking what
they were laughing at, everyone laughed all the more.

"I'll go back downstairs and put the kettle on," said Barbara, when she finally
stopped laughing. "Come on everyone. Leave them be." She mouthed the word
sorry to Bill as she pulled the door shut.

Bill tickled Joey. "Next time, young man, close the door behind you."

"Joey, your daddy is going to take me back to my house this morning so
I can get some more clothes." Joey didn't answer. Sally glanced at Bill. "Joey
sweetheart, is something wrong?"

His eyes welled with tears. "You're going to come back aren't you Mummy?"
he said, his lip quivering as he spoke.

"Of course I am, silly. Look, why don't you come with us? You can see inside
the little house where I used to live and you can help me to pack my suitcase.
Would you like that?"

Joey looked up at his father. "Can I, Daddy? Please?"

"I don't see why not. Mummy has said so, hasn't she?" Bill replied. "As long
as you are ready in time and have eaten all your breakfast."

Joey jumped out of bed and ran through to the en-suite and began to run a
bath. Bill leaned over Sally and kissed her.

"Will Joey be alright in the bathroom by himself?" she asked.

"He won't get into the bath unless I'm there," answered Bill. "He knows he
mustn't do that." He kissed her again.

"Daddy the bath is ready," called out Joey.

"Okay. I'm coming," said Bill.

Climbing out of bed, he turned to Sally said, "Don't you move a muscle."

In no time at all Joey was washed, dried and dressed. "Go downstairs and
tell Nanna we'll be down shortly. Ask her nicely for some orange juice... and
don't forget to say please." Bill waited until heard Joey was safely downstairs
before he closed the door and turned the key. "We don't want to be disturbed,
do we?" He climbed back into bed. "Now then, sweetheart, where were we?"

"You know something darling?" said Sally. "The more I think about it, the
more I believe Colin is right. You are a randy devil!"

Bill was showered and dressed before Sally. Barbara grinned when he walked into the kitchen alone. "You're a crafty pair," she said.

"What on earth do you mean?" Bill replied, trying to look innocent.

"You know perfectly well what I mean," laughed Barbara. "Sending Joey down here so you and Sally could stay in bed and…" She broke off as her mother came into the room with Joey.

"Ah! You're up, Bill," said Anne. "Joey tells me you're going to Sally's this morning to bring some of her things here."

"Yes, Mum. She needs some more clothes. I said I'd run her over there after breakfast. We'll take Joey with us. It shouldn't take very long."

"Good morning everyone," said Sally, walking into the kitchen.

Then looking at Barbara, she added. "Did you sleep well?"

"Yes, thank you," answered Barbara. "Jack and Dad have gone out for a stroll before breakfast. It looks quite a nice morning. Giving her brother a sideways glance, she added, "Did you have a good night?"

Her mother frowned.

Sally took Bill's hand and squeezed it. "Well," she said, before Bill could answer. "I can't speak for Bill, but I certainly did!"

"What exactly do you want to take today?" asked Bill, opening a suitcase.

There was no reply. Since arriving at the flat, Sally had wandered around looking at various items of furniture and ornaments. Bill went through to the lounge and found her sitting on the sofa looking at a photograph of herself and Jo. It had been taken a few years back. The two friends were walking along the promenade at the coast. In the background was the lighthouse she and Bill had visited the weekend before.

Bill sat down beside her and put his arm around her. "Sally, darling, you aren't having second thoughts, are you?"

"Good heavens no," she replied, quickly. "Whatever gave you that idea? I'm simply looking at a chapter of my life that's now ended." She looked around the room. "It doesn't even feel like home anymore. I was even thinking of phoning

Vera to let her know what the situation is. Unless of course, you're having doubts."

"No, Sally, none at all. Like I said to your father, I love you and always will."

"I know Bill, I'm teasing you." She leant over and kissed him. "I'll give Vera the good news."

Vera was delighted to hear about the engagement, saying she was happy for them both. Sally went on to tell her that she and Tom could either rent or buy the flat if they still wanted it. Vera was thrilled and promised to get back to her on which option they chose.

It didn't take long to pack a couple of cases of clothes for Sally. "That should do to be going on with." She took Joey by the hand. "Come on, let's go home. We'll give Nanna a hand with the lunch."

She and Joey walked around the flat once more before going down the stairs. Bill was outside waiting by the car. He had already put the cases in the boot. "Come on you two. I was beginning to think you were both going to stay here."

"Not on your life," Sally laughed. "You don't get rid of us that easily."

When they arrived back at the house, Anne and Barbara had started preparing the lunch. Anne told them it wouldn't be long. "Providing Barbara doesn't forget to put something in the oven again. I thought we could get lunch over early. Then we can relax a little before your friends come. You go upstairs and unpack your things, Sally. There's nothing for you to do here, everything's under control."

Sally went upstairs, leaving Bill and Joey playing a game in the sitting room. The phone rang and Barbara went to answer it.

"Hello. Oh hello, Colin," she said. Yes, he's here somewhere. Hang on a minute." She called Bill over to the phone.

"Hello, Bill. I didn't interrupt anything of a… shall we say… personal nature, this time, did I?" Colin laughed down the phone.

"No you didn't. If you had, I wouldn't have come to the phone. I'm playing a game with my son if you must know. You're such a nosey devil, Colin, I bet you only telephoned to see what I was doing." Bill laughed. "What can I do for you?"

"I thought I'd let you know my parents are going to stay here with the kids. I spoke to Alan yesterday and they're both coming. I told you he'd come. He's probably sitting there with his coat on as we speak, waiting for four o'clock."

"Don't be stupid Colin, give the lad a break," said Bill. He hesitated for a moment. "I'm thinking of moving him up from a junior, what do you think?"

"Well Bill, obviously it's up to you, but I don't see why not. I've been watching him closely since he was appointed and I like what I've seen. You'll have noticed my reports have all been favourable. He's very capable and shows willing and he does want to pull his weight, he told me that on Friday, which is more than can be said for some of your staff."

"Yes I've read all your reports carefully and it doesn't seem fair to leave someone so keen in a junior position. Anyway, don't say anything to him, let me give it some more thought, I just wanted to run it past you. Thanks for letting me know whose coming, I'll tell Mum. She'll probably organise some sandwiches. See you later."

Once the lunch was over and a few sandwiches had been made for the tea, everyone settled down to a quiet afternoon. Joey was playing with his toys. He could hardly wait to tell his friends at the nursery all about his new mummy from Santa.

Sally asked Bill if she could ring her brothers. She thought Paul would still be at Tom's and she wanted to take the opportunity to speak to them both.

"Of course you can, Sally. This is your home now. You don't have to ask to use the telephone." Out in the hall, she dialled the number.

"Sally. How wonderful to hear you. Paul and Maureen have gone out for a walk. He's going to be sorry he missed you. Have you had a nice Christmas?"

"It's been wonderful." She thought it best not to say anything about the upset on Christmas morning. After all, it had been a stupid misunderstanding. "Bill and I got engaged. He gave me the most beautiful ring. I didn't know anything about it until Christmas Day. I'm so happy, Tom. I can't tell you how happy I am and how much I love him."

"We're all very pleased for you Sally. Dad said he liked Bill very much. At least he told Paul. I wasn't around to see him before he and Mum went to Tenerife. I took the consignment up north. That was a tight spot, Bill got us out of." He paused for a moment, feeling a little embarrassed about what he had to say next. "Actually, Sally, Paul and I are really sorry we messed up your life. We did boss you around a lot, didn't we? And then we tried to push you into marrying Peter. I still can't believe we did that." Their father had made a point of telling Paul what Sally had said to him.

"Don't worry Tom. It all worked out well in the end. I would like you and Paul to meet Bill sometime soon. Perhaps when Mum and Dad get back we could come over for lunch or something, or you could all come here."

"We'll look forward to that. I think Dad is going to ask Bill to look at the books sometime. I hear he's a financial wizard."

"He is," said Sally. "You have absolutely no idea how clever he is. His firm is terrified of losing him."

"Yes Dad told Paul about it; something about a large cheque to keep him sweet."

Sally lowered her voice and told him briefly what had happened at the office the previous week. After a few more pleasantries, she gave him the phone number. "I really would like us all to keep in touch."

"I will Sally. I promise. We would have called you this weekend, but Dad went away without giving us the number or Bill's surname so we couldn't even look it up."

"It's Roberts," she told him before putting down the phone.

Sally then made a quick phone call to Jo and told her of her engagement to Bill.

Jo commented she wasn't really surprised, but she was very happy for them both. "You will keep in touch, won't you?" She had an awful feeling she mightn't see Sally again.

"Of course I will, I want you to be a bridesmaid, if it doesn't go against your principles too much. I insist you wear a dress though. None of that khaki gear you favour so much."

"Sally, I would love it," replied Jo. "My principles have taken a battering lately, I've met someone and he's not unlike Bill actually, kind and considerate. We met at the lecture on Wednesday night. He sat next to me and then gave me a lift home afterwards. I've seen him twice since then. Perhaps you and I could get together sometime soon and I'll tell you all about him."

"I'll look forward to it." Sally was amazed at the sudden change in Jo. Some-one kind and considerate didn't sound like Jo's type at all. She gave her Bill's phone number before she hung up.

Returning to the sitting room, she found Joey trying to persuade his grand-parents to take him out on his new bike. They weren't very keen. The room was warm and cosy and the sofa was so inviting. However, in the end they gave in. After all they may be going home tomorrow and it would probably be a while before they saw him again.

Barbara decided to take Wendy upstairs for a feed, leaving Jack asleep in an armchair. "He might as well get some sleep now. It's his turn to pace the floor tonight. I'll probably get changed while I'm up there. It won't be long before Colin and the others get here."

"We'll relax here for half an hour then follow you up," said Bill. "Mum and Dad will be worn out by the time they get back. Joey will insist on going to the park. At least we three will be ready."

Bill had just come downstairs at three-thirty when he heard a car pull onto the drive. He opened the front door to find their four guests spilling out of Alan's car. "Sally, darling, they're here. They've all come together." He called up the stairs." He shook Colin's hand and kissed the two ladies.

Alan came in last. He felt a little awkward at meeting Bill for the first time since the episode on Friday. However Bill greeted him warmly.

"Merry Christmas, Alan. Come in and make yourself at home."

"Sorry we're so early," said Colin, taking off his coat. "But you can blame Alan for that. He phoned me back later this morning to say he would pick us up. I told him to come at four but he couldn't wait to see you again and arrived a little after three."

Alan turned beetroot red. "I thought it would have taken longer to get here."

"Don't worry, Alan, It's not too early," said Bill, shaking his head at Colin.

"Let me take your coats," said Sally, coming downstairs.

"I'll see to it," said Bill. "You show every one into the sitting room. Colin can give me a hand."

"Am I going to get a lecture already?" Colin said, once they were in the bed-room. He grinned at Bill.

"No, not really," Bill replied. "I was only going to ask you not to say anything too embarrassing. Okay?"

"Like, how much time you and Sally spend up here in the bedroom?" Colin grinned broadly.

"Oh, so you've noticed that, too." Barbara laughed. She was on her way downstairs with Wendy and had overheard the conversation.

"Well – yes. That as well, actually," said Bill, frowning at his sister. "But I was thinking of Alan. Don't upset him too much, especially in front of Judy. I'm used to your teasing but he's not, so try to be a little tactful. He's probably still reeling from Friday."

"Why, what happened on Friday?" Barbara pounced. She could tell something was going on.

"Nothing you'd be interested in," answered Bill sharply. "It's only office business."

Barbara looked at Colin and screwed her eyes up. There was something they weren't telling her. "Office business?" she enquired.

"Yes, it was simply a little business in the office." Colin nodded his head vigorously in agreement with Bill.

He wasn't proud of his part in the incident and didn't want the subject brought up again today – especially with Rachel sitting downstairs. Not having mentioned it to her, he certainly didn't want her hearing about it now. But even worse, if Barbara learned of it she would be extremely angry and no doubt deliver several cutting remarks of her own.

Though Colin looked away, he still felt Barbara's eyes piercing through him. He hadn't fooled her. He needed to say something – and quickly!

"Well, as Bill said, it's nothing really." He forced a grin. "It seems Alan absolutely hero worships your brother. The lad was already impressed last Monday with a contract Bill had produced for one of the clients, but when he saw him do some large calculations in his head on Friday, he went over the top…" He paused for effect. "Well, you know me, Barbara; I had to say something. Bill thought I was being cruel… But watch Alan for yourself. You'll see what I mean."

Barbara's eyes had never left Colin. He could tell she wasn't convinced and he was relieved when Bill interrupted.

"Come on, we'd better go downstairs." Bill moved over to the door. "They'll be wondering what's going on up here. But remember, Colin no wisecracks.

And Babs, that goes for you too. Don't you start on Alan as well, he can do without it."

Barbara was sure Colin hadn't told her everything. Yet she realised she wasn't going to get any further at the moment. She looked at her brother. "Who? Me make wisecracks? As if!"

Holding back for a moment, Colin allowed Barbara to leave first. Once she was out of earshot, he nudged Bill's arm. "Did you tell Sally about Friday?" he whispered.

"Of course not. Why would I?"

Relieved, Colin nodded and smiled. He'd had a sudden thought that Sally might mention the incident to Rachel, believing she knew about it already.

They reached the bottom of the stairs, as Bill's parents came in with Joey. "Daddy, I've been to the park." Then he saw Colin. "Uncle Colin I've been to the park with my new bike." He ran over to Colin and took him by the hand. "Is Auntie Rachel here? I want to show her my new Mummy."

"Yes Joey, she is. We'll go in to see her in a minute, I want to say hello to your nanna and granddad first."

Going across to Anne and John he wished them a Merry Christmas and asked if they were enjoying their stay. He waited until Bill had gone into the sitting room before adding, "You must be very pleased about Bill and Sally."

"Yes we are. You know how long we've waited for this day," replied Anne, smiling. "Sally's a lovely girl, Bill adores her and so does Joey."

"They're made for each other," said Colin. "Rachel and I are happy for them both. Did you know he turned down extra work at the office because she asked him to?

"Yes, he told us and we're delighted someone is able to make him see sense at last," said John.

Colin glanced towards the sitting room door. "We'd better go in otherwise they'll all come looking for us."

Joey was hugging Rachel. But when he saw Alan and Judy sitting next to Sally, he ran back to his father and clung to him.

"He's very shy with strangers," explained Bill.

"And we know who he gets that from," said Barbara. "Bill was just the same when he was small," she said to Alan and Judy. "He still is actually."

"I don't think they need to know that." Bill frowned at his sister.

"Come over here, Joey and sit beside me," said Sally gently. "These are your daddy and mummy's friends and we would like you to meet them."

Joey ventured across to Sally and she pulled him up onto her knee. Sally introduced Alan and Judy as Uncle and Aunt. She told him it would be nice if he would say hello to them. Joey climbed down and went across to Judy and Alan. He kept looking back at his father and Sally, but he did manage a "hello" in a very quiet voice before running back to Bill.

"Well, that's a start," said Sally. "Now, what would everyone like to drink?"

"Mine's a whisky," said Bill's father.

"Is that your engagement ring?" asked Judy, noticing the ring for the first time.

Sally nodded. She held out her hand for them all to see.

"It's absolutely, beautiful," said Judy and Rachel together.

"You have very good taste," said Rachel.

"Bill chose it. I didn't know anything about it until he gave it to me yesterday," said Sally, going over to Bill. She slipped her arm around his waist. "It was such a lovely surprise. Yet I'm curious to know how you knew my size."

Bill explained how he had found a ring belonging to her lying on the floor. "Joey walked into the bedroom, so I slipped it into my pocket. I forgot all about it until I was in the jewellers." He put his arm around her and kissed her. "Well now, what about those drinks?"

"Mine is still a whisky," said Bill's father. "Is anyone going to join me? I hope you have some more, son. I don't know if you've noticed, but this bottle is nearly finished."

"And we all know why that is, Dad," said Bill, raising his eyes to the ceiling. "Yes there's some more in the cupboard in the kitchen."

"I'll get it, son. You see to everyone else." He went out and came back with the bottle. "Well, we whisky drinkers are alright. I don't know about the rest of you."

When he had made sure everyone had a drink, Bill sat down next to Sally. They all drank a toast, wishing everyone all the best for the future.

"But most especially Bill and Sally," added Colin. He wanted to know when the wedding was going to be.

"We haven't had time to think about it yet," said Bill. "But I'd like it to be soon. What do you say, Sally? I'll go along with whatever you want."

"Yes, I'd like for us to be married very soon," said Sally. "I don't want anything too grand, but Bill, I really would like a church wedding. Would you mind very much?" She was a little concerned it may remind Bill of his first marriage and open sore wounds.

"Sally, darling, whatever you want is fine by me," Bill replied. After all, this was the first time for her and a church wedding was what most young women dreamed about. "Colin, would you be my Best Man?"

"I would be honoured, Bill. I really would."

"Of course, both you and Judy will be invited," Bill said to Alan.

Sally nodded in agreement.

"Thank you, we'd love **Day Twelve**to attend," said Alan.

"I bet he would," whispered Colin to Rachel.

"What about you and Judy?" asked Sally. "You must be starting to think about your wedding. I know you have to wait a few months, but you could start planning it now."

"Oh yes. We have the church and the reception booked for September. But when we went to the Building Society on Friday afternoon to ask about a mortgage, they weren't very helpful," said Alan. "We haven't saved with them for very long so we aren't a good risk. Or so they say and of course I haven't been in my job for very long, which doesn't help. From there we went on to a bank but were told we'd have to pay an extra five and a half per cent above the normal interest rate and on a mortgage of... Wait a minute I have it all written down somewhere."

He took out the leaflet the bank had given him and showed it to Bill. "Now on those figures we would have to pay an extra..." He pulled a calculator from his pocket.

"An extra £271,507.52p over a twenty five year term," said Bill after glancing at the leaflet. "And if the rates go up in the meantime, it would be more."

Alan gazed at Bill in admiration. He looked at the calculator and then at Colin. "That's absolutely brilliant. I haven't even got the first figure in yet, I wish I could do that."

"Don't bother with the calculator," said Colin. "Bill will be right. He always is." He looked at Barbara and mouthed the words 'see what I mean?'

She grinned and nodded.

"How long are you planning to stay at Websters?" asked Bill.

"Well, I hope to stay there long term," said Alan. "They seem to be a good company to work for and I hope to do well and work my way up the ladder, make something of myself."

"Sounds to me as though you're going to have to look out for your job, Bill," said Colin, grinning. "We may be looking at the new head of finance."

Colin was only joking, but Alan took him seriously. "Oh no Bill, I didn't mean… It wouldn't ever come to that." He blushed. He didn't want Bill to think he was after his job. "I'll never be good enough for a position like yours. I simply want to do well. I like working with figures and enjoy being in the finance office. The firm also have a very good pension scheme and…"

"And of course you have an extremely clever boss in the shape of Bill Roberts. Who I might add, you simply idolise," interrupted Colin, grinning at Barbara.

"Yes. I do have a very clever boss," said Alan quietly. He went red again and looked down at the floor. Seeing his discomfort, Judy slipped her hand into his and squeezed. She wished Colin would stop picking on him. Why did he always have to keep putting him down?

Rachel gave Colin a dig in the ribs. She loved him dearly, but on some occasions she could quite happily disown him. Colin looked at Alan and felt guilty when he saw how upset he was.

"I'm sorry, Alan, don't take any notice of me, I don't mean anything by it." It was true. He didn't mean anything nasty, but he couldn't resist teasing anyone who was so easily embarrassed and Alan's hero worship of Bill made him a prime target.

Noticing Bill's frown, Colin shrugged his shoulders and mouthed the word, 'sorry'.

Alan continued looking at the floor. Colin was right; he did admire Bill a great deal and saw him as someone he could learn a lot from. But he hadn't realised he had been so obvious. What on earth would Bill think of him now? Not only will he think him an idiot, but an idiot, who was after his job.

"Well, Alan, you know you could always ask Websters for a mortgage," Bill said, still glaring at Colin. "The interest rate would only be between one and two per cent, which as you know is a great deal less than either the bank or building society. They sometimes lend money to reliable, loyal staff. But of course you must understand if you were to leave before it was paid, you would have to pay the going interest rate or get a regular Building Society mortgage to cover it.

However, paying less interest gives you the chance to look for a more expensive house or pay the mortgage off quickly."

"That sounds too good to be true," said Alan. "Dare I ask if you are buying this house through Websters?"

"Yes I bought it through the firm," said Bill. "Though it's paid for now. A few of the staff have tried to take up the offer and while some have been accepted, most are turned down. Not because of salary, though of course salary is taken into account when deciding the amount of the loan. They are turned down because they have no real commitment to the firm."

Alan looked at Colin. "What about you?" While Colin's house was not in the same league as Bill's, it was large and certainly a lot more than he and Judy could afford.

"Yes, said Colin. "I'm buying mine the same way. Although in my case, it's not paid for yet."

Alan turned back to Bill. "What are the possibilities of me being accepted? After all, I haven't been with the firm for very long."

"Very optimistic I'd say," said Bill. "Wouldn't you agree, Colin?"

"Well, you certainly know more about it than I do Bill. But yes, from what I'm hearing this afternoon, I'd be inclined to agree."

Alan looked at Judy, who was still gripping his hand. "It's worth a try, isn't it?"

"After what we went through on Friday, anything is worth a try," she replied.

"Okay Bill," said Alan. "So tell me. To whom do I have to grovel, to get this loan?"

Bill looked across at Colin and grinned, before turning back to Alan. "Well now, let me see. That would be... Me!"

Alan looked around the room when everyone burst out laughing. They had all known where this conversation was going.

"Right! Now Alan's mortgage is settled. What about another drink?" Bill's father leapt to his feet.

"Okay Dad," said Bill. "You top up the whisky glasses and I'll see to the others."

Alan was stunned. He was still looking at Bill. "Seriously?" he asked, when he found his voice.

"Yes, seriously," said Bill, refilling Judy's glass. "But you don't need to grovel. When we get back to the office after the holiday, we'll fill in the forms together. I don't have any here."

"Thanks Bill," said Alan. "I don't know what to say."

"You don't have to say anything. If I didn't believe in you, I wouldn't have mentioned it in the first place. Actually there's something else I want to talk to you about. I should really wait until we're back in the office, but as you're here I'll tell you now. I've decided to move you up from a junior to a full member of staff. I discussed it with Colin on the telephone this morning and he agrees with me."

"Well done, Alan," said Colin. "Being promoted before the statutory two years are up is something, which very seldom occurs. It has only happened to two other people in all the years I've been at Websters and as it turns out, you know them both quite well." He looked at Bill and winked before continuing. "It's a real achievement and I'm very pleased for you. You deserve it."

Alan was so overwhelmed he couldn't speak. He knew it meant a dramatic rise in salary. "Thank you, Bill," he said eventually. "I won't let you down." He glanced across at Colin and added, "Either of you."

"I'm sure you won't," said Bill.

"That's absolutely wonderful, Alan. I'm so very proud of you. You've always dreamed of a chance like this." Full of excitement, Judy glanced a**Day Twelve**cross at Bill. "Thank you so much."

"He's earned it," replied Bill. "We could do with more like Alan in the office."

Alan was still shaking when Bill's father came to refill his glass. Only last Friday he had thought Bill was going to dismiss him through a stupid prank and now today, even after Colin's silly remarks, he was offering him a mortgage and a promotion. It was too much for him to take in.

"Put your glass on the table lad, or else I'll have this all over you."

"Not too much," said Alan. "I'm the driver. Although I must say I feel like celebrating."

"Well you could all stay the night," said Bill. "We could work something out. The three ladies in one bed, and the men in another."

"That would cramp your style a bit, Bill," said Colin, winking at Alan. "It would give Sally a rest though."

Alan gave a slight grin back. He didn't want to get too involved in Colin's jokes. Especially those aimed at Bill.

"It certainly would," said Barbara, laughing. If you only knew what went on here."

"Tell us more Bar…" said Colin.

"Colin, Barbara," interrupted Bill's mother. "Behave yourselves. Joey's listening."

"What does Uncle Colin mean?" asked Joey, looking at his father.

"You tell him Colin," said Bill laughing.

"Well… err…err…" said Colin, thinking quickly. "Well Joey. I meant they would all be cramped and squashed together, if there were three in one bed."

He looked at Bill and raised his eyes to the ceiling. "It's the best I could come up with," he whispered.

"No they wouldn't, Uncle Colin," said Joey. "I was in bed with my mummy and daddy this morning and we weren't squashed at all, were we Daddy?"

"No we weren't Joey, you're quite right," said Bill.

"Sorry Joey, I thought they would have been," said Colin, grinning at Bill. "Well then young man, tell us what you have been doing today. We know you went to the park with your nanna and granddad this afternoon. What did you do this morning?"

"Well, Uncle Colin," said Joey importantly. "Daddy helped me to get dressed and I went downstairs to see Nanna. But I think Daddy was tired because he went back to bed with my mummy for a little while."

Everyone grinned at Bill and Sally while Joey carried on telling them about the rest of his morning.

"Out of the mouths of babes!" Colin winked at Bill.

Sally buried her head in Bill's shoulder to hide her embarrassment.

"Exactly how much time do you two spend…?" continued Colin.

"Leave it," interrupted Bill, shaking his head.

"Sorry, Bill, I get carried away sometimes."

"There are times, Colin, when I wish you would." Rachel laughed.

"What are your plans now Sally?" said Bill's mother, quickly changing the subject. "Are you going to finish your course?"

"I don't know. I must say I've lost interest recently. I've had so much more on my mind. What do you think, Bill?"

"It's entirely up to you. But you aren't too far behind. Jo has taped the lectures for you, hasn't she?"

"Yes and I could miss **Day Twelve**one assignment. Oh! What shall I do?"

"Well," said Bill. "You wouldn't need to work in the offices at the college and Joey could still continue at the nursery school. That would give you more time to catch up."

"You have it all worked out," said Sally.

"I simply don't want you to do something you'll regret later."

Sally looked at Bill and grinned. "Haven't we been here before?" She was referring to the last time Bill had said those words. It was the night she had told him she wanted to sleep with him. He grinned back at her and nodded. He knew what she meant.

"Are we missing something here?" asked Colin.

"Don't be so nosey," said Rachel. "It might be private."

"It is. Very private," replied Bill.

"Would you like something to eat?" Anne changed the subject again. "I've laid out a buffet in the dining room. Go and help yourselves. I'll put the kettle on in case anyone wants some tea or coffee."

"Is anyone ready for another drink – apart from my father?" asked Bill.

"I think your father's had enough," said Anne.

"Nonsense," said John. "We're celebrating our son's engagement. Not to mention Alan's mortgage and promotion."

"Well I'd better not, Bill," said Alan. "I'll have some of your mother's tea."

"It's up to you. You can stay the night if you like," said Bill. "Don't take any notice of Colin. He likes to wind me up, he always has."

"I was starting to notice that," said Alan, shyly. He was recalling last Friday morning. "But no. Thanks all the same, I'd better get Judy home tonight. We're off to meet some of her relatives early tomorrow morning. Not something we're looking forward to, but it'll keep her parent's sweet. Otherwise I would certainly take you up on your offer."

"I bet he would," whispered Colin to Barbara and Rachel. "I don't know how he's going to tear himself away tonight. No doubt we'll hear how wonderful Bill is all the way home."

Barbara covered her mouth to hide a smile.

"Okay, Alan, but if you change your mind, say the word," said Bill. "Now then, shall we go and have something to eat?"

During the evening, Bill's mother suggested they should bring some of the food into the lounge. "There's plenty left in the dining room."

"I'll get it for you, Mrs Roberts... I mean, Anne," said Sally.

"And I'll give you a hand." Bill hurried after her.

"Mind what you two are doing out there. No sneaking off upstairs to the... Ouch! That hurt," said Colin, as Rachel kicked his foot.

"Nanna," said Joey, "Why did Auntie Rachel kick Uncle Colin?"

"I think her foot slipped, Joey." Anne grinned at Rachel.

In the dining room, Sally began putting plates of food on to a tray. "I think that should be enough, don't you?"

Bill didn't answer so she repeated the question.

"I'm sorry Sally, but I was miles away. I was thinking, only two weeks ago today I hadn't even met you. In the space of that short time you've turned my life around. Looking back, I see how bleak my life was."

"This morning I was thinking the very same thing," replied Sally. "There were only twelve days 'til Christmas when I first met you and here I find myself engaged and planning my wedding to the most wonderful man. And it's all down to Jane Miller having to take time off at the nursery because of a dose of 'flu. We must invite her to the wedding."

"Sally, I want to take you somewhere wonderful for our honeymoon. Where would you like to go? The Bahamas? California? You name it."

"Anywhere would be wonderful, as long we're together and I don't have to go to the college or you to the office," replied Sally.

Bill pulled Sally to him and kissed her, but they were interrupted by a voice from the lounge.

"It's gone very quiet out there. What are you both up to?" Colin laughed. "Put her down Bill, you randy...Ouch! ...What did you do that for?"

Rachel had given him another kick.

"Look Nanna, Auntie Rachel's foot has slipped again, Nanna," giggled Joey.

Everyone burst out laughing, as Colin rubbed his injured ankle.

"I think we'd better go back to our guests before Rachel breaks Colin's foot." said Bill. "But later, I'd like to carry on where we've left off."

"That's fine by me," replied Sally, running her fingers slowly up and down his back. "I can't wait."

"Neither can I now," said Bill, smiling at her. He kissed her again before carrying the tray of food into the lounge.

"About time too," Colin laughed. "I was about to come and look for you." He thought of making another comment about what they had been up to, but decided against it. Instead, he turned to Joey and asked what he thought of his new mummy.

"I think she's lovely, Uncle Colin. Santa brought her for Daddy and me."

"Yes. Your daddy told me all about it, you're both very lucky." He looked over to Bill. "You are, you know."

"Yes, Joey and I both know that." Bill put down the tray. "And we are going to take good care of her."

"That's right." Joey went over to Sally and climbed up onto her knee.

She put her arms around him and hugged him. "And I'm going to look after both of you."

"Tell me, Joey, what do you think of your Auntie Barbara's new baby?" asked Rachel.

"I think she's lovely as well," he said. He glanced at his father. "Next year, Daddy, I'm going to ask Santa for one of those."

Colin burst out laughing. "Well Joey, the way your daddy's going I don't think you'll need to wait that long." He moved his feet out of Rachel's reach to avoid another kick.

"I'll second that," said Barbara, ignoring her mother's frown.

"Daddy, what does Uncle Colin mean?" asked Joey.

"Why don't you explain it to him Colin?" said Bill, laughing. "You're very good at that sort of thing."

Colin looked around the room for support, but none was forthcoming. "Alan," he pleaded. "Help me out here."

"No, Colin, you're on your own with this one," he said, grinning.

"Well, go on then, Colin," said Rachel. "Joey's waiting, explain it to him."

Colin turned back to Joey, who was still staring up at him.

"What do you mean, Uncle Colin?"

"Well... err..." said Colin, glancing at everyone again. "It's like this Joey... err..."

About the Author

Born on Tyneside, Eileen Thornton now lives in the pretty town of Kelso in the Scottish Borders with her husband, Phil. She has been writing on a freelance basis for the past twelve years, and her illustrated articles and short stories have appeared in several national magazines.

A selection of Eileen's work can be found on her website:
http://www.eileenthornton.com/

CPSIA information can be obtained
at www.ICGtesting.com
Printed in the USA
BVHW030949250121
598677BV00010B/242/J

9 781034 269700